Brian Lu...

Brian Lumley is the internationally bestselling author of the *Necroscope* and *Vampire World* series. Both of these epics have gained a huge and loyal following and have demonstrated a breadth of imagination and scope to rival the greats: Poe, Lovecraft and King. A career British Army Military Policeman for over twenty years, he has been a full-time writer since the army and lives in Torquay, South Devon.

Brian has just been awarded the title of 'Grandmaster of Horror' by the 1998 World Horror Convention. Previous winners of this accolade include Clive Barker, Stephen King and Peter Straub.

His new *Necroscope* series – *E-Branch* – will be launched early in 1999.

Coven of Vampires

Brian Lumley

NEW ENGLISH LIBRARY
Hodder and Stoughton

Copyright © 1998 by Brian Lumley

First published in Great Britain in 1998 Hodder and Stoughton
A division of Hodder Headline PLC
First published in paperback in 1998 by Hodder and Stoughton

The right of Brian Lumley to be identified as the Author of the
Work has been asserted by him in accordance with the
Copyright, Designs and Patents Act 1988.

A New English Library Paperback

10 9 8 7 6 5 4 3 2 1

A CIP catalogue record is available from the British Library

ISBN 0 340 71542 1

Typeset by Hewer Text Limited, Edinburgh
Printed and bound in Great Britain by
Clays Ltd, St Ives PLC

Hodder and Stoughton
A division of Hodder Headline PLC
338 Euston Road
London NW1 3BH

ACKNOWLEDGEMENTS

'What Dark God?', *Nameless Places* ed. Gerald W. Page, Arkham House, 1975.

'Back Row', *Terror Australis*, Autumn 1988.

'The Strange Years', *Fantasy Tales*, No. 9, Spring 1982.

'Kiss of the Lamia', *Weirdbook*, No. 20, Spring 1985.

'Recognition', *Weirdbook*, No. 15, 1981.

'The Thief Immortal', *Weirdbook*, No. 25, 1990.

'Necros', *The Second Book of After Midnight Stories*, ed. Amy Myers, Wm. Kimber, 1986.

'The Thing from the Blasted Heath,' *The Caller of the Black*, Arkham House, 1971.

'Uzzi', *Fear*, September/October 1988.

'Haggopian', *The Magazine of Fantasy and Science Fiction*, June 1973.

'The Picknickers', *Final Shadows*, ed. Charles L. Grant, Doubleday, 1991.

'Zack Phalanx *is* Vlad the Impaler', *Weirdbook*, No. 11, March 1977.

'The House of the Temple', *Weird Tales*, Vol. 48, No. 3, Fall 1981.

CONTENTS

FOREWORD

I've been hooked (or should that be impaled?) on vampires ever since I was a kid. But don't ask me to be exact, because when I was a kid was a long time ago. It was probably those old books my father used to keep on a high shelf he knew I couldn't reach . . . without the aid of stepladders.

The stepladders would come out whenever Mom and Dad would make one of their rare excursions out into the world, maybe to the Picturehouse or the Ritz or the Empress, to see the latest big picture – the latest 'movie', to you American cousins. It would be something with Betty Grable, maybe, or Dick Haymes.

But ah, those books! Do you remember all those big, heavy, black-bound books? *Fifty Great Mysteries! Fifty Great Tales of Terror and the Imagination!* Fifty This and Fifty That. Perhaps those weren't the precise titles – it's hard to remember now – but I'll never forget the weight and the looks, and the *smell*, of those books; they were musty even then. The black bat embossed into the binding cloth; the claw-like hand drawing back the curtains, and the sinister figure *beyond* the curtains. And the interior illustrations. The *horrid* interior illustrations! The naked black girl wrapped in a carnivorous tree's tendrils, being hoisted to her doom like a cocooned fly. That one stuck in my boy's mind for a long time; it's still there, in fact, just as fresh (and as monstrous) as ever.

All those books, and some of them must have contained vampire stories, I'm sure . . .

I had a library ticket when I was eight, and I think I was maybe halfway through Bram Stoker's *Dracula* before 'they' even noticed. But that was okay . . . *Dracula* was a classic after all. Then my big brother, Harry – just about to be drafted for National Service – started to read it, and he asked the Old Folks: 'Do you really think he should be reading this? Won't it give him nightmares?' Thanks a bunch, big brother! After that I had to read it chapter by chapter in the library.

Before I was sixteen, I was out of school and had a job as an apprentice machinist. That meant a bus ride into town every workday, and there was a newsagent opposite where I got off the bus. It must have been the early to mid-50s, and one morning I saw this garish magazine cover glaring at me through the window of the shop. *Weird Tales*, And the 's' looked like it was about to fall off the end of the title.

Those British edition WT were – *wow!* – a whole shilling each in those days. That was good money. In pristine condition they'd easily fetch two hundred times that amount now. *That* is really good money! But just looking at the cover of that first of many issues (*my* first issue, anyway) was like seeing one of those ancient mariner maps with the legend 'Here be Monsters,' stamped over uncharted waters. And in WT's terms, 'Here be Vampires,' too! Oh, yes, those magazines were definitely my blood group. And I used to suck 'em bone dry.

1958. The year I was drafted. And *that* was a horror story in its own right . . . well, until I got to like it. And I liked it so much I signed on for twenty-two years. But that's not the only reason I remember '58. Not a bit of it, for it's also the year they released *Dracula* on film again – only this time with Christopher Lee as the bloodthirsty Count. Now tell me, isn't that scene where he strides past the castle's battlements with his cloak belling behind him just one of your favourites? It's one of mine, be sure!

But whoah – I've missed something! And a very important something at that. Do you remember EC? No, of course you don't, 'cos you were a little kid then and your big brother would probably have told on you. *Tales From the Crypt*, and *The Vault of Horror*, and . . . God, there was a whole gaggle of them! Not only EC but other publishers, too. *Frankenstein, Black Magic* – man, I *remember* those titles! And they were called 'comics' . . .?

You know, I'm frequently accused of using too many exclamation marks. But honestly, how could I write this without them? I *need* exclamation marks to make my point. Which is that EC was Vampire Wonderland to me. Was there ever an issue without a vampire story? Well, maybe, but I can't remember one. (Or maybe I just don't want to.)

Even worse, I can't remember where or when I first read Richard Matheson's *I Am Legend*, but I do know I've read it half a dozen times since. It probably delayed my attempts to write my own vampire novels by, oh, twenty years . . . Because it was that damned good! But that wasn't a bad thing (in a couple of decades I'd learned a lot, not only about authorship but about the world). And if I was going to do it at all, I knew it would have to be wide-screen.

And eventually I did do it, let all of that stuff I'd once soaked up so avidly leak back out of me, and even occasionally splatter. The *Necroscope* novels and *Vampire World Trilogy* are the end results.

Between times, though, I had worked up to it in a host of shorter stories that explored the vampire myth and came at it from many diverse angles, some of them so far removed from the original that even I didn't realize what I was really writing until the stories were finished.

A host of them? Well, a coven of them, in fact. Thirteen tales that dance widdershins around the central concept, and occasionally rock 'n' roll with it, too. Stories that are more or less traditional, some less so, and others straight out of Lovecraft's Cthulhu Mythos.

So there you go. I 'blame' this collection on EC Comics, *Weird Tales*, Christopher Lee, Richard Matheson, *et al*, whose stories in this sub-genre really bit me. To all of them and to others long forgotten I offer my thanks. They all have a stake in this collection . . .

Brian Lumley
Devon, England,
February 1997.

WHAT DARK GOD?

'. . . *Summanus* – whatever power he may be . . .'

Ovid's *Fasti*

The Tuscan Rituals? Now where had I heard of such a book or books before? Certainly very rare . . . Copy in the British Museum? Perhaps! Then what on earth were *these* fellows doing with a copy? And such a strange bunch of blokes at that.

Only a few minutes earlier I had boarded the train at Bengham. It was quite crowded for a night train and the boozy, garrulous, and vociferous 'Jock' who had boarded it directly in front of me had been much upset by the fact that all the compartments seemed to be fully occupied.

'Och, they bleddy British trains,' he had drunkenly grumbled, 'either a'wiz emp'y or a'wiz fool. No orgyniza-tion whatsayever – ye no agree, ye sassenach?' He had elbowed me in the ribs as we swayed together down the dim corridor.

'Er, yes,' I had answered. 'Quite so!'

Neither of us carried cases and as we stumbled along, searching for vacant seats in the gloomy compartments, Jock suddenly stopped short.

'Noo what in hell's this – will ye look here? A compart-ment wi' the bleddy blinds doon. Prob'ly a young laddie an' lassie in there wi' six emp'y seats. Privacy be damned. Ah'm no standin' oot here while there's a seat in there . . .'

The door had proved to be locked – on the inside – but that had not deterred the 'bonnie Scot' for a moment. He had banged insistently upon the wooden frame of the door until it was carefully, tentatively opened a few inches; then he had stuck his foot in the gap and put his shoulder to the frame, forcing the door fully open.

3

'No, no . . .' The scrawny, pale, pin-stripe jacketed man who stood blocking the entrance protested. 'You can't come in – this compartment is reserved . . .'

'Is that so, noo? Well, if ye'll kindly show me the reserved notice,' Jock had paused to tap significantly upon the naked glass of the door with a belligerent fingernail, 'Ah'll bother ye no more – meanwhile, though, if ye'll hold ye're blether, *Ah'd appreciate a bleddy seat . . .*'

'No, no . . .' The scrawny man had started to protest again, only to be quickly cut off by a terse command from behind him:

'*Let them in . . .*'

I shook my head and pinched my nose, blowing heavily and puffing out my cheeks to clear my ears. For the voice from within the dimly-lit compartment had sounded hollow, unnatural. Possibly the train had started to pass through a tunnel, an occurrence which never fails to give me trouble with my ears. I glanced out of the exterior corridor window and saw immediately that I was wrong; far off on the dark horizon I could see the red glare of coke-oven fires. Anyway, whatever the effect had been which had given that voice its momentarily peculiar – resonance? – it had obviously passed, for Jock's voice sounded perfectly normal as he said: 'Noo tha's *better*; excuse a body, will ye?' He shouldered the dubious looking man in the doorway to one side and slid clumsily into a seat alongside a second stranger. As I joined them in the compartment, sliding the door shut behind me, I saw that there were four strangers in all, six people including Jock and myself; we just made comfortable use of the eight seats which faced inwards in two sets of four.

I have always been a comparatively shy person so it was only the vaguest of perfunctory glances which I gave to each of the three new faces before I settled back and took out the pocket-book I had picked up earlier in the day in London.

Those merest of glances, however, were quite sufficient to put me off my book and to tell me that the three friends of the pin-stripe jacketed man appeared the very strangest of travelling companions – especially the extremely tall and thin member of the three, sitting stiffly in his seat beside Jock. The other two answered to approximately the same description as Pin-Stripe – as I was beginning mentally to tag him – except that one of them wore a thin moustache; but that fourth one, the tall one, was something else again.

Within the brief duration of the glance I had given him I had seen that, remarkable though the rest of his features were, his mouth appeared decidedly odd – almost as if it had been painted onto his face – the merest thin red line, without a trace of puckering or any other depression to show that there was a hole there at all. His ears were thick and blunt and his eyebrows were bushy over the most penetrating eyes it has ever been my unhappy lot to find staring at me. Possibly that was the reason I had glanced so quickly away; the fact that when I had looked at him I had found *him* staring at *me* – and his face had been totally devoid of any expression whatsoever. *Fairies?* The nasty thought had flashed through my mind unbidden; none the less, that would explain why the door had been locked.

Suddenly Pin-Stripe – seated next to me and directly opposite Funny-Mouth – gave a start, and, as I glanced up from my book, I saw that the two of them were staring directly into each other's eyes.

'*Tell them* . . .' Funny-Mouth said, though I was sure his strange lips had not moved a fraction, and again his voice had seemed distorted, as though his words passed through weirdly angled corridors before reaching my ears.

'It's, er – almost midnight,' informed Pin-Stripe, grinning sickly first at Jock and then at me.

'Aye,' said Jock sarcastically, 'happens every nicht aboot this time . . . Ye're very observant . . .'

5

'Yes,' said Pin-Stripe, choosing to ignore the jibe, 'as you say – but the point I wish to make is that we three, er, that is, we *four*,' he corrected himself, indicating his companions with a nod of his head, 'are members of a little-known, er, religious sect. We have a ceremony to perform and would appreciate it if you two gentlemen would remain quiet during the proceedings . . .' I heard him out and nodded my head in understanding and agreement – I am a tolerant person – but Jock was of a different mind.

'Sect?' he said sharply. 'Ceremony?' He shook his head in disgust. 'Well; Ah'm a member o' the Church o' Scotland and Ah'll tell ye noo – Ah'll hae no truck wi' bleddy heathen *ceremonies* . . .'

Funny–Mouth had been sitting ram-rod straight, saying not a word, doing nothing, but now he turned to look at Jock, his eyes narrowing to mere slits; above them, his eyebrows meeting in a black frown of disapproval.

'Er, perhaps it would be better,' said Pin-Stripe hastily, leaning across the narrow aisle towards Funny-Mouth as he noticed the change in that person's attitude, 'if they, er, *went to sleep* . . . ?'

This preposterous statement or question, which caused Jock to peer at its author in blank amazement and me to wonder what on earth he was babbling about, was directed at Funny-Mouth who, without taking his eyes off Jock's outraged face, nodded in agreement.

I do not know what happened then – it was as if I had been suddenly *unplugged* – I was asleep, yet not asleep – in a trance-like condition full of strange impressions and mind-pictures – abounding in unpleasant and realistic sensations, with dimly-recollected snatches of previously absorbed information floating up to the surface of my conscious mind, correlating themselves with the strange people in the railway compartment with me . . .

And in that dream-like state my brain was still very active; possibly *fully* active. All my senses were still working; I could hear the clatter of the wheels and smell the acrid tang of burnt tobacco from the compartment's ash-trays. I saw Moustache produce a folding table from the rack above his head – saw him open it and set it up in the aisle, between Funny-Mouth and himself on their side and Pin-Stripe and his companion on my side – saw the designs upon it, designs suggestive of the more exotic work of Chandler Davies, and wondered at their purpose. My head must have fallen back until it rested in the corner of the gently rocking compartment, for I saw all these things without having to move my eyes; indeed, I doubt very much if I *could* have moved my eyes and do not remember making any attempt to do so.

I saw that book – a queerly bound volume bearing its title, *The Tuscan Rituals*, in archaic, burnt-in lettering on its thick spine – produced by Pin-Stripe and opened reverently to lie on that ritualistic table, displayed so that all but Funny-Mouth, Jock, and I could make out its characters. But Funny-Mouth did not seem in the least bit interested in the proceedings. He gave me the impression that he had seen it all before, many times . . .

Knowing I was dreaming – or was I? – I pondered that title, *The Tuscan Rituals*. Now where had I heard of such a book or books before? The *feel* of it echoed back into my subconscious, telling me I recognized that title – but in what connection?

I could see Jock, too, on the fixed border of my sphere of vision, lying with his head lolling towards Funny-Mouth – in a trance similar to my own, I imagined – eyes staring at the drawn blinds on the compartment windows. I saw the lips of Pin-Stripe, out of the corner of my right eye, and those of Moustache, moving in almost perfect rhythm and imagined those of Other – as I had named the fourth who was completely out of my periphery of vision – doing the same, and heard the low and intricate liturgy which they were chanting in unison.

Liturgy? Tuscan rituals? Now what dark 'God' was this they worshipped? . . . And what had made *that* thought spring to my dreaming or hypnotized mind? And what was Moustache doing now?

He had a bag and was taking things from it, laying them delicately on the ceremonial table. Three items in all; in one corner of the table, that nearest Funny-Mouth. Round cakes of wheat-bread in the shape of wheels with ribbed spokes. Now who had written about offerings of round cakes of— . . . ?

Festus? Yes, *Festus* – but, again, in what connection?

Then I heard it. A *name*: chanted by the three worshippers, but not by Funny-Mouth who still sat aloofly upright.

'Summanus, Summanus, Summanus . . .' they chanted; and suddenly, it all clicked into place.

Summanus! Of whom Martianus Capella had written as being The Lord of Hell . . . I remembered now. It was Pliny who, in his *Natural History*, mentioned the dreaded *Tuscan Rituals*, 'books containing the Liturgy of Summanus . . .' Of course; Summanus – Monarch of Night – The Terror that Walketh in Darkness; Summanus, whose worshippers were so few and whose cult was surrounded with such mystery, fear, and secrecy that according to St Augustine even the most curious enquirer could discover no particular of it.

So Funny-Mouth, who stood so aloof to the ceremony in which the others were participating, must be a priest of the cult.

Though my eyes were fixed – my centre of vision being a picture, one of three, on the compartment wall just above Moustache's head – I could still clearly see Funny-Mouth's face and, as a blur to the left of my periphery, that of Jock.

The liturgy had come to an end with the calling of the 'God's' name and the offering of bread. For the first time Funny-Mouth seemed to be taking an interest. He turned his head to look at the table and just as I was certain that he was going to reach out and take the bread-cakes the train lurched and Jock slid sideways in his seat, his face coming into clearer perspective as it came to rest about half-way down Funny-Mouth's upper right arm. Funny-Mouth's head snapped round in a blur of hate. *Hate*, livid and pure, shone from those cold eyes, was reflected by the bristling eyebrows and tightening features; only the strange, painted-on mouth remained sterile of emotion. But he made no effort to move Jock's head.

It was not until later that I found out what happened then. Mercifully my eyes could not take in the whole of the compartment – or what was happening in it. I only knew that Jock's face, little more than an outline with darker, shaded areas defining the eyes, nose, and mouth at the lower rim of my fixed 'picture,' became suddenly contorted; twisted somehow, as though by some great emotion or pain. He said nothing, unable to break out of that damnable trance, but his eyes bulged horribly and his features writhed. If only I could have taken my eyes off him, or closed them even, to shut out the picture of his face writhing and Funny-Mouth staring at him so terribly. Then I noticed the change in Funny-Mouth. He had been a chalky-grey colour before; we all had, in the weak glow from the alternatively brightening and dimming compartment ceiling light. Now he seemed to be *flushed*; pinkish waves of unnatural colour were suffusing his outré features and his red-slit mouth was fading into the deepening blush of his face. It almost looked as though . . . *My God! He did not have a mouth.* With that unnatural reddening of his features the painted slit had vanished completely; his face was *blank* beneath the eyes and nose.

What a God-awful dream. I knew it must be a dream now – it *had* to be a dream – such things do not happen in real life. Dimly I was aware of Moustache putting the bread-cakes away and folding the queer table. I could feel the rhythm of the train slowing down. We must be coming into Grenloe. Jock's face was absolutely convulsed now. A white, twitching, jerking, bulge-eyed blur of hideous motion which grew paler as quickly as that of Funny-Mouth – if that name applied now – reddened. Suddenly Jock's face stopped its jerking. His mouth lolled open and his eyes slowly closed. He slid out of my circle of vision towards the floor.

The train was moving much slower and the wheels were clacking over those groups of criss-crossing rails which always warn one that a train is approaching a station or depot. Funny-Mouth had turned his monstrous, nightmare face towards me. He leaned across the aisle, closing the distance between us. I mentally screamed, physically incapable of the act, and strained with every fibre of my being to break from the trance which I suddenly knew beyond any doubting *was not a dream and never had been* . . .

The train ground to a shuddering halt with a wheeze of steam and a squeal of brakes. Outside in the night the station-master was yelling instructions to a porter on the unseen platform. As the train stopped Funny-Mouth was jerked momentarily back, away from me, and before he could bring his face close to mine again Moustache was speaking to him.

'There's no time, Master – this is our stop . . .' Funny-Mouth hovered over me a moment longer, seemingly undecided, then he pulled away. The others filed past him out into the corridor while he stood, tall and eerie, just within the doorway. Then he lifted his right hand and snapped his fingers.

I could move. I blinked my eyes rapidly and shook myself, sitting up straight, feeling the pain of the cramp between my shoulder-blades.

'I say . . .' I began.

'*Quiet!*' ordered that echoing voice from unknown spaces – and of course, his painted, false mouth never moved. I was right; I had been hypnotized, not dreaming at all. That false mouth – Walker in Darkness – Monarch of Night – Lord of Hell – the Liturgy to Summanus . . .

I opened my mouth in amazement and horror, but before I could utter more than one word – '*Summanus*' – *something happened.*

His waist-coat slid to one side near the bottom and a long, white, tapering tentacle with a blood-red tip slid into view. That tip hovered, snake-like, for a moment over my petrified face – and then struck. As if someone had taken a razor to it, my face opened up and the blood began to gush. I fell to my knees in shock, too terrified even to yell out, automatically reaching for my handkerchief; and when next I coweringly looked up, Funny-Mouth had gone.

Instead of seeing him – *It* – I found myself staring, from where I knelt dabbing uselessly at my face, into the slack features of the sleeping Jock.

Sleeping?

I began to scream. Even as the train started to pull out of the station I was screaming. When no one answered my cries, I managed to pull the communication-cord. Then, until they came to find out what was wrong, I went right on screaming. Not because of my face – *because of Jock* . . .

A jagged, bloody, two-inch hole led clean through his jacket and shirt and into his left side – the side which had been closest to . . . to that *thing – and there was not a drop of blood in his whole, limp body*. He simply lay there – half on, half off the seat – victim of 'a bleddy heathen ceremony' – substituted for the bread-cakes simply because the train had chosen an inopportune moment to lurch – a sacrifice to Summanus . . .

BACK ROW

I'll tell it exactly the way it happened.

They were showing a love story at the Odeon, a classic from years dead and all but forgotten. The first time I'd seen this picture had been with my wife – would you believe, thirty years ago? The picture had outlasted her, if not our love. Maybe that's why I wanted to see it again.

I picked a rainy Wednesday afternoon. No kids hooting and gibbering in the back rows, maybe a pair or two of lovers in the double seats back there, snuggling up to each other and blissfully, deliciously secure and secretive in the dark. I'd been young myself, once. But what with this ancient film and the middle of the week, and the miserable weather, the old Odeon should be just about empty; maybe a few dodderers like myself, down at the front where their eyes wouldn't feel the strain.

But not me, I'd be up in the gods, in the next but back row. Along with my memories, my eyes seemed to be the only things that hadn't faded on me.

I was there waiting for the doors to open, my collar turned up, a fifty-pence piece ready in my hand. That's one mercy: we oldies can get in cheap. Cheap? *Hah!* I remember when it was thruppence! And these two kids in front of me, why, they'd be paying maybe two pounds *each!* For a bit of privacy, if you can call it that, in a mouldy old flea-trap like the Odeon.

Behind me a handful of people had gathered: Darby and Joans, some of them, but mainly singles. Most of them were pensioners like myself, out chasing memories of their own, I supposed. And we all stood there waiting for the doors to open.

I had to look somewhere, and so I looked ahead of me, at these two kids. Well, I didn't actually look *at* them – I mean you don't, do you? I looked around them, over them, through them, the way you do. But something of them stuck to my mind – not very much, I'm afraid.

The lad would be eighteen, maybe nineteen, and the girl a couple of years younger. I didn't fix her face clearly, mind you, but she was what they call a looker: all pink and glowing, and a bit giggly, with a mass of shiny black hair under the hood of her bright red plastic rain-mac. White teeth and a stub of a nose, and eyes that sparkled when she smiled. A right Little Red Riding-Hood! And all of it in little more than sixty-two or -three inches; but then again they say nice things come in small packages. Damned if I could see what she saw in *him!* But she clung to him so close it was like he'd hypnotized her. And you know, I had to have a little smile to myself? Jealousy, at my age!

About the lad: he was pale, gangly – or 'gawky' as we'd say in my neck of the woods – hollow-cheeked; he looked like someone had been neglecting him. A good feed would fix him up no end. But it probably wouldn't fix the fishy, unblinking stare that came through those thick-lensed spectacles of his. He wore a black mac a bit small for him, which made his wrists stick out like pipe-stems. A matched couple? Hardly, but they do say that opposites attract . . .

Anyway, before I could look at them more closely, if I'd wanted to, we went in.

The Odeon's a dowdy place. It always has been. Twenty years ago it was dowdy, since when it's well past the point of no return. The glitter's gone, I'm afraid and no putting it back. But I'll say one thing for it: they've never called bingo there. When telly came in and the cinemas slumped, the old Odeon continued to show films; somehow it came through it, but not without its share of scars.

These days . . . well, you could plaster and paint all you liked, and you still wouldn't cover up all the wrinkles. It would be like an old woman putting on her war-paint: she'd still come out mutton dressed as lamb. But that's the old Odeon: even with the lights up full, the place seems so dim as to be almost misty. Misty, yes, with that clinging miasma of old places. Not haunted, no, but old and creaking and about ready to be pulled down. Or maybe my eyes weren't so good after all, or perhaps there's a layer of dust on the light-bulbs in the high ceiling . . .

I went upstairs (taking it easy, you know, and leaning on my stick a bit) and headed for my usual seat near the back. And sure enough the young 'uns were right there ahead of me, not in my row but the one behind, at the very back – all very quiet and coy, they were – where they'd chosen one of the double seats. But I hadn't noticed them buying sweets or popcorn at the kiosk in the shabby foyer, so maybe they'd stay that way right through the show: nice and quiet.

Other patrons came upstairs, all heading for the front where there was a little more leg-room and they could lean on the mahogany balcony and look down on the screen. When the lights started to go down in that slow way of theirs, there couldn't have been more than two dozen people in all up there, and most of them in the front two rows. Me and the kids, we had the back entirely to ourselves. It was a poor showing even for a Wednesday; maybe there'd be more people in the cheap seats downstairs.

In the old days this was the part I'd liked the best: the lights dimming, organ music (but only recorded, even in my time), and the curtains on stage slowly swishing open to reveal a dull, pearly, vacant screen. Then there'd be The Queen and the curtains would close again while the lights died completely. Followed by a supporting film, a cartoon, the trailers, and finally the feature film. Oh, yes – and between the cartoon and the main show there'd be an intermission, when the ice-cream ladies would come down the aisles with their trays. And at the end, The Queen again. Funny thing, but I can't go back as far as The King. I mean, I can, but my memory can't or won't! And even remembering what I can, I'm not sure I have it exactly right. That's what getting old does to you. Anyway, the whole thing from going in to coming out would last two and a half to maybe three whole hours! *That* was value.

Nowadays . . . you get the trailer, local advertisements, the feature film – and that's it. Or if you're lucky there *might* be a short supporting picture. And here's me saying I was surprised at the poor turnout.

Well, the trailers weren't much, and the local ads were totally colourless and not even up to date – Paul's Unisex Hairdressing Salon had shut down months ago! Then the briefest of brief intervals when the lights came half-way up; and suddenly it dawned on me that I hadn't heard a peep out of the young couple behind me in the back row. Well, maybe the very faintest whisper or giggle or two. Certainly nothing to complain about.

The seats were stepped down in tiers from the back to the balcony, so that my row of seats was maybe six inches lower than theirs. I sneaked a backward glance and my eyes trapped just a snapshot of the two sitting there very close, wasting half their seat, the girl crammed in one corner with the pale lad's black-clad arm thrown lightly round her red-clad shoulders. And his fish-eyes behind their thick lenses, swivelling to meet mine, expressionless but probably wishing I'd go away. Then it was dark again and the titles rolling, and me settling down to enjoy this old picture, along with one or two old-fashioned memories.

That was when it started; the carrying-on in the back row. Of course I had seen it coming: when I'd glanced back at them, those kids had still been wearing their rain-macs. You don't have to be a dirty old man to see through that old ploy. It's amazing what can go on – or come off – under a rain-mac.

Very soon buttons would slowly be giving way, one by one, to trembly, groping fingers under the shiny plastic; garments would be loosened, warm, naked flesh cautiously exposed – but not to view. No usherette's torch beam would find them out, and certainly not the prying eyes of some old duffer in the row in front. Indeed, the fact that I was there probably added to their excitement. It amused me to think of myself as a prop in their loveplay, a spanner in their wet works, whom they must somehow deceive even knowing that I wasn't deceived.

And all the time this sick-looking excuse for a youth pretending the exploratory hand had nothing to do with him, and the girl pretending to be completely unaware of its creeping advance toward her nipples. And they'd only be its first objective. All of this assuming, of course, that they were just beginners. Oh, yes – it's a funny business, love in the back row of a cinema.

First there was the heavy breathing. Ah, but there's heavy breathing and there's heavy breathing! And the moaning, very low at first but gradually becoming more than audible. I quickly changed my mind, restructured the scenario I'd devised for them. They weren't new to it, these two; by now *all* the buttons would be loose, and just about everything else for that matter! No exploratory work here. This was old ground, gone over many, many times before, together or with others; no prelude but a full-blown orchestration, which would gradually build to a crescendo.

Would they actually do it, I wondered? Right there in the back row? Fifteen minutes ago I'd seen myself as some sort of obstacle they'd have to overcome; now I was thinking they didn't give a damn about me, didn't care that I was there at all. I might as well not exist for these two, not here, not tonight. They had the darkness and each other – what the hell was the presence of one old man, who was probably deaf anyway?

A knee had found its way up onto the curved collar of my seat back; I felt its gentle pressure, then its vibration starting up like a mild electric current, building to a throb that came right through the wood and the padding to my shoulders. A knee-trembler, we'd called it in my day, when the body's passion is too great to be contained. And all the time the moaning increasing in pitch, until it rose just a little above the whirring of the projector where it aimed its white, flickering curtain of beams at the screen to form the moving pictures.

It dawned on me that I was a voyeur. Without even looking at them I was party to their every action. But an unwilling party . . . wasn't I? I had come here to watch a film, not to be caught up in the animal excitement of lusting lovers. And yet I was caught up in it!

They'd aroused me – *me*, an old man. With their panting and moaning and slobbering. I was sweating with their sweat and shaking with their vibrations; and all I could do was sit there, stricken and trembling like a man immobilized as by the touch of some strange female's hand in his most private place; yes, actually *feeling* as if some unknown woman had taken the seat next to mine and started to fondle me! That's how engrossed I had become with what was happening behind me, there in the back row.

Suddenly I was startled to realize that we were into the last reel. My God! – but what had happened here? Where had my film and my memories gone? A little bit of nostalgia was all I had wanted. And I'd missed it all, everything, because of them.

Them . . .

Why, I could even smell them now! Musty, sweet, sweaty, sexual, biological! I could *smell* sex! And a mouth gobbling away at flesh only inches from my ears! And a frantic gasping coming faster and faster, bringing pictures of some half-exhausted dog steaming away on a bitch!

Lovers? Animal excitement? They *were* animals! Young animals – and right now they were feasting on each other like . . . like vampires! Oh, I *suppose* you could call it petting, kissing, 'canoodling' – but it wasn't the kind I used to do. Not the kind me and my lass had indulged in, all those years ago. Kissing? I could hear them *sucking* at each other, foaming away like hard acid eating into soft wood. And suddenly I was angry.

Angry with myself, with them, with everything. The film had only fifteen minutes to run and everything felt . . . ruined. Well, now I'd ruin it for them. For him, anyway. *You won't come, you young bugger!* I thought. *You've denied me my pleasure, and now I'll deny you yours.*

Abruptly I turned the top half of my body, my head, and spat out: 'Now listen, you two—'

They were like one person, fused together, almost prone on their long seat. The hoods of their macs were up and crushed together, and I swear that I saw steam – the smoke of their sex – escaping from the darkness where their faces were locked like tightly-clasped hands. The slobbering stopped on the instant, and a moment later . . . I heard a growl!

No, a snarl! A warning not to interfere.

Oh, pale and sickly he might have seemed, but he was young and I was old. His bones would bend where mine would break like twigs. I could feel his contempt like a physical thing; I *had been* feeling it for the last ninety minutes. Of course, for who else but a contemptuous lout would have dared all of this with me sitting there right in front of him? And the girl was just as bad if not worse!

'I . . . I . . . I'm disgusted!' I mumbled. And then I quickly turned my face back to the screen, and watched the rest of the film through a wash of hot, shameful tears.

Just before the lights went up I thought I heard them leave. At least I heard light footsteps treading the carpet along the back row, receding. Of course it could be the girl, on her own, going to 'tidy herself up' in the Ladies. And because he might still be there behind me, sneering at me, I didn't look to see.

Then the film was over, and as the people down front began filing out, still I sat there. Because I could still feel someone behind me, hot and salty. Because it might be him and he'd look at me, fishy-eyed and threatening, through those steamed-up glasses of his.

Eventually I had to make a move. Maybe they'd both gone after all and I was just an old coward. I stood up, glanced into the back row, and saw—

God! What had he done to her?

The rain mac was open top to bottom. She – what was left of her – was slumped down inside it. There was very little flesh on her face, just raw red. Breasts had gone, right down to steaming ribs. The belly was open, eviscerated, a laid back gash that opened right down to the spread thighs. There were no innards, no sexual parts left at all down there. If I hadn't seen her before, I couldn't even have said it was a girl at all.

These were my thoughts before I noticed the true colour of the mac. I had only thought it was red at first glance, because my mind hadn't been able to accept so much red that wasn't plastic. And I saw his specs, crushed and broken on the blackened, blood-soaked baize of the double seat . . .

That's my statement, Sergeant, and there's nothing else I can tell you – except that there's something terrible loose in this town that eats living guts and looks like a pretty girl.

THE STRANGE YEARS

He lay face-down on the beach at the foot of a small dune, his face turned to one side, the summer sun beating down upon him. The clump of beach-grass at the top of the dune bent its spikes in a stiff breeze, but down here all was calm, with not even a seagull's cry to break in upon the lulling *hush, hush* of waves from far down the beach.

It would be nice, he thought, to run down the beach and splash in the sea, and come back dripping salt water and tasting it on his lips, and for the very briefest of moments be a small boy again in a world with a future. But the sun beat down from a blue sky and his limbs were leaden, and a great drowsiness was upon him.

Then . . . a disturbance. Blown on the breeze to climb the far side of the dune, flapping like a bird with broken wings, a slim book – a child's exercise book, with tables of weights and measures on the back – flopped down exhausted in the sand before his eyes. Disinterested, he found strength to push it away; but as his fingers touched it so its cover blew open to reveal pages written in a neat if shaky adult longhand.

He had nothing else to do, and so began to read . . .

'When did it begin? Where? How? Why?

'The Martians we might have expected (they've been frightening us long enough with their tales of invasion from outer space) and certainly there have been enough threats from our Comrades across the water. But this?'

'Any ordinary sort of plague, we would survive. We

always have in the past. And as for war: Christ! – when has there not been a war going on somewhere? They've irradiated us in Japan, defoliated us in Vietnam, smothered us in DDT wherever we were arable and poured poison into us where we once flowed sweet and clean – and we always bounced right back.

'Fire and flood – even nuclear fire and festering effluent – have not appreciably stopped us. For "They" read "We", Man, and for "Us" read "the World", this Earth which once was ours. Yes, there have been strange years, but never a one as strange as this.

'A penance? The ultimate penance? Or has Old Ma Nature finally decided to give us a hand? Perhaps she's stood off, watching us try our damnedest for so damned long to exterminate ourselves, and now She's sick to death of the whole damned scene. "OK," She says, "have it your own way." And She gives the nod to Her Brother, the Old Boy with the scythe. And He sighs and steps forward, and—

'And it is a plague of sorts; and certainly it is DOOM; and a fire that rages across the world and devours all . . . Or will that come later? The cleansing flame from which Life's bright phoenix shall rise again? There will always be the sea. And how many ages this time before something gets left by the tide, grows lungs, jumps up on its feet and walks . . . and reaches for a club?

'*When* did it begin?

'I remember an Irish stoker who came into a bar dirty and drunk. His sleeves were rolled up and he scratched at hairy arms. I thought it was the heat. "Hot? Damned right, sur," he said, "an' hotter by far down below – an' lousy!" He unrolled a newspaper on the bar and vigorously brushed at his matted forearm. Things fell on to the newsprint and moved, slowly. He popped them with a cigarette. "Crabs, sur!" he cried. "An' Christ – they suck like crazy!" '

'*When?*'

'There have always been strange years – plague years, drought years, war and wonder years – so it's difficult to pin it down. But the last twenty years . . . they have been *strange*. When, *exactly*? Who can say? But let's give it a shot. Let's start with the '70s – say, '76? – the drought.

'There was so little water in the Thames that they said the river was running backwards. The militants blamed the Soviets. New laws were introduced to conserve water. People were taken to court for watering flowers. Some idiot calculated that a pound of excreta could be satisfactorily washed away with six pints of water, and people put bricks in their WC cisterns. Someone else said you could bathe comfortably in four inches of water, and if you didn't use soap the resultant mud could be thrown on the garden. The thing snowballed into a national campaign to "Save It!" – and in October the skies were still cloudless, the earth parched, and imported rainmakers danced and pounded their tom-toms at Stonehenge. Forest and heath fires were daily occurrences and reservoirs became dustbowls. Sun-worshippers drank Coke and turned very brown . . .

'And finally it rained, and it rained, and it rained. Widespread flooding, rivers bursting their banks, gardens (deprived all summer) inundated and washed away. Millions of tons of water, and not a pound of excreta to be disposed of. A strange year, '76. And just about every year since, come to think.

'77, and stories leak out of the Ukraine of fifty thousand square miles turned brown and utterly barren in the space of a single week. Since then the spread has been very slow, but it hasn't stopped. The Russians blamed "us" and we accused "them" of testing a secret weapon.

"79 and '80, and oil tankers sinking or grounding themselves left, right and centre. Miles-long oil slicks and chemicals jettisoned at sea, and whales washed up on the beaches, and Greenpeace, and the Japanese slaughtering dolphins. Another drought, this time in Australia, and a plague of mice to boot. Some Aussie commenting that "The poor 'roos are dying in their thousands – and a few aboes, too . . ." And great green swarms of aphids and the skies bright with ladybirds.

'Lots of plagues, in fact. We were being warned, you see?

'And '84! Ah – 1984! Good old George!

'He was wrong, of course, for it wasn't Big Brother at all. It was Big Sister – Ma Nature Herself. And in 1984 She really started to go off the rails. '84 was half of India eaten by locusts and all of Africa down with a mutant strain of beriberi. '84 was the year of the poisoned potatoes and sinistral periwinkles, the year it rained frogs over wide areas of France, the year the cane-pest shot sugar beet right up to the top of the crops.

'And not only Ma Nature but Technology, too, came unstuck in '84. The Lake District chemically polluted – permanently; nuclear power stations at Loch Torr on one side of the Atlantic and Long Island on the other melting down almost simultaneously; the Americans bringing back a "bug" from Mars (see, even a *real* Martian invasion); oil discovered in the Mediterranean, and new fast-drilling techniques cracking the ocean floor and allowing it to leak and leak and leak – and even Red Adair shaking his head in dismay. How do you plug a leak two hundred fathoms deep and a mile long? And that jewel of oceans turning black, and Cyprus a great white tombstone in a lake of pitch. "Aphrodite Rising From The High-Grade."

'Then '85 and '86; and they were strange, too, because they were so damned quiet! The lull before the storm, so to speak. And then—'

'Then it was '87, '88 and '89. The American space-bug leaping to Australia and New Zealand and giving both places a monstrous malaise. No one doing any work for six months; cattle and sheep dead in their millions; entire cities and towns burning down because nobody bothered to call out the fire services, or they didn't bother to come . . . And all the world's beaches strewn with countless myriads of great dead octopuses, a new species (or a mutant strain) with three rows of suckers to each tentacle; and their stink utterly unbearable as they rotted. A plague of great, fat seagulls. All the major volcanoes erupting in unison. Meteoric debris making massive holes in the ionosphere. A new, killer-cancer caused by sunburn. The common cold cured! – and uncommon leprosy spreading like wildfire through the Western World.

'And finally—

'Well, that was "When?". It was also, I fancy, "Where?" and "How?". As to "Why" – I give a mental shrug. I'm tired, probably hungry. I have some sort of lethargy – the spacebug, I suppose – and I reckon it won't be long now. I had hoped that getting this down on paper might keep me active, mentally if not physically. But . . .

'*Why?*

'Well, I think I've answered that one, too.

'Ma Nature strikes back. Get rid of the human vermin. They're lousing up your planet! And maybe *that's* what gave Her the idea. If fire and flood and disease and disaster and war couldn't do the trick, well, what else could She do? They advise you to fight fire with fire, so why not vermin with vermin?

'They appeared almost overnight, five times larger than their immediate progenitors and growing bigger with each successive hatching; and unlike the new octopus they didn't die; and their incubation period down to less than a week. The superlice. All Man's little body parasites, all of his tiny, personal vampires, growing in the space of a month to things as big as your fist. Leaping things, flying things, walking sideways things. To quote a certain Irishman: "An' Christ – they suck like crazy!"'

31

'They've sucked, all right. They've sucked the world to death. New habits, new protections – new immunities and near-invulnerability – to go with their new size and strength. The meek inheriting the Earth? Stamp on them and they scurry away. Spray them with lethal chemicals and they bathe in them. Feed them DDT and they develop a taste for it. "An' Christ – they suck like crazy!"

'And the whole world down with the creeping, sleeping sickness. We didn't even *want* to fight them! Vampires, and they've learned new tricks. Camouflage . . . Clinging to walls above doors, they look like bricks or tiles. And when you go through the door . . . And their bite acts like a sort of LSD. Brings on mild hallucinations, a feeling of well-being, a kind of euphoria. In the cities, amongst the young, there were huge gangs of "bug-people!" My God!

'They use animals, too; dogs and cats – as mounts, to get them about when they're bloated. Oh, they kill them eventually, but they know how to use them first. Dogs can dig under walls and fences; cats can climb and squeeze through tiny openings; crows and other large birds can fly down on top of things and into places . . .

'Me, I was lucky – if you can call it that. A bachelor, two dogs, a parakeet and an outdoor aviary. My bungalow entirely netted in; fine wire netting, with trees, trellises and vines. And best of all situated on a wild stretch of the coast, away from mankind's great masses. But even so, it was only a matter of time.

'They came, found me, sat outside my house, outside the wire and the walls, and they waited. They found ways in. Dogs dug holes for them, seagulls tore at the mesh overhead. Frantically, I would trap, pour petrol, burn, listen to them pop! But I couldn't stay awake for ever. One by one they got the birds, leaving little empty bodies and bunches of feathers. And my dogs, Bill and Ben, which I had to shoot and burn. And this morning when I woke up, Peter parakeet.

'So there's at least one of them, probably two or three, here in the room with me right now. Hiding, waiting for night. Waiting for me to go to sleep. I've looked for them, of course, but—

'Chameleons, they fit perfectly into any background. When I move, they move. And they imitate perfectly. But they do make mistakes. A moment ago I had two hairbrushes, identical, and I only ever had one. Can you imagine brushing your hair with something like *that*? And what the hell would I want with *three* fluffy slippers? A left, a right – and a centre?

. . . I can see the beach from my window. And half a mile away, on the point, there's Carter's grocery. Not a crust in the kitchen. Dare I chance it? Do I want to? Let's see, now. Biscuits, coffee, powdered milk, canned beans, potatoes – no, strike the potatoes. A sack of carrots . . .'

The man on the beach grinned mirthlessly, white lips drawing back from his teeth and freezing there. A year ago he would have expected to read such in a book of horror fiction. But not now. Not when it was written in his own hand.

The breeze changed direction, blew on him, and the sand began to drift against his side. It blew in his eyes, glazed now and lifeless. The shadows lengthened as the sun started to dip down behind the dunes. His body grew cold.

Three hairy sacks with pincer feet, big as footballs and heavy with his blood, crawled slowly away from him along the beach . . .

KISS OF THE LAMIA

Bully boys out of Chlangi they were, desperadoes riding forth from that shunned city of yeggs and sharpers, on the lookout for quick profits in the narrow strip twixt Lohmi's peaks and the Desert of Sheb. And the lone Hrossak with his team of camels easy meat where they caught him in ambush, by the light of blind old Gleeth, god of the moon. Or at least, he *should* have been easy meat.

But the master and sole member of that tiniest of caravans was Tarra Khash, and meat were rarely so tough. For all his prowess, however (which one day would be legendary in all of Theem'hdra), the brawny bronze steppe-man was, on this occasion, caught short. With only the stump of a jewelled, ceremonial scimitar to defend himself, and nodding in the saddle as he let his mount pick out the way through badland rockpiles and gulleys, Tarra was hardly prepared for the three where they saw him coming and set their snare for him.

Indeed the first he knew of it was when a sighing arrow plunked through the polished leather of the scabbard across his back, sank an inch into his shoulder and near knocked him out of his saddle. Then, as a second feathered shaft whistled by his ear, he was off the camel and tumbling in dust and grit, his hand automatically grasping the jewelled hilt of his useless sword. In the darkness all was a chaos of shock and spurting blood and adrenalin; where wide awake now Tarra heard the terrified snorting and coughing of his beasts, huddled to avoid their kicking hooves as they ran off; where the moonlight silvered the stony bones of some ruined, long-deserted pile, and where the dust of Hrossak's fall was still settling as stealthy shadows crept in upon him.

Out of the leering dark they came, eyes greenly ablaze in greed and blood-lust, darting in the shadows, and fleet as the moonbeams themselves where the way was lit by Gleeth's cold light and by the blue sheen of far stars. Men of the night they were, as all such are, as one with the darkness and silhouetted dunes.

Tarra lay still, his head down, eyes slitted and peering; and in a little while a booted foot appeared silently before his face, and he heard a hoarse voice calling: 'Ho! He's finished – feathered, too! 'Twas my arrow nailed him! Come on, you two!'

Your arrow, hey, dog? Tarra silently snarled, coming from huddle to crouch, straightening and striking all in the same movement. The stump of his not-so-useless sword was a silver blur where it arced under a bearded jackal's chin, tearing out his taut throat even as he screamed: 'He's al – *ach-ach-ach!*'

Close behind the Hrossak, someone cursed and gripped the arrow in his back, twisting it sharply. He cried out his agony – cut off as a mountain crashed down on the back of his skull – and without further protest crumpled to the earth.

Tarra was not dead, not even unconscious, though very nearly so. Stunned he lay there, aware only of motion about him in the night, and of voices gruff as grit, coming it seemed from far, far away:

'Gumbat Chud was ever a great fool. "My arrow!" he yells, "my arrow!" And this fellow meanwhile slitting his throat nice as that!'

And a different voice: 'Is he dead?'

'Gumbat? Aye. See, he now has two mouths – and one of 'em scarlet!'

'Not him, no – the stranger.'

'Him too, I fancy, I gave him such a clout. I think it almost a shame, since he's done us such a favour. Why, with Gumbat gone there's just the two of us now to share the spoils! So waste no time on this one. If arrow and clout both haven't done for him, the badlands surely will. Come on, let's get after his beasts and see what goods he hauled.'

The other voice was harder, colder: 'Best finish him, Hylar. Why spoil a good night's work by leaving this one, perchance to tell the tale?'

'To whom? But . . . I suppose you're right, Thull. We have had a good night, haven't we? First that girl, alone in the desert, wandering under the stars. Can you believe it?'

A coarse chuckle. 'Oh, I believe it, all right. I was first with her, remember?'

'You were last with her, too – pig!' spat the first voice. 'Well, get on with it, then. If you want this fellow dead, get it done. We've beasts to chase and miles to cover back to Chlangi. Pull out the arrow, that'll do for him. His life – if any's left – will leak out red as wine!'

Thull did as Hylar suggested, and shuddering as fresh waves of agony dragged him under, the Hrossak's mind shrank down into pits of the very blackest jet . . .

Tarra Khash, the Hrossak, inveterate wanderer and adventurer, had a lust for life which drove him ever on where other men would fail. And it was that bright spark, that tenacious insistence upon life, which now roused him up before he could bleed to death. That and the wet, frothy ministrations of his camel, kneeling beside him in starlit ruins, where it washed his face and grunted its camel queries. This was the animal Tarra had used as mount, which, over the two hundred miles now lying in their wake, had grown inordinately fond of him. Eluding its pursuers, it had returned to its master much as a dog might do, and for the past half-hour had licked his face, kneed him in the ribs, and generally done whatever a camel might for a man.

Finally coming awake, Tarra gave its nose an admonitory slap and propped himself up into a seated position. He was cold but his back felt warm, stiff and sticky; aye, and he could feel a trickle of fresh blood where his movements had cracked open a half-formed scab. In the dirt close at hand lay the man he'd killed, Gumbat Chud, and between them a bloody arrow where it had been wrenched from his back and thrown down. Tarra's scabbard lay within reach, empty of its broken sword. They'd taken it for its jewels, of course.

Staring at the arrow, his blood dry on its point, Tarra remembered the conversation he'd heard before he blacked out. He especially remembered the names of the two who had stood over him: Hylar and Thull, Gumbat Chud's bandit brothers. Rogues out of Chlangi, aye – and dead ones when he caught up with them!

But for now . . . the Hrossak was fortunate and he knew it. Only a most unlikely set of circumstances had spared him. The ambushers might easily have slit his throat, but they hadn't wanted to waste time. Indeed, Chud's arrow might have missed the scabbard and hit his heart, which would have ended things at once! Also, the reavers could have caught instead his camel – this one, which carried food, water, blankets, all those things necessary for the maintenance of life – and probably had caught the three pack animals, which were far more heavily laden.

Heavily laden indeed!

Tarra thought about all the gold and jewels those animals carried: twelve full saddle bags! And wouldn't those badland marauders lose their eyeballs when they turned them on that lot! What a haul! Tarra almost wished he was one of his ambushers – except that wasn't his line of work. Ah,

40

well: easy come, easy go – for now. Until he caught up with those two. Anyway, it was his own fault. Only a damn fool would have tried to take a king's ransom through a den of thieves and out the other side. And he'd known well enough Chlangi's reputation.

Tomb-loot – *hah!* Ill-gotten gains. And hadn't his father always warned him that anything you didn't work hard for wasn't worth having? Trouble was, he'd never heeded his father anyway. Also, he *had* worked hard for it. Damned hard! He thought of the subterranean sarcophagi of ancient, alien kings whose tombs were a source of loot – and of his narrow escape from that place – and shuddered. And again: tomb-loot, *hah!*

Tarra's head argued with his back as to which of them hurt worst. Climbing groggily to his feet, he gently shrugged his blanket robe from his shoulders, wincing a little where it had adhered to drying scab of blood, then washed the wound as best he could with clean water from a skin in the camel's packs. The arrow had not gone deep; his broken sword's leather scabbard had saved him. Now he wrapped that scabbard in a soft cloth and re-strapped it tight in former position across his back, thus staunching the flow of blood. Then . . . a kerchief soaked in water round his head, and a bite of dried meat and gulp of sour wine, and Tarra was ready to take up the chase. It wasn't a wise pursuit, he knew – indeed it might well be the last thing he ever did – but that's the way it was with Tarra Khash. Hylar and Thull, whoever they were, had hurt him deliberately and for no good reason, and now he would hurt them. Or die trying . . .

The night was still young, not long past the midnight hour, when he struggled up into his mount's ridgy saddle and goaded the beast once more in the direction of Chlangi, cursing low under his breath as each smallest jolt set his head to ringing and his back to dull, angry throbbing. And

41

so, at a pace only a little faster than walking, Tarra Khash, the Hrossak journeyed again under moon and stars.

He went wary now, his eyes tuned to the night, but for a mile or two there was nothing. Then—

Tarra was not aware what it was *exactly* which drew his eyes to the cross lying silvered on the side of a dune; in other circumstances (were his senses not so alert for strange smells, sights or sounds) then he might have passed it by. It could have been a figure of white stone, or a scattering of bones, or simply the bleached roots of an olive or carob tree long drowned in the desert's ergs and sandpapered to a reflective whiteness; but whichever, he turned his camel's head that way.

And as he drew closer . . . what he saw then brought him down from the back of his beast in a blur of painful motion, tossing his blanket over the naked, ravaged figure of a girl pegged down on the gentle slope of the dune. A moment more and he pressed water-soaked kerchief to cracked, puffed lips, then breathed a sigh of relief as the girl's throat convulsed in a choke, and breathed more deeply as she first shook her head and finally sucked at the cloth where he held it to her mouth. Then she gazed at Tarra through eyes bruised as fallen fruit and dusted with fine sand, wriggled a little way back from him, affrightedly, and tried to ask:

'Who—?'

But he cut her off with, '*Shh!* Be still. I'll not harm you.'

Even as she continued to cringe from him, he tore up the long pegs and ties which bound her to the earth and broke them, then wiped her fevered face with damp rag and wrapped her in the blanket. A moment later and she lay across the camel's saddle, face down, while he swiftly led the beast from this brutal place in search of some rude shelter.

In a little while he found low, broken walls with sand drifted against them, and to one of these pegged a sheet of tentage to form a refuge. Therein he lay the unprotesting girl and propped up her head so that she could watch him while he built a fire in the lee of the wall just outside the tent. Over the fire he boiled up soup from a pouch of herbs and dried vegetables, and likewise fried several near-rancid strips of bacon in their own fat on a flat stone until they were crisp and sweet. These he offered to the girl, but having merely tasted the soup and sniffed at the bacon she then refused both, offering a little shake of her head.

'Well, I'm sorry, lass,' Tarra told her, squatting down and satisfying his own hunger, 'but this is the best I can do. If you're used to finer fare I'm sure I don't know where I'll find it for you in these parts!' He went to the camel and brought her the last of his wine, and this she accepted, draining the skin to the last drop. Then, while Tarra finished his food she watched him closely, so that he was ever aware of her eyes upon him. For his own part, however obliquely, he watched her, too.

He little doubted that this was the girl those curs out of Chlangi had laughed about, which in itself would form a bond between them, who had both suffered at the hands of those dogs; but just as the bandits had done before him, he too marvelled at the mystery of it: a girl like this, wandering alone beneath the stars in so desolate a place. She seemed to read his thoughts, and said:

'I make . . . a pilgrimage. It is a requirement of my . . . order, that once in a five-year I go to a secret place in the Nameless Desert, there to renew my . . . vows.'

Tarra nodded. 'Who is your god?' he asked, thinking: *for he's let you down sorely this night, and no mistake!*

'His name is . . . secret,' she answered in a moment. 'I may not divulge it.'

'Myself,' said Tarra, 'I'm partial to Old Gleeth, blind god of the moon. He's out tonight in all his glory – do you see?'

And he lifted up the skirt of the tent, so that moonbeams fell within. The girl shrank back into shadow.

'The light,' she said. 'So silvery . . . bright.'

Tarra let fall the flap, sat staring at her through eyes narrowed just a fraction. 'Also,' he said, 'I'll not have anything said against Ahorra Izz, god of—'

'—scarlet scorpions,' she finished it for him, the hint of a hiss in her voice.

Slowly Tarra nodded. 'He's a rare one,' he said, 'Ahorra Izz. I wouldn't have thought many would know of him. Least of all a young sister of—'

'In my studies,' she whispered, cutting him off, 'I have concerned myself with all the gods, ancient and modern, of all the peoples of Theem'hdra. A god is a god, black or white – or scarlet. For how may one conceive of Good if one has no knowledge of Evil?'

And vice versa, thought Tarra, but he answered: 'How indeed? Truth to tell, I didn't find Ahorra Izz at all evil. In fact I'm in his debt!'

Before he could say more or frame another question, she asked: 'Who are you?'

'Tarra Khash,' he answered at once, in manner typically open. 'A Hrossak. I was set upon by the same pack of hairies who . . . happened your way. They robbed me. Aye, and they put an arrow in my back, too. Hence my stiffness. I was tracking them back to Chlangi when I found you. Which makes you a complication. Now I have your skin to consider as well as my own. Mine's not worth a lot to anyone, but yours . . . ?' He shrugged.

She sat up, more stiffly than Tarra, and the blanket fell away from her. Under the bruises she was incredibly lovely. Her beauty was . . . unearthly.

'Come,' she held out a marble arm. 'Let me see your back.'

'What can you do?' he asked. 'It's a hole, that's all.' But he went to her anyway. On hands and knees he looked at her, close up, then turned his back and sat down. He unfastened the straps holding his empty scabbard in place, and her hands were so gentle he didn't even feel her take the scabbard away.

And anyway – what *could* she do? She had no unguents or salves, not even a vinegar-soaked pad.

And yet . . . Tarra relaxed, sighed, felt the pain going out of his shoulder as easy as the air went out of his lungs. Well, now he knew what she could do. Ointments, balms? – *hah!* She had fingers, didn't she? And now Tarra believed he knew her order: she was a healer, a very special sort of physician, a layer on of hands. He'd heard of such but never seen one at work, never really believed. But seeing – or rather, feeling – was believing!

'A pity you can't do this for yourself,' he told her.

'Oh, I shall heal, Tarra Khash,' she answered, her voice sibilant. 'Out there in the desert, under the full moon, I was helpless, taken by surprise no less than you. Now I grow stronger. Your strength has become mine. For this I thank you.'

Tarra's voice was gruff now. 'Huh! If you'd take some food you'd grow stronger faster!'

'There is food and food, Tarra Khash,' she answered, her voice hypnotic in its caress. 'For all you have offered, I am grateful.'

Tarra's senses were suddenly awash in warm, languid currents. Her hands had moved from his shoulder to his neck, where now they drew out every last trace of tension. Her head on his shoulder, she cradled his back with her naked breasts. He slumped – and at once jerked his head erect, or tried to. What had she been saying? Grateful for what he'd offered? 'You're welcome to whatever I have,' he mumbled, scarcely aware of her sharp intake of breath. 'Not that there's much . . .'

'Oh, but there is! There is!' she whispered. 'Much more

than I need, and though I'm hungry I shall take very little. Sleep now, sleep little mortal, and when you wake seek out those men and take your vengeance – while yet you may. For if I find them first there'll be precious little left for you!'

Sweet sister of mercy? A healer? Layer on of hands? Nay, none of these. Even sinking into uneasy slumbers, Tarra tried to turn his drowsy head and look at her, and failed. But he did force out one final question: '*Who . . . are you?*'

She lifted her mouth from his neck and his blood was fresh on her pale lips. 'My name is Orbiquita!' she said – which was the last thing he heard before the darkness rolled over him. The last thing he *felt* was her hot, salty kiss . . .

'Lamia!' snapped Arenith Han, seer and rune-caster to the robber-king, Fregg, of doomed Chlangi. 'She was a lamia, a man-lusting demon of the desert. You two are lucky to be alive!'

It was Fregg's dawn court, held in the open courtyard of his 'palace', once a splendid place but now a sagging pile in keeping with most of Chlangi's buildings. Only the massive outer walls of the city itself were undecayed, for Fregg insisted that they at least be kept in good order. To this end he used 'felons' from his court sessions, on those rare occasions when such escaped his 'justice' with their lives intact.

Chlangi's monarch was one Fregg Unst, a failed con man long, long ago hounded out of Klühn on the coast for his frauds and fakeries. His subjects – in no wise nicer persons than Fregg himself – were a rabble of yeggs, sharpers, scabby whores and their pimps, unscrupulous taverners and other degenerates and riff-raff blown here on the winds of chance, or else fled from justice to Chlangi's doubtful refuge. And doubtful it was.

Chlangi the Doomed – or the Shunned City, as it is elsewhere known – well deserved these doleful titles. For of all places of ill-repute, this were perhaps the most notorious in all the Primal Land. And yet it had not always been this way.

In its heyday the city had been opulent, its streets and markets bustling with merchants, its honest taverners selling vintages renowned throughout the land for their clean sweetness. With lofty domes and spires all gilded over, walls high and white, and roofs red with tiles baked in the ovens of Chlangi's busy builders, the city had been the veriest jewel of Theem'hdra's cities. Aye, and its magistrates had had little time for members of the limited criminal element.

Now . . . all good and honest men shunned the place, and had done so since first the lamia Orbiquita builded her castle in the Desert of Sheb. Now the gold had been stripped from all the rich roofs, the grapevines had returned to the wild, producing only small, sour grapes and flattening their rotten trellises, arches and walls had toppled into disrepair, and the scummy water of a many-fractured aqueduct was suspect indeed. Only the rabble horde and their robber-king now lived here, and outside the walls a handful of hungry, outcast beggars.

Now, too, Fregg kept the land around well scouted, where day and night men of his were out patrolling in the badlands and along the fringe of the desert, intent upon thievery and murder. Occasionally there were caravans out of Eyphra or Klühn; or more rarely parties of prospectors out of Klühn headed for the Mountains of Lohmi, or returning therefrom; and exceeding rare indeed lone wanderers and adventurers who had simply strayed this way. Which must surely elevate the occurrences of last night almost to the fabulous. Fabulous in Fregg's eyes, anyway, which was one of the reasons he had brought his scouts of yester-eve to morning court.

Their tale had been so full of fantastic incident that Fregg could only consider it a fabrication, and the tale wasn't all he found suspect.

Now the court was packed; battle-scarred brigands rubbed shoulders with nimble thieves and cut-throats, and Fregg's own lieutenants formed a surly jury whose only concern was to 'get the thing over, the accused hanged, and on with the day's gaming, scheming and back-stabbing.' Which did not bode well for transgressors against Fregg's laws!

Actually, those laws were simple in the extreme:

Monies and goods within the city would circulate according to barter and business, with each man taking his risks and living, subsisting or existing in accordance with his acumen. Monies and so on. from without would be divided half to Fregg and his heirs, one third to the reaver or reavers clever enough to capture and bring it in, and the remaining one sixth part to the city in general, to circulate as it might. More a code than a written law proper. There was only one real law and it was this: Fregg's subjects could rob, cheat, even kill each other; they could sell their swords, souls or bodies; they could bully, booze and brawl all they liked and then some . . . *except* where it would be to annoy, inconvenience, pre-empt or otherwise interfere with, or displease, Fregg. Simple.

Which meant that on this occasion, in some way as yet unexplained, last night's far-scavenging scouts had indeed displeased Fregg; a very strange circumstance, considering the fantastic haul they'd brought back for him!

Now they were here, dragged before Fregg's 'courtiers' and 'council' and 'jury' for whatever form of inquisition he had in mind, and Arenith Han – a half-breed wizard of doubtful dexterity, one time necromancer and failed alchemist in black Yhem, now Fregg's right-hand man – had opened the proceedings with his startling revelation.

'What say you?' Burly, bearded Fregg turned a little on

his wooden stool of office behind a squat wooden table, to peer at his wizard with raised eyebrows. 'Lamia? This girl they ravaged was a lamia? Where's your evidence?'

Central in the courtyard, where they were obliged to stand facing into a sun not long risen, Hylar Arf and Thull Drinnis shuffled and grimaced, surly at Fregg's treatment of them. But no use to protest, not at this stage; they were here and so must face up to whatever charge Fregg brought against them. The fallen wizard's examination of their spoils, and his deductions concerning the same and the nature of at least one of their previous owners, that was simply for openers, all part of the game.

Sharing space in the central area were two camels, a pair of white yaks and, upon the ground, blankets bearing various items. Upon one: tatters of sorely dishevelled female apparel; upon the other, eight saddle bags, their contents emptied out in a pile of gleam and glitter and golden, glancing fire. Treasure enough to satisfy even the most avaricious heart – almost. Probably. Possibly.

'Observe!' Arenith Han, a spidery, shrivelled person in a worn, rune-embellished cloak scuttled about, prodding the yaks and examining their gear. 'Observe the rig of these beasts – especially this one. Have you ever seen the like? A houdah fixed upon the back of a yak? A *houdah*? Now, some tiny princess of sophisticate kingdom might well ride such gentle, canopied beast through the gardens of her father's palace – for her pleasure, under close scrutiny of eunuchs and guards – and the tasselled shade to protect her precious skin from sun's bright ray. But here, in the desert, the badlands, the merest trajectory of a good hard spit away from Chlangi's walls? Unlikely! And yet so it would appear to be . . .'

He turned and squinted at the uncomfortable ruffians. 'Just such a princess, our friends here avow, was out riding in the desert last night. She rode upon this yak, beneath this shade, while the other beast carried her toiletries and trinkets, her prettiest things, which is in the nature of princesses when they go abroad: frivolously to take small items of comfort with them. Ah! – but I have *examined* the beasts' packs. Behold!'

He scattered what was contained in the packs on to the dust and cracked flags of the courtyard – contents proving to be, with one exception, ample handfuls of loamy soil – stooped to pick up the single extraneous item, and held it up. 'A book,' he said. 'A leather-bound rune-book. A book of spells!'

Oohs! and *Aahs!* went up from the assemblage, but Han held up a finger for silence. 'And *such* spells!' he continued. 'They are runes of transformation, whose purpose I recognize e'en though I cannot read the glyphs in which they're couched – for of course they're writ in the lamia tongue! As to their function: they permit the user to alter her form at will, becoming a bat, a dragon, a serpent, a hag, a wolf, a toad – even a beautiful girl!'

Hylar Arf, a hulking Northman with mane of blue-black hair bristling the length of his spine, had heard enough. Usually jovial – especially when in a killing mood – his laughter now welled up in a great booming eruption of sound. One-handed, he picked the skinny sorcerer up by the neck and dangled him before the court. 'This old twig's a charlatan!' he derided. 'Can't you all see that? Why! – here's Thull Drinnis and me alive and kicking, no harm befallen us – and this fool says the girl was lamia? *Bah!* We took her yaks and we took *her*, too – all three of us, before Gumbat Chud, great fool, got himself slain – and you can believe me when I tell you it was *girl*-flesh we had, sweet and juicy. Indeed, because he's a pig, Thull here had her twice! He was both first and last with her; and does he look any the worse for wear?'

'We're not pleased!' Fregg came to his feet, huge and

round as a boulder. 'Put down our trusted sorcerer at once!' Hylar Arf spat in the dust but did as Fregg commanded, setting Arenith Han upon his feet to stagger to and fro, clutching at his throat.

'Continue,' Fregg nodded his approval.

The wizard got well away from the two accused and found the fluted stone stump of an old column to sit on. Still massaging his throat, he once more took up the thread – or attempted to:

'About . . . lamias,' he choked. And: 'Wine, wine!' A court attendant took him a skin, from which he drank deeply. And in a little while, but hurriedly now and eager to be done with it:

'About lamias. They are desert demons, female, daughters of the pit. Spawned of unnatural union be-twixt, *ahem*, say a sorcerer and a succubus – or perhaps a witch and incubus – the lamia is half-caste. Well, I myself am a "breed" and see little harm in that; but in the case of a lamia things are very much different. The woman in her lusts after men for satisfaction, the demon part for other reasons. Men who have bedded lamias and survived are singularly rare – but *not* fabulous, not unheard of! Mylakhrion himself is said to have had several.'

Fregg was fascinated. Having seated himself again following Hylar Arf's outburst, he now leaned forward. 'All very interesting,' he said. 'We would know more. We would know, for example, just exactly *how* these two escaped with their lives from lamia's clutches. For whereas the near-immortal Mylakhrion was – some might say "is" – a legended magician, these men are merely—' (he sniffed) '—*men*. And pretty scabby specimens of men at that!'

'Majesty,' said Arenith Han, 'I am in complete agreement with your assessment of this pair. Aye, and Gumbat Chud was cut, I fear, of much the same cloth. But first let me say a little more on the nature of lamias, when all should become quite clear.'

'Say on,' Fregg nodded.

'Very well.' Han stood up from column seat, commenced to pace, kept well away from the hulking barbarian and his thin, grim-faced colleague. 'Even lamias, monstrous creatures that they are, have their weaknesses; one of which, as stated, is that they lust after men. Another is this: that once in a five-year their powers wane, when they must needs take them off to a secret place deep in the desert, *genius loci* of lamias, and there perform rites of renewal. During such periods, being *un*-natural creatures, all things of nature are a bane, a veritable poison to them. At the very best of times they cannot abide the sun's clean light – in which abhorrence they are akin to ghouls and vampires – but at the height of the five-year cycle the sun is not merely loathed but lethal in the extreme! Hence they must needs travel by night. And because the moon is also a thing of nature, Old Gleeth in his full is likewise a torment to them, whose cold silvery light will scorch and blister them even as the sun burns men!'

'Ah!' Fregg came once more erect in his seat. He leaned forward, great knuckles supporting him where he planted them firmly on the table before him. 'The houdah on the yak!' And he nodded, 'Yes, yes – I see!'

'Certainly,' Arenith Han smiled. 'It is a shade against the moon – which was full last night, as you know well enow.'

Fregg sat down with a thump, banged upon the table with heavy hand, said: 'Good, Han, good! And what else do you divine?'

'Two more things, Majesty,' answered the mage, his voice low now. 'First, observe the contents of her saddle bags: largely, soil! And does not the lamia, like the vampire, carry her native earth with her for bed? Aye, for she likes to lie

down in the same charnel earth which her own vileness has
cursed . . .'

'And finally?' Fregg grunted.

'Finally – observe the *motif* graven in the leather of the
saddle bags, and embroidered into the canopy of yon
houdah, and blazoned upon binding of rune-book.
And . . .' Han narrowed his eyes, '—carved in the jade
inset which Thull Drinnis even now wears in the ring of
gold on the smallest finger of his left hand! *Is it not indeed
the skull and serpent crest of the Lamia Orbiquita herself?'*

Thull Drinnis, a weaselish ex-Klühnite, at once thrust his
left hand deep into the pocket of his baggy breeks, but not
before everyone had seen the ring of which the wizard made
mention. In the stony silence which ensued, Drinnis realized
his error – his admittance of guilt of sorts – and knew that
was not the way to go. So now he drew his hand into view
and held it up so that the sun flashed from burnished gold.

'A trinket!' he cried. 'I took it from her and I claim it as a
portion of my share. What's wrong with that? Now enough
of this folly. Why are we here, Hylar and me? Last night we
brought more wealth into this place than was ever dreamed
of. Chlangi's share alone will make each man and dog of
you rich!'

'He's right!' Hylar Arf took up the cry. 'All of you rich –
or else—' he turned accusingly to Fregg, '—or else our
noble king would take it all for himself!'

And again the stony silence, but this time directed at
Fregg where he sat upon his stool of office at his table of
judgement. But Fregg was wily, more than a match for two
such as Arf and Drinnis, and he was playing this game with
loaded dice. Now he decided the time was ripe to let those
dice roll. He once again came to his feet.

'People of Chlangi,' he said. 'Loyal subjects. It appears to
me that there are three things here to be taken into
consideration. Three, er – shall we say "discrepancies"? –

upon which, when they are resolved, Hylar and Thull's guilt or innocence shall be seen to hang. Now, since my own interest in these matters has been brought into question, I shall merely present the facts as we know them, and you – *all* of you – shall decide the outcome. A strange day indeed, but nevertheless I now put aside my jury, my wizard, even my own perhaps self-serving opinions in this matter, and let *you* make the decision.' He paused.

'Very well, these are the facts:

'For long and long the laws of Chlangi have stood, and they have served us moderately well. One of these laws states that all – I repeat *all* – goods of value stolen without and fetched within these walls are to be divided in pre-determined fashion: half to me, Chlangi's rightful king, one third to them responsible for the catch, the remainder to the city. And so to the first discrepancy. Thull Drinnis here has seen fit to apportion himself a little more than his proper share, namely the ring upon his finger.'

'A trinket, as he himself pointed out!' someone at the back of the crowd cried.

'But a trinket of value,' answered Fregg, 'whose worth would feed a man for a six-month! Let me say on:

'The second "discrepancy" – and one upon which the livelihoods and likely the very lives of each and every one of us depends – is this: that if what we have heard is true, good Hylar and clever Thull here have rid these parts forever of a terrible bane, namely the Lamia Orbiquita.'

'Well done, lads!' the cry went up. And: 'What's that for a discrepancy?' While someone else shouted, 'The monster's dead at last!'

'*Hold!*' Fregg bellowed. 'We do not know that she is dead – and it were better for all if she is not! Wizard,' he turned to Arenith Han, 'what say you? They beat her, ravished her, pegged her out under the moon. Would she survive all that?'

'The beating and raping, aye,' answered Han. 'Very likely

she would. The staking out 'neath a full bright Gleeth: that would be sore painful, would surely weaken her nigh unto death. And by now—' he squinted at the sun riding up out of the east. 'Now in the searing rays of the sun – now she is surely dead!'

'Hoorah!' several in the crowd shouted.

When there was silence Fregg stared all around. And sadly he shook his head. 'Hoorah, is it? And how long before word of this reaches the outside world, eh? How long before the tale finds its way to Klühn and Eyphra, Yhem and Khrissa and all the villages and settlements between? Have you forgotten? Chlangi the Shunned – this very Chlangi the Doomed – was once Chlangi the bright, Chlangi the beautiful! Oh, all very well to let a handful of outcast criminals run the place now, where no right-minded decent citizen would be found dead; but with Orbiquita gone, her sphere of evil ensorcelment removed forever, how long before some great monarch and his generals decide it were time to bring back Chlangi within the fold, to make her an honest city again? Not long, you may rely upon it! And what of *your* livelihoods then? And what of *your* lives? Why, there's a price on the head of every last one of you!'

No cries of 'bravo' now from the spectators but only the hushed whispers of dawning realization, and at last a sullen silence which acknowledged the ring of truth in Fregg's words.

And in the midst of this silence:

'We killed a lamia!' Hylar Arf blustered. 'Why, all of Theem'hdra stands in our debt!'

'Theem'hdra, aye,' answered Fregg, his voice doomful. 'But not Chlangi, and certainly not her present citizens.'

'But—' Thull Drinnis would have taken up the argument.

'—But we come now to the third and perhaps greatest discrepancy,' Fregg cut him off. 'Good Thull and Hylar returned last night with vast treasure, all loaded on these camels here and now displayed upon the blanket for all to see. And then they took themselves off to Dilquay Noth's brothel and drank and whored the night away, and talked of how, with their share, they'd get off to Thandopolis and set up in legitimate business, and live out their lives in luxury undreamed . . .

'But being a suspicious man, and having had news of this fine scheme of theirs brought back to me, I thought: 'What? And are they so displeased with Chlangi, then, that they must be off at once and gone from us? Or is there something I do not yet know? And I sent out trackers into the badlands to find what they could find.'

(Thull and Hylar, until this moment showing only a little disquietude, now became greatly agitated, fingering their swords and peering this way and that. Fregg saw this and smiled, however grimly, before continuing.)

'And lo! – at a small oasis known only to a few of us, what should my trackers find there but a *third* beast, the very brother of these two here – and four more saddle bags packed with choicest items!' He clapped his great hands and the crowd gave way to let through a pair of dusty mountain men, leading into view the beast in question.

'We are all rich, all of us!' cried Fregg over the crowd's rising hum of excitement and outrage. 'Aye, and after the share has been made, now we can *all* leave Chlangi for lands of our choice. That is to say, all save these two . . .'

Thull Drinnis and Hylar Arf waited no longer. The game was up. They were done for. They knew it.

As a man they went for Fregg, swords singing from scabbards, lips drawn back in snarls from clenched teeth. And up on to his table they leaped, their blades raised on high – but before they could strike there came a great sighing of arrows which stopped them dead in their tracks. From above and behind Fregg on the courtyard walls, a party of crossbowmen had opened up, and their massed bolts not only transfixed the cheating pair but knocked them down from the table like swatted flies. They were dead before they hit the ground.

Fregg gently took it from him. 'But I *do* mind, Tarra Khash!'

'But—'

'Wait, lad, hear me out. See, I've nothing against you, but you simply don't understand our laws. You see, upon the instant loot is brought into the city, said loot belongs to me, its finders, and to the city itself. And no law at all, I'm afraid, to cover its retrieval by rightful owner. Not even the smallest part of it. Also, I perceive these stones set in the hilt to be valuable, a small treasure in themselves.' He shrugged almost apologetically, adding: 'No, I'm sorry, lad, but at least two men – and likely a good many more – have died for this little lot. And so—' And he tossed the jewelled hilt back with the other gems.

'Actually,' Tarra chewed his lip, eyed the swords and crossbows of Fregg's bodyguards, 'actually it's the hilt I treasure more than the stones. Before it was broken there were times that sword saved my miserable life!'

'Ah!' said Fregg. 'It has sentimental value, has it? Why didn't you say so? You shall have it back, of course! Only come to me tonight, in my counting room atop the tower, and after I've prised out the stones, then the broken blade is yours. It seems the least I can do. And my thanks, for in your way you've already answered a riddle I'd have asked of you.'

'Oh?' Tarra raised an eyebrow.

'Indeed. For if you were rightful owner of this hoard in the first place, why surely you'd agonize more over the bulk of the stuff than the mere stump of a sword, not so?'

Tarra shrugged, grinned, winked, and tapped the side of his nose with forefinger. 'No wonder you're king here,

Fregg. Aye, and again you've gauged your man aright, I fear.'

Fregg roared with laughter. 'Good, good!' he chortled. 'Very good. So you're a reaver, too, eh? Well, and what's a reaver if not an adventurer, which is what you said you were? You took this lot from a caravan, I suppose? No mean feat for a lone wanderer, even a brave and brawny Hrossak.'

'You flatter me,' Tarra protested, and lied: 'No, there were ten of us. The men of the caravan fought hard and died well, and I was left with treasure.'

'Well then,' said Fregg. 'In that case you'll not take it so badly. It seems you're better off to the extent of one camel. As for the treasure: it was someone else's, became yours, and now has become mine – er, Chlangi's.'

Tarra sucked his teeth. 'So it would seem,' he said.

'Aye,' Fregg nodded. 'So count your blessings and go on your way. Chlangi welcomes you if you choose to stay, will not detain you should you decide to move on. The choice is yours.'

'Your hospitality overwhelms me,' said Tarra. 'If I had the change I'd celebrate our meeting with a meal and a drink.'

'Pauper, are you?' said Fregg, seeming surprised. And: 'What, penniless, an enterprising lad like you? Anyway, I'd warn you off Chlangi's taverns. Me, I kill my own meat and brew my own wine! But if you're desperately short you can always sell your blanket. Your camel will keep you warm nights . . .' And off he strode, laughing.

Which seemed to be an end to that.

Almost . . .

Tarra was one of the last to pass out through the courtyard's gates, which were closed at once on his heels. On his way he'd given the place a narrow-eyed once-over, especially the tumbledown main building and its central tower. So that standing there outside the iron-banded gates, staring up thoughtfully at the high walls, he was startled when a voice barked in his ear:

'Hrossak, I overheard your conversation with Fregg. Quickly now, tell me, d'you want a meal and a wineskin? And then maybe a safe place to rest your head until tonight? For if your're thinking of leaving, it would be sheerest folly to try it in broad daylight, despite what Fregg says!'

The speaker was a tiny man, old and gnarly, with an eye-patch over his left eye and a stump for right hand. The latter told a tale in itself: he was a failed thief, probably turned con man. But . . . Tarra shrugged. 'Any port in a storm,' he said. 'Lead on.'

And when they were away from Fregg's sorry palace and into the old streets of the city proper: 'Now what's all this about not leaving in daylight? I came in daylight, after all.'

'I'm Stumpy Adz,' the old-timer told him. 'And if it's to be known, Stumpy knows it. Odds are you're watched even now. You're a defenceless stranger and you own blanket, saddle, camel and gear, and leather scabbard. That's quite a bit of property for a lad with no friends here, save me.'

'I wear loincloth and sandals, too,' Tarra pointed out. 'Are they also lusted after?'

'Likely,' Stumpy Adz nodded. 'This is Chlangi, lad, not Klühn. Anyway, I've pillow for your head, cabbage tops and shade for the beast, food and drink for your belly. Deal?'

'What'll I pay?'

'Blanket'll do. It's cold here nights. And as Fregg pointed out: you've your camel to keep you warm.'

Tarra sighed but nodded. 'Deal. Anyway, I wasn't planning on leaving till tonight. Fregg's invited me to call on him in his tower counting house. I have to get my sword back – what's left of it.'

'Heard that, too,' said Stumpy. '*Huh!*'

He led the way into a shady alley and from there through a heavy oak door into a tiny high-walled yard, planked over for roof with a vine bearing grapes and casting cool shade. 'Tether your beast there,' said Stumpy. 'Will he do his business?'

'Likely,' said Tarra. 'He doesn't much care where he does it.'

'Good! A treat for the grapevine . . .'

Tarra looked about. Half-way up one wall was a wooden platform, doubtless Stumpy's bed (Tarra's for the rest of the day), and behind the yard a low, tiled hovel built between the walls as if on afterthought. It might one time have been a smithy; cooking smells now drifted out of open door.

'Gulla,' Stumpy called. 'A meal for two – and a skin, if you please. Quick, lass, we've a visitor.'

Tarra's ears pricked up. 'Lass'? If not the old lad's wife, then surely his daughter. The latter proved to be the case, but Tarra's interest rapidly waned. Gulla Adz was comely enough about the face but built like a fortress. Tarra could feel his ribs creaking just looking at her. Looking at *him*, as she dished out steamy stew in cracked plates atop a tiny table, she made eyes and licked her lips in a manner that made him glad his bed was high off the ground.

Stumpy chased her off, however, and as they ate Tarra asked:

'Why the "*huh!*", eh? Don't you think Fregg'll give me back my sword, then?'

'His own, more likely – between your ribs! No, lad, when Fregg takes something it stays took. Also, I fancy he makes his own plans for leaving, and sooner rather than later. I'd make book we're kingless within a week. And there'll be no share out, that's for sure! No, this is just what Fregg's been waiting for. Him and his bullies'll take the lot – and then he'll find a way to ditch them, too.'

'Why should he want to leave?' asked Tarra Khash, innocently. 'It seems to me he's well set up here.'

'He was, he was,' said Stumpy. 'But—' and he told Tarra about the Lamia Orbiquita and her assumed demise. Hearing all, Tarra said nothing – but he fingered twin sores on his neck, like the tiny weeping craters of mosquito bites. Aye, and if what this old lad said about lamias were true, then he must consider himself one very fortunate Hrossak. Fortunate indeed!

'That treasure,' he said when Stumpy was done, 'was mine. I'll not leave without a handful at least. And I want that sword-hilt, with or without its jewels! Can I buy your help, Stumpy, for a nugget of gold? Or perhaps a ruby big enough to fit the socket behind your eye-patch?'

'Depends what you want,' said Stumpy carefully.

'Not much,' Tarra answered. 'A good thin rope and grapple, knowledge of the weakest part of the city's wall, details of Fregg's palace guards – how many of them, and so forth – and a plan of quickest route from palace, through city, to outer wall. Well?'

'Sounds reasonable,' the oldster nodded, his good eye twinkling.

'Lastly,' said Tarra, 'I'll want a sharp knife, six-inch blade and well balanced.'

'Ah! That'll cost you an extra nugget.'

'Done! – if I make it. If not . . . you can keep the camel.' They shook on it left-handed, and each felt he'd met a man to be trusted – within limits.

Following which the Hrossak climbed rickety ladder to shady platform, tossed awhile making his plans, and finally fell asleep . . .

Tarra slept until dusk, during which time Stumpy Adz was busy. When the Hrossak awoke Stumpy gave him a throwing knife and sat down with him, by light of oil lamp and floating wick, to study several parchment sketches. There was meat sizzling over charcoal, too, and a little weak wine in a stone jar beaded with cold moisture. Stumpy lived pretty well, Tarra decided.

As for the Hrossak: he was clear-headed; the stiffness was still in his shoulder but fading fast; the two-pronged bite on his neck had scabbed over and lost its sting. What had been taken out of him was replacing itself, and all seemed in working order.

He took leave of Stumpy's place at the hour when all cats turn grey and headed for the south gate. At about which time, some three hundred and more miles away in the heart of the Nameless Desert . . .

Deep, deep below the furnace sands, cooling now that the sun was caught once more in Cthon's net and drawn down, and while the last kites of evening fanned the air on high in a crimson cavern with a lava lake, where red imps danced nimbly from island to island in the reek and splash of molten rock – there the Lamia Orbiquita came awake at last and stretched her leathery wings and breathed gratefully of the hot brimstone atmosphere.

She lay cradled in smoking ashes in the middle of a smouldering island which itself lay central in the lava lake; and over her warty, leathery, loathsome form hunched a mighty black lava lump glowing with a red internal life of its own and moulded in perfect likeness of – what else but another lamia? And seeing that infernally fossilized thing crouching over her she knew where she was and remembered how she got here.

The whole thing had been a folly, a farce. First: that she failed to make adequate preparation for her journey when she knew full well that the five-year cycle was nearing its peak, when her powers would wane even as the hated moon waxed. Next: that having allowed the time to creep too close, and most of her powers fled, still she had not used the last of them to call up those serfs of the desert, the djinn, to transport her here; for she scorned all imps – even bottle imps, and even the biggest of them – and hated the thought of being in their debt. Finally: that as her choice of guise under which to travel she had chosen that of beautiful human female, for once the change was made she'd been stuck with that shape and all the hazards that went with it. The choice, however, had not been completely arbitrary; she could take comfort in that, at least. The human female form was small and less cumbersome than that of a dragon; and where girls sometimes got molested and raped, dragons were usually slain! She could have been a lizard, but lizards making a beeline across the desert are easy prey for hawks and such, and anyway she hated crawling on her belly. Flying creature such as harpy or bat were out of the question; since they must needs flit, they could not shade themselves against sun and moon. Her true lamia form was likewise problematic: impossible to shade in flight and cumbersome afoot. And so she had chosen the shape of a beautiful human girl. Anyway, it was her favourite and had served her well for more than a century. The victims she had lured with it were without number. Moreover, yaks and camels did not shy from it.

Ah, well, a lesson learned – but learned so expensively. A veritable string of errors never to be repeated. The ravishment had been bad enough and the beating worse, but the loss of her rune-book and ring were disasters of the first magnitude. Orbiquita's memory was not the best and the runes of metamorphosis were anything but easy. As for the ring: that had been gifted to her by her father, Mylakhrion of Tharamoon. She could not bear to be without it. Indeed, of the entire episode the one thing she did not regret was the Hrossak. Odd, that . . .

Stretching again and yawning hideously, she might perhaps have lingered longer over thoughts of Tarra

Khash, but that was a luxury not to be permitted. No, for she was in serious trouble and she knew it, and now must prepare whatever excuses she could for her lateness and unseemly mode of arrival here in this unholy place.

Aye, for the eyes in the lava lamia's head had cracked open and now glared sulphurously, and from the smoking jaws came the voice of inquisitor, demanding to be told all and truthfully:

'What have you to say for yourself, Orbiquita, borne here by djinn and weary nigh unto death, and late by a day so that all your sisters have come and gone, all making sport over the idleness or foolhardiness of the hated Orbiquita? You know, of course, the penalty?'

'I hate my sisters equally well!' answered Orbiquita unabashed. 'Let them take solace from that. As to your charges, I cannot deny them. Idle and foolhardy I have been. And aye, I know well enow the price to pay.' Then she told the whole, miserable tale.

When she reached the part concerning Tarra Khash, however, the lava lamia stopped her in something approaching astonishment: 'What? And you took not this Hrossak's life? But this is without precedence!'

'I had my reasons!' Orbiquita protested.

'Then out with them at once,' ordered the lava lamia, 'or sit here in stony silence for five long years – which is, in any case, your fate. Of what "reasons" do you speak?'

'One,' said Orbiquita, 'he saved me from Gleeth's scorching beams.'

'What is that? He is a man!'

'My father was a man, and likely yours too.'

'*Hah!* Do not remind me! Say on, Orbiquita.'

'Two, though I suspect he guessed my nature – or at least that I was more than I appeared – still he offered no offence, no harm, but would have fed and protected me.'

'Greater fool he!' the lava lamia answered.

'And three,' (Orbiquita would not be browbeaten) 'I sensed, by precognition, that in fact I would meet this one again, and that he would be of further service to me.'

And, '*Hah!*' said lava lamia more vehemently yet. 'Be sure it will not happen for a five-year at least, Orbiquita! "Precognition", indeed! You should have gorged on him, and wrapped yourself in his skin to protect your own from the moon, and so proceeded here without let and indebted to no one. Instead you chose merely to sip, summoning only sufficient strength to call up detested desert djinn to your aid. All in all, most foolish. And are you ready now to take my place, waiting out your five years until some equally silly sister's deed release you?'

'No,' said Orbiquita.

'*It is the law!*' the other howled. 'Apart from which, I'm impatient of this place.'

'And the law shall be obeyed – and you released, as is only right – eventually . . . But first a boon.'

'What? You presume to—'

'Mylakhrion's ring!' cried Orbiquita. 'Stolen from me. My rune-book, too. Would you deny me time to right this great wrong? Must I wait a five-year to wipe clean this smear on *all* lamias? Would you suffer the scorn of *all* your sisters – and not least mine – for the sake of a few hours, you who have centuries before you?'

After long moments, calmer now but yet bubbling lava from every pore, the keeper of this place asked, 'What is it you wish?'

'My powers returned to me – fully!' said Orbiquita at once. 'And I'll laugh in Gleeth's face and fly to Chlangi, and find Mylakhrion's ring and take back my rune-book. Following which—'

'You'll return here?'

'Or be outcast forever from the sisterhood, aye,' Orbiquita

bowed her warty head. 'And is it likely I'll renege, to live only five more years instead of five thousand?'

'So be it,' said the lava lamia, her voice a hiss of escaping steam. 'You are renewed, Orbiquita. Now get you hence and remember your vow, and return to me here before Cthon releases the sun to rise again over Theem'hdra. On behalf of all lamias, I have spoken.'

The sulphur pits which were her eyes lidded themselves with lava crusts, but Orbiquita did not see. She was no longer there . . .

Tarra Khash left Chlangi by the south gate, two hours after the sun's setting. By then, dull lights glowed in the city's streets in spasmodic pattern, flickering smokily in the taverns, brothels, and a few of the larger houses and dens – and (importantly) in Fregg's palace, particularly his apartments in the tower. It was a good time to be away, before night's thieves and cutthroats crawled out of their holes and began to work up an interest in a man.

Out of the gate the Hrossak turned east for Klühn, heading for the pass through the Great Eastern Peaks more than two hundred miles away. Beyond the pass and fording the Lohr, he would cross a hundred more miles of grassland before the spires and turrets of coastal Klühn came into view. Except that first, of course, he'd be returning – however briefly, and hopefully painlessly – to Chlangi.

Jogging comfortably east for a mile or more, the Hrossak never once looked back – despite the fact that he knew he was followed. Two of them, on ponies (rare beasts in Theem'hdra), and keeping their distance for the nonce. Tarra could well imagine what was on their minds: they wondered about the contents of his saddle bags, and of course the camel itself was not without value. Also they knew – or thought they knew – that he was without weapon.

Well, as long as he kept more than arrow or bolt's flight distance between he was safe, but it made his back itch for all that.

Then he spied ahead the tumbled ruins of some ghost town or other on the plain, and urged his mount to a trot. It was quite dark now, for Gleeth sailed low as yet, so it might be some little time before his pursuers twigged that he'd quickened his pace. That was all to the good. He passed along the ghost town's single skeletal street, dismounted and tethered his beast by a heap of stones, then fleet-footed it back to the other end and flattened himself to the treacherous bricks of an arch where it spanned the narrow street. And waited.

And waited . . .

Could they have guessed his next move? Did they suspect his ambush? The plan had been simple: hurl knife into the back of one as they passed beneath, and leap on the back of the other; but what now?

Ah! – no sooner the question than an answer. Faint sounds in the night growing louder. Noise of their coming at last. But hoofbeats, a beast at gallop? What was this? No muffled, furtive approach this, but frenzied flight! A pony, snorting its fear, fleeing riderless across the plain; and over there, silhouetted against crest of low hill, another. Now what in—?

Tarra slid down from the arch, held his breath, stared back hard the way he had come, toward Chlangi, and listened. But nothing, only the fading sounds of drumming hooves and a faint whinny in the dark.

Now instinct told the Hrossak he should count his blessings, forget whatever had happened here, return at once to his camel and so back to Chlangi by circuitous route as previously planned; but his personal demon, named Curiosity, deemed it otherwise. On foot, moving like a shadow among shadows, his bronze skin aiding him considerably in the dark, he loped easily back along his own route until—

It was the smell stopped him, a smell he knew at once from its too familiar reek. Fresh blood!

More cautiously now, nerves taut as a bowstring, almost in a crouch, Tarra moved forward again; and his grip on the haft of his knife never so tight, and his eyes never so large where they strained to penetrate night's canopy of dark. Then he was almost stumbling over them, and just as smartly drawing back, his breath hissing out through clenched teeth.

Dead, and not merely dead but gutted! Chlangi riff-raff by their looks, unpretty as the end they'd met. Aye, and a butcher couldn't have done a better job. Their entrails still steamed in the cool night air.

The biters bit: Tarra's trackers snared in advance of his own planned ambush; and what of the unseen, unheard killers themselves? Once more the Hrossak melted into shadow, froze, listened, stared. Perhaps they had gone in pursuit of the ponies. Well, Tarra wouldn't wait to find out. But as he turned to speed back to his camel—

Another smell in the night air? A sulphur reek, strangely laced with cloying musk? And where had he smelled that dubious perfume before? A nerve jumped in his neck, and twin scabs throbbed dully as if in mute answer.

To hell with it! They were all questions that could wait . . .

Half a mile from Chlangi Tarra dismounted and tethered his camel out of sight in a shallow gulley, then proceeded on foot and as fast as he could go to where the east wall was cracked as by some mighty tremor of the earth. Here boulders and stones had been tumbled uncemented into the gap, so that where the rest of the wall was smooth, offering little of handholds and making for a difficult climb, here it was rough and easily scaleable. Fregg knew this too, of course, for which reason there was normally a guard positioned atop the wall somewhere in this area. Since Chlangi was hardly a place people would want to break *into*, however, chances were the guard would have his belly wrapped around the contents of a wineskin by now, snoring in some secret niche.

The wall was high at this point, maybe ten man-lengths, but Old Gleeth was kind enough to cast his rays from a different angle, leaving the east wall in shadow. All should be well. Nevertheless—

Before commencing his climb Tarra peered right and left, stared long and hard back into the night toward the east, listened carefully to see if he could detect the slightest sound. But . . . nothing. There were bats about tonight, though – and big ones, whole roosts of them – judging from the frequent flappings he'd heard overhead.

Satisfied at last that there were no prying eyes, finally the Hrossak set fingers and toes to wall and scaled it like a lizard, speeding his ascent where the crack widened and the boulders were less tightly packed. Two-thirds of the way up he rested briefly, where a boulder had long since settled and left a man-sized gap, taking time to get his breath and peer out and down all along the wall and over the scraggy plain, and generally checking that all was well.

And again the stirring of unseen wings and a whipping of the air as something passed briefly across the starry vault. Bats, yes, but a veritable cloud of them! Tarra shivered his disgust: he had little time for night creatures of any sort. He levered himself out of his hole, began to climb again – and paused.

A sound from on high, atop the wall? The scrape of heel against stone? The shuffle of bored or disconsolate feet? It came again, this time accompanied by wheezy grunt!

Tarra flattened himself to wall, clung tight, was suddenly aware of his vulnerability. At which precise moment he felt the coil of rope over his shoulder slip a little and heard his hook clang against the wall down by his waist. Quickly he trapped the thing, froze once more. Had it been heard?

'Huh?' came gruff inquiry from above. And: *'Huh?'* Then, in the next moment, a cough, a whirring sound diminishing, a gurgle – and at last silence once more.

For five long minutes Tarra waited, his nerves jumping and the feeling going out of his fingers and toes, before he dared continue his upward creep. By then he believed he had it figured out – or hoped so, anyway. The guard was, as he had suspected might be the case, asleep. The grapple's clang had merely caused him to start and snort into the night, before settling himself down again more comfortably. And perhaps the incident had been for the best at that; at least Tarra knew now that he was there.

With infinite care the Hrossak proceeded, and at last his fingertips went up over the sill of an embrasure. Now, more slow and silent yet, he drew up his body until—

Seated in the deep embrasure with his back to one wall and his knees against the other, a bearded guardsman grinned down on Tarra's upturned face and aimed a crossbow direct into the astonished 'O' of his gaping mouth!

Tarra might simply have recoiled, released his grip upon the rim and fallen. He might have (as some men doubtless would) fainted. He might have closed his eyes tight shut and pleaded loud and desperate, promising anything. He did none of these but gulped, grinned and said:

'Ho! No fool you, friend! Fregg chooses his guards well. He sent me here to catch you asleep – to test the city's security, d'you see? – but here you are wide awake and watchful, obviously a man who knows his duty. So be it; help me up from here and I'll go straight to our good king and make report how all's . . . well?'

For now the Hrossak saw that all was indeed well – for him if not for the guard. That smell was back, of fresh blood, and a dark pool of it was forming and sliming the stone where Tarra's fingers clung. It dripped from beneath the guard's chin – where his throat was slit from ear to ear!

Aye, for the gleam in his eyes was merely glaze, and his fixed grin was a rictus of horror! Also, the crossbow's groove was empty, its bolt shot; and now Tarra remembered the whirring sound, the cough, the gurgle . . .

Adrenalin flooded the Hrossak's veins as a flash flood fills dry river beds. He was up and into the embrasure and across the sprawling corpse in a trice, his flesh ice as he stared all about, panting in the darkness. He had a friend here for sure, but who or what he dared not think. And now, coming to him across the reek of spilled blood . . . *again* that sulphurous musk, that fascinating yet strangely fearful perfume.

Then, from the deeper shadows of a shattered turret:

'Have you forgotten me then, Tarra Khash, whose life you saved in the badlands? And is not the debt I owed you repaid?'

And oh the Hrossak knew that sibilant, whispering voice, knew only too well whose hand – or claw – had kept him safe this night. Aye, and he further knew now that Chlangi's bats were no bigger than the bats of any other city; knew *exactly* why those ponies had fled like the wind across the plain; knew, shockingly, how close he must have come last night to death's sharp edge! The wonder was that he was still alive to know these things, and now he must ensure no rapid deterioration of that happy circumstance.

'I've not forgotten,' he forced the words from throat dry as the desert itself. 'Your perfume gives you away, Orbiquita – and your kiss shall burn on my neck and in my memory forever!' He took a step toward the turret.

'*Hold!*' she hissed from the shadows, where now a greater darkness moved uncertainly, its agitation accompanied by scraping as of many knives on stone. 'Come no closer,

Hrossak. It's no clean-limbed, soft-breasted girl stands here now.'

'I know that well enow,' Tarra croaked. 'What do you want with me?'

'With you – nothing. But with that pair who put me to such trial in the desert—'

'They are dead,' Tarra stopped her.

'What?' (Again the clashing of knives.) 'Dead? That were a pleasure I had promised myself!'

'Then blame your disappointment on some other, Orbiquita,' Tarra spoke into darkness. 'Though certainly I would have killed them, if Fregg hadn't beaten me to it.'

'Fregg, is it?' she hissed. 'Scum murders scum. Well, King Fregg has robbed me, it seems.'

'Both of us,' Tarra told her. 'You of your revenge, me of more worldly pleasures – a good many of them. Right now I'm on my way to take a few back.'

The blackness in the turret stirred, moved closer to the door. Her voice was harsher now, the words coming more quickly, causing Tarra to draw back from brimstone breath. 'What of my rune-book?'

'Arenith Han, Fregg's sorcerer, will have that,' the Hrossak answered.

'And where is he?'

'He lives in Fregg's palace, beneath his master's tower.'

'Good! Show me this place.' She inched forward again and for a moment the moonlight gleamed on something unbearable. Gasping, Tarra averted his eyes, pointed a trembling hand out over the city.

'There,' he said, his voice breaking a little. 'That high tower there with the light. That's where Fregg and his mage dwell, well guarded and central within the palace walls.'

'What are guards and walls to me?' she said, and he heard the scrape of her clawed feet and felt the heat of her breath on the back of his neck. 'What say you we visit this pair together?'

Rooted to the spot, not daring to look back, Tarra answered: 'I'm all for companionship, Orbiquita, but—'

'So be it!' she was closer still. 'And since you can't bear to look at me, close your eyes. Also, put away that knife – it would not scratch my scales.'

Gritting his teeth, Tarra did both things – and at once felt himself grasped, lifted up, crushed to a hot, stinking, scaly body. Wings of leather creaked open in the night; wind rushed all about; all was dizzy, soaring, whirling motion. Then—

Tarra felt his feet touch down and was released. He staggered, sprawled, opened his eyes and sprang erect. Again he stood upon a parapet; on one hand a low balcony wall, overlooking the city, and on the other an arabesqued archway issuing warm, yellow light. Behind him, stone steps winding down, where even now something dark descended on scythe feet! Orbiquita, going in search of her rune-book.

'Who's there?' came sharp voice of inquiry from beyond the arched entrance. 'Is that you, Arenith? And didn't I say not to disturb me at my sorting and counting?'

It was Fregg – Fregg all alone, with no bully boys to protect him now – which would make for a meeting much more to Tarra's liking. And after all, he'd been invited, hadn't he?

Invited or not, the shock on Fregg's face as Tarra entered showed all too clearly how the robber-king had thought never to see him again. Indeed, it was as if Fregg gazed upon a ghost, which might say something about the errand of the two who'd followed Tarra across the plain; an errand unfulfilled, as Fregg now saw. He half came to his feet, then slumped down again with hands atop the huge oak table that stood between.

'Good evening, Majesty,' said Tarra Khash, no hint of

malice in his voice. 'I've come for my broken sword, remember?' He looked all about the circular, dome-ceilinged room, where lamps on shelves gave plenty of light. And now the Hrossak saw what a magpie this jowly bandit really was. Why, 'twere a wonder the many shelves had room for Fregg's lamps at all – for they were each and every one stacked high with stolen valuables of every sort and description! Here were jade idols and goblets, and more jade in chunks unworked. Here were silver statuettes, plates, chains and trinkets galore. Here were sacklets of very precious gems, and larger sacks of semi-precious stones. Here was gold and scrolls of gold-leaf, bangles of the stuff hanging from nails like so many hoops on pegs, and brooches, and medallions on golden chains, and trays of rings all burning yellow. But inches deep on the great table, and as yet unsorted, there lay Fregg's greatest treasure – which, oh so recently, had belonged to Tarra Khash.

'Your sword?' Fregg forced a smile more a grimace on to his face, fingered his beard, continued to stare at his visitor as if hypnotized. But at last animation: he stood up, slapped his thigh, roared with laughter and said, 'Why of course, your broken sword!' Then he sobered. 'It's here somewhere, I'm sure. But alas, I've not yet had time to remove the gems.' His eyes rapidly swept the table, narrowing as they more slowly returned to the Hrossak's face.

Tarra came closer, watching the other as a cat watches a mouse, attuned to every breath, to each slightest movement. 'Nor will there be time, I fancy,' he said.

'Eh?' said Fregg; and then, in imitation of Tarra's doomful tone: 'Is that to be the way of it? Well, before we decide upon all that – first tell me, Hrossak, how it is you've managed to come here, to this one place in all Chlangi which I had thought impregnable?'

Before Tarra could answer there came from below a shrill, wavering cry borne first of shock, then disbelief, finally terror – cut off most definitely at zenith. Skin prickling, knowing that indeed Orbiquita had found Arenith Han, Tarra commenced an involuntary turn – and and knew his mistake on the instant. Already he had noted, upon a shelf close to where Fregg sat a small silver crossbow, with silver bolt loaded in groove and string ready-nocked. Turning back to robber-king he fell to one knee, his right hand and arm a blur of motion. Tarra's knife thrummed like a harp where its blade was fixed inches deep in shelf's soft wood, pinning Fregg's fat hand there even as it reached for weapon. And upon that pinned hand, glinting on the smallest finger, a ring of gold inset with jade cut in a skull and serpent crest.

Blood spurted and Fregg slumped against the shelves – but not so heavily that his weight put stress on the knife. 'M-mercy!' he croaked, but saw little of mercy in the hulking steppe-man's eyes. Gasping his pain, he reached trembling free-hand toward the knife transfixing the other.

In a scattering of gems and baubles Tarra vaulted the table, his heels slamming into Fregg's face. The bandit was hurled aside, his hand split neatly between second and third fingers by the keen blade! Screaming Fregg fell, all thought of fighting back relinquished now to agony most intense from riven paw. Gibbering he sprawled upon the floor amidst scattering gems and nuggets, while Tarra stood spread-legged and filled the scabbard at his back, then topped his loot with hilt of shattered sword.

Until, 'Enough!' he said. 'I've got what I came for.'

'But *I* have not!' came Orbiquita's monstrous hiss from the archway.

Tarra turned, saw her, went weak at the knees. Now he looked full upon a lamia, and knew all the horror of countless others gone before him. And yet he found the strength to answer her as were she his sister: 'You did not find your rune-book?'

'The book, aye,' her breath was sulphur. 'Mylakhrion's ring, no. Have you seen it, Tarra Khash? A ring of gold with skull and serpent crest?'

Edging past her, Tarra gulped and nodded in Fregg's direction where he sat, eyes bugging, his quivering back to laden shelves. 'Of that matter, best speak to miserable monarch there,' he told her.

Orbiquita's claws flexed and sank deep into the stone floor as she hunched toward the now drooling, keening robber-king.

'Farewell,' said Tarra, leaping out under the archway and to the parapet wall, and fixing his grapnel there.

From below came hoarse shouts, cries of outrage, the clatter of many feet ascending the tower's corkscrew stairs. 'Farewell,' came Orbiquita's hiss as Tarra swung himself out and down into the night. 'Go swiftly, Hrossak, and fear no hand at your back. I shall attend to that.'

After that—

All was a chaos of flight, of hideous screams fading into distance behind, of climbing, falling, of running and riding, until Chlangi was a blot, then less than a blot, then vanished altogether into distance behind him. Somewhere along the way Stumpy Adz dragged him to a gasping, breathless halt, however brief, gawped at a handful of gems, disappeared dancing into shadows; and somewhere else Tarra cracked a head when unknown assailant leaped on him from hiding; other than which he remembered very little.

And through all of that wild panic flight, only once did Tarra Khash look back – of which he wished he likewise had no recall.

For then . . . he had thought to see against the face of the moon a dark shape flying, whose outlines he knew well. And dangling beneath, a fat flopping shape whose silhouette seemed likewise familiar. And he thought the dangling thing screamed faintly in the thin, chill air of higher space, and he thought he saw its fitful kicking. Which made him pray it was only his imagination, or a dark cloud fleeing west.

And after that he put it firmly out of his mind.

As for Orbiquita:

She hated being in anyone's debt. This should square the matter. Fregg would make hearty breakfast for a hungry sister waking up from five long years of stony vigil . . .

RECOGNITION

I

'As to why I asked you all to join me here, and why I'm making it worth your while by paying each of you five hundred pounds for your time and trouble, the answer is simple: the place appears to be haunted, and I want rid of the ghost.'

The speaker was young, his voice cultured, his features fine and aristocratic. He was Lord David Marriot, and the place of which he spoke was a Marriot property: a large, ungainly, mongrel architecture of dim and doubtful origins, standing gaunt and gloomily atmospheric in an acre of brooding oaks. The wood itself stood central in nine acres of otherwise barren moors borderland.

Lord Marriot's audience numbered four: the sprightly octogenarian Lawrence Danford, a retired man of the cloth; by contrast the so-called 'mediums' Jonathan Turnbull and Jason Lavery, each a 'specialist' in his own right; and myself, an old friend of the family whose name does not really matter since I had no special part to play. I was simply there as an observer – an adviser, if you like – in a matter for which, from the beginning, I had no great liking.

Waiting on the arrival of the others, I had been with David Marriot at the old house all afternoon. I had long known something of the history of the place . . . and a little of its legend. There I now sat, comfortable and warm as our host addressed the other three, with an excellent sherry in my hand while logs crackled away in the massive fireplace. And yet suddenly, as he spoke, I felt chill and uneasy.

'You two gentlemen,' David smiled at the mediums, 'will employ your special talents to discover and define the malignancy, if indeed such an element exists; and you, sir,' he spoke to the elderly·cleric, 'will attempt to exorcise the unhappy – creature? – once we know who or what it is.' Attracted by my involuntary agitation, frowning, he paused and turned to me. 'Is something troubling you, my friend . . . ?'

'I'm sorry to have to stop you almost before you've started, David,' I apologized, 'but I've given it some thought and – well, this plan of yours worries me.'

Lord Marriot's guests looked at me in some surprise, seeming to notice me for the first time, although of course we had been introduced; for after all they were the experts while I was merely an observer. Nevertheless, and while I was never endowed with any special psychic talent that I know of (and while certainly, if ever I had been, I never would have dabbled), I did know a little of my subject and had always been interested in such things.

And who knows? – perhaps I do have some sort of sixth sense, for as I have said, I was suddenly and quite inexplicably chilled with a sensation of foreboding that I knew had nothing at all to do with the temperature of the library. The others, for all their much-vaunted special talents, apparently felt nothing.

'My plan worries you?' Lord Marriot finally repeated. 'You didn't mention this before.'

'I didn't know before just how you meant to go about it. Oh, I agree that the house requires some sort of exorcism, that something is quite definitely wrong with the place, but I'm not at all sure that you should concern yourself with finding out exactly what it is you're exorcizing.'

'Hmm, yes, I think I might agree,' Old Danford nodded his grey head. 'Surely the essence of the, *harumph*, matter, is to be rid of the thing – whatever it is. Er, not,' he hastily added, 'that I would want to do these two gentlemen out of a job – however much I disagree with, *harumph*, spiritualism and its trappings.' He turned to Turnbull and Lavery.

'Not at all. sir,' Lavery assured him, smiling thinly. 'We've been paid in advance, as you yourself have been paid, regardless of results. We will therefore – *perform* – as Lord Marriot sees fit. We are not, however, spiritualists. But in any case, should our services no longer be required . . .' He shrugged.

'No, no question of that,' the owner of the house spoke up at once. 'The advice of my good friend here has been greatly valued by my family for many years, in all manner of problems, but he would be the first to admit that he's no expert in matters such as these. I, however, am even less of an authority, and my time is extremely short; I never have enough time for anything! That is why I commissioned him to find out all he could about the history of the house, in order to be able to offer you gentlemen something of an insight into its background.

And I assure you that it's not just idle curiosity that prompts me to seek out the source of the trouble here. I wish to dispose of the property, and prospective buyers just will not stay in it long enough to appreciate its many good features! And so, if we are to lay something to rest here, something which ought perhaps to have been laid to rest long ago, then I want to know what it is. Damn me, the thing's caused me enough trouble!

So let's please have no more talk about likes and dislikes or what should or should not be done. It will be the way I've planned it.' He turned again to me. 'Now, if you'll be so good as to simply outline the results of your research . . . ?'

'Very well,' I shrugged in acquiescence. 'As long as I've made my feelings in the matter plain . . .' Knowing David the way I did, further argument would be quite fruitless: his mind was made up. I riffled through the notes lying in my lap, took a long pull on my pipe, and commenced:

'Oddly enough, the house as it now stands is comparatively modern, no more than two hundred and fifty years old, but it was built upon the shell of a far older structure, one whose origin is extremely difficult to trace. There are local legends, however, and there have always been chroniclers of tales of strange old houses. The original house is given brief mention in texts dating back almost to Roman times, but the actual site had known habitation – possibly a Druidic order or some such – much earlier. Later it became part of some sort of fortification, perhaps a small castle, and the remnants of earthworks in the shape of mounds, banks and ditches can be found even today in the surrounding countryside.

'Of course the present house, while large enough by modern standards, is small in comparison with the original: it's a mere wing of the old structure. An extensive cellar – a veritable maze of tunnels, rooms, and passages – was discovered during renovation some eighty years ago, when first the Marriots acquired the property, and then several clues were disclosed as to its earlier use.

'This wing would seem to have been a place of worship of sorts, for there was a crude altar-stone, a pair of ugly, font-like basins, a number of particularly repugnant carvings of gargoyles or 'gods', and other extremely ancient tools and bric-à-brac. Most of this incunabula was given into the care of the then curator of the antiquities section of the British Museum, but the carved figures were defaced and destroyed. The records do not say why . . .

'But let's go back to the reign of James I.

Then the place was the seat of a family of supposed nobility, though the line must have suffered a serious decline during the early years of the seventeenth century – or perhaps fallen foul of the authorities or the monarch himself – for its name simply cannot be discovered. It would seem that for some reason, most probably serious dishonour, the family name has been erased from all contemporary records and documents!

'Prior to the fire which razed the main building to the ground in 1618, there had been a certain intercourse and intrigue of a similarly undiscovered nature between the nameless inhabitants, the de la Poers of Exham Priory near Anchester, and an obscure esoteric sect of monks dwelling in and around the semi-ruined Falstone Castle in Northumberland. Of the latter sect, they were wiped out utterly by Northern raiders – a clan believed to have been outraged by the 'heathen activities' of the monks – and the ruins of the castle were pulled to pieces, stone by stone. Indeed, it was so well destroyed that today only a handful of historians could even show you where it stood!

'As for the de la Poers, well, whole cycles of ill-omened myth and legend revolve around that family, just as they do about their Anchester seat. Suffice it to say that in 1923 the Priory was blown up and the cliffs beneath it dynamited, until the deepest roots of its foundations were obliterated. Thus the Priory is no more, and the last of that line of the family is safely locked away in a refuge for the hopelessly insane.

'It can be seen then that the nameless family that lived here had the worst possible connections, at least by the standards of those days, and it is not at all improbable that they brought about their own decline and disappearance through just such traffic with degenerate or ill-advised cultists and demonologists as I have mentioned.

'Now then, add to all of this somewhat tenuously connected information the local rumours, which have circulated on and off in the villages of this area for some three hundred years – those mainly unspecified fears and old wives' tales that have sufficed since time immemorial to

keep children and adults alike away from this property, off
the land and out of the woods – and you begin to understand something of the aura of the place. Perhaps you can
feel that aura even now? I certainly can, and I'm by no
means psychic . . .'

'Just what is it that the locals fear?' Turnbull asked.
'Can't you enlighten us at all?'

'Oh, strange shapes have been seen on the paths and
roads; luminous nets have appeared strung between the
trees like great webs, only to vanish in daylight; and, yes, in
connection with the latter, perhaps I had better mention the
bas-reliefs in the cellar.'

'Bas-reliefs?' queried Lavery.

'Yes, on the walls. It was writing of sorts, but in a
language no one could understand – glyphs almost.'

'My great-grandfather had just bought the house,'
David Marriot explained. 'He was an extremely well-
read man, knowledgeable in all sorts of peculiar subjects. When the cellar was opened and he saw the glyphs,
he said they had to do with the worship of some strange
deity from an obscure and almost unrecognized myth
cycle. Afterwards he had the greater area of the cellar
cemented in – said it made the house damp and the
foundations unsafe.'

'Worship of some strange deity?' Old Danford spoke up.
'What sort of deity? Some lustful thing that the Romans
brought with them, d'you think?'

'No, older than that,' I answered for Lord Marriot.
'Much older. A spider-thing.'

'A spider?' This was Lavery again, and he snorted the
words out almost in contempt.

'Not quite the thing to sneer at,' I answered. 'Three years
ago an ageing but still active gentleman rented the house for
a period of some six weeks. An anthropologist and the
author of several books, he wanted the place for its solitude;

and if he took to it he was going to buy it. In the fifth week he was taken away raving mad!'

'Eh? *Harumph!* Mad, you say?' Old Danford repeated after me.

I nodded. 'Yes, quite insane. He lived for barely six months, all the while raving about a creature named Atlach-Nacha – a spider-god from the Cthulhu Cycle of myth – whose ghostly avatar, he claimed, still inhabited the house and its grounds.'

At this Turnbull spoke up. 'Now really!' he spluttered. 'I honestly fear that we're rapidly going from the sublime to the ridiculous!'

'Gentlemen, please!' There was exasperation now in Lord Marriot's voice. 'What does it matter? You know as much now as there is to know of the history of the troubles here – more than enough to do what you've been paid to do. Now then, Lawrence –' he turned to Danford. 'Have you any objections?'

'*Harumph!* Well, if there's a demon here – that is, something other than a creature of the Lord – then of course I'll do my best to help you. *Harumph!* Certainly.'

'And you, Lavery?'

'Objections? No, a bargain is a bargain. I have your money, and you shall have your noises.'

Lord Marriot nodded, understanding Lavery's meaning. For the medium's talent was a supposed or alleged ability to speak in the tongue of the ghost, the possessing spirit. In the event of a non-human ghost, however, then his mouthings might well be other than speech as we understand the spoken word. They might simply be – noises.

'And that leaves you, Turnbull.'

'Do not concern yourself, Lord Marriot,' Turnbull answered, flicking imagined dust from his sleeves. 'I, too, would be loath to break an honourable agreement. I have promised to do an automatic sketch of the intruder, an art in which I'm well practised, and if all goes well, I shall do just that. Frankly, I see nothing at all to be afraid of. Indeed, I would appreciate some sort of explanation from our friend here – who seems to me simply to be doing his best to frighten us off.' He inclined his head inquiringly in my direction.

I held up my hands and shook my head. 'Gentlemen, my only desire is to make you aware of this feeling of mine of . . . yes, premonition! The very air seems to me imbued with an aura of –' I frowned. 'Perhaps disaster would be too strong a word.'

'Disaster?' Old Danford, as was his wont, repeated after me. 'How do you mean?'

'I honestly don't know. It's a feeling, that's all, and it hinges upon this desire of Lord Marriot's to know his foe, to identify the nature of the evil here. Yes, upon that, and upon the complicity of the rest of you.'

'But –' the young Lord began, anger starting to make itself apparent in his voice.

'At least hear me out,' I protested. 'Then –' I paused and shrugged. 'Then . . . you must do as you see fit.'

'It can do no harm to listen to him,' Old Danford pleaded my case. 'I for one find all of this extremely interesting. I would like to hear his argument.' The others nodded slowly, one by one, in somewhat uncertain agreement.

'Very well,' Lord Marriot sighed heavily. 'Just what is it that bothers you so much, my friend?'

'Recognition,' I answered at once. 'To recognize our – opponent? – that's where the danger lies. And yet here's Lavery, all willing and eager to speak in the thing's voice, which can only add to our knowledge of it; and Turnbull, happy to fall into a trance at the drop of a hat and sketch the thing, so that we may all know exactly what it looks like. And what comes after that? Don't you see? The more we learn of it, the more it learns of us!

'Right now, this *thing* – ghost, demon, "god", apparition, whatever you want to call it – lies in some deathless limbo, extra-dimensional, manifesting itself rarely, incompletely, in our world. But to *know* the thing, as our lunatic anthropologist came to know it and as the superstitious villagers of these parts think they know it – that is to draw it from its own benighted place into this sphere of existence. That is to give it substance, to participate in its materialization!'

'Hah!' Turnbull snorted. 'And you talk of superstitious villagers! Let's have one thing straight before we go any further. Lavery and I do *not* believe in the supernatural, not as the misinformed majority understand it. We believe that there are other planes of existence, yes, and that they are inhabited; and further, that occasionally we may glimpse alien areas and realms beyond the ones we were born to. In this we are surely nothing less than scientists, men who have been given rare talents, and each experiment we take part in leads us a little further along the paths of discovery. No ghosts or demons, sir, but scientific phenomena which may one day open up whole new vistas of knowledge. Let me repeat once more: there is nothing to fear in this, nothing at all!'

'There I cannot agree,' I answered. 'You must be aware, as I am, that there are well-documented cases of . . .'

'Self-hypnotism!' Lavery broke in. 'In almost every case where medium experimenters have come to harm, it can be proved that they were the victims of self-hypnosis.'

'And that's not all,' Turnbull added. 'You'll find that they were all believers in the so-called supernatural. We, on the other hand, are not—'

'But what of these well-documented cases you mentioned?' Old Danford spoke up. 'What sort of cases?'

'Cases of sudden, violent death!' I answered. 'The case of the medium who slept in a room once occupied by a murderer, a strangler, and who was found the next morning strangled – though the room was windowless and locked from the inside! The case of the exorcist,' (I paused briefly to glance at Danford) 'who attempted to seek out and put to rest a certain grey thing which haunted a Scottish graveyard. Whatever it was, this monster was legended to crush its victims' heads. Well, his curiosity did for him: he was found with his head squashed flat and his brains all burst from his ears!'

'And you think that all of–' Danford began.

'I don't know what to think,' I interrupted him, 'but certainly the facts seem to speak for themselves. These men I've mentioned, and many others like them, all tried to understand or search for things which they should have left utterly alone. Then, too late, each of them recognized . . . something . . . and it recognized them! What *I* think really does not matter; what matters is that these men are no more. And yet here, tonight, you would commence just such an *experiment*, to seek out something you really aren't meant to know. Well, good luck to you. I for one want no part of it. I'll leave before you begin.'

At that Lord Marriot, solicitous now, came over and laid a hand on my arm. 'Now you promised me you'd see this thing through with me.'

'I did not accept your money, David,' I reminded him.

'I respect you all the more for that,' he answered. 'You were willing to be here simply as a friend. As for this change of heart . . . At least stay a while and see the thing under way.'

I sighed and reluctantly nodded. Our friendship was a bond sealed long ago, in childhood. 'As you wish – but if and when I've had enough, then you must not try to prevent my leaving.'

'My word on it,' he immediately replied, briskly pumping my hand. 'Now then: a bite to eat and a drink, I think, another log on the fire, and then we can begin . . .'

II

The late autumn evening was setting in fast by the time we gathered around a heavy, circular oak table set centrally upon the library's parquet flooring, in preparation for Lavery's demonstration of his esoteric talent. The other three guests were fairly cheery, perhaps a little excited – doubtless as a result of David's plying them unstintingly with his excellent sherry – and our host himself seemed in very good spirits; but I had been little affected and the small amount of wine I had taken had, if anything, only seemed to heighten the almost tangible atmosphere of dread which pressed in upon me from all sides. Only that promise wrested from me by my friend kept me there; and by it alone I felt bound to participate, at least initially, in what was to come.

Finally Lavery declared himself ready to begin and asked us all to remain silent throughout. The lights had been turned low at the medium's request and the sputtering logs in the great hearth threw red and orange shadows about the spacious room.

The experiment would entail none of the usual paraphernalia beloved of mystics and spiritualists; we did not sit with the tips of our little fingers touching, forming an unbroken circle; Lavery had not asked us to concentrate or to focus our minds upon anything at all. The antique clock on the wall ticked off the seconds monotonously as the medium closed his eyes and lay back his head in his high-backed chair. We all watched him closely.

Gradually his breathing deepened and the rise and fall of his chest became regular. Then, almost before we knew it and coming as something of a shock, his hands tightened on the leather arms of his chair and his mouth began a silent series of spastic jerks and twitches. My blood, already cold, seemed to freeze at the sight of this, and I had half risen to my feet before his face grew still. Then Lavery's lips drew back from his teeth and he opened and closed his mouth several times in rapid succession, as if gnashing his teeth through a blind, idiot grin. This only lasted for a second or two, however, and soon his face once more relaxed. Suddenly conscious that I still crouched over the table, I forced myself to sit down.

As we continued to watch him, a deathly pallor came over the medium's features and his knuckles whitened as he gripped the arms of his chair. At this point I could have sworn that the temperature of the room dropped sharply, abruptly. The others did not seem to note the fact, being far too fascinated with the motion of Lavery's exposed Adam's apple to be aware of anything else. That fleshy knob moved slowly up and down the full length of his throat, while the column of his windpipe thickened and contracted in a sort of slow muscular spasm. And at last Lavery spoke. He spoke – and at the sound I could almost feel the blood congealing in my veins!

For this was in no way the voice of a man that crackled, hissed and gibbered from Lavery's mouth in a – language? – which surely never originated in this world or within our sphere of existence. No, it was the voice of . . . something else. Something monstrous!

Interspaced with the insane cough, whistle and stutter of harshly alien syllables and cackling cachinnations, occasionally there would break through a recognizable combination of sounds which roughly approximated our pronunciation of 'Atlach-Nacha'; but this fat had no sooner made itself plain to me than, with a wild shriek, Lavery hurled himself backwards – or was *thrown* backwards – so violently that he overturned his chair, rolling free of it to thrash about upon the floor.

Since I was directly opposite Lavery at the table, I was the last to attend him. Lord Marriot and Turnbull on the other hand were at his side at once, pinning him to the floor and steadying him. As I shakily joined them I saw that Old Danford had backed away into the furthest corner of the room, holding up his hands before him as if to ward off the very blackest of evils. With an anxious inquiry I hurried towards him. He shook me off and made straight for the door.

'Danford!' I cried. 'What on earth is –' But then I saw the way his eyes bulged and how terribly he trembled in every limb. The man was frightened for his life, and the sight of him in this condition made me forget my own terror in a moment. 'Danford,' I repeated in a quieter tone of voice. 'Are you well?'

By this time Lavery was sitting up on the floor and staring uncertainly about. Lord Marriot joined me as Danford opened the library door to stand for a moment facing us. All the blood seemed to have drained from his face; his hands fluttered like trapped birds as he stumbled backwards out of the room and into the passage leading to the main door of the house.

'Abomination!' he finally croaked, with no sign of his customary '*Harumph!*' 'A presence – monstrous – ultimate abomination – *God help us . . .* !'

'Presence?' Lord Marriot repeated, taking his arm. 'What is it, Danford? What's wrong, man?'

The old man tugged himself free. He seemed now somewhat recovered, but still his face was ashen and his trembling unabated. 'A presence, yes,' he hoarsely answered, 'a monstrous presence! I could not even try to exorcise . . . *that*!' And he turned and staggered along the corridor to the outer door.

'But where are you going, Danford?' Marriot called after him.

'Away,' came the answer from the door. 'Away from

here. I'll – I'll be in touch, Marriot – but I cannot stay here now.' The door slammed behind him as he stumbled into the darkness and a moment or two later came the roar of his car's engine.

When the sound had faded into the distance, Lord Marriot turned to me with a look of astonishment on his face. He asked: 'Well, what was that all about? Did he see something, d'you think?'

'No, David,' I shook my head, 'I don't think he *saw* anything. But I believe he sensed something – something perhaps apparent to him through his religious training and he got out before it could sense him!'

We stayed the night in the house, but while bedrooms were available we all chose to remain in the library, nodding fitfully in our easy chairs around the great fireplace. I, for one was very glad of the company, though I kept this fact to myself, and I could not help but wonder if the others might not now be similarly apprehensive.

Twice I awoke with a start in the huge quiet room, on both occasions feeding the red-glowing fire. And since that blaze lasted all through the night, I could only assume that at least one of the others was equally restless . . .

In the morning, after a frugal breakfast (Lord Marriot kept no retainers in the place; none would stay there, and so we had to make do for ourselves), while the others prowled about and stretched their legs or tidied themselves up, I saw and took stock of the situation. David, concerned about the aged clergyman, rang him at home and was told by Danford's housekeeper that her master had not stayed at home overnight. He had come home in a tearing rush at about nine o'clock, packed a case, told her that he was off 'up North' for a few days' rest, and had left at once for the railway station. She also said that she had not liked his colour.

The old man's greatcoat still lay across the arm of a chair in the library where he had left it in his frantic hurry of the night before. I took it and hung it up for him, wondering if he would ever return to the house to claim it.

Lavery was baggy-eyed and dishevelled and he complained of a splitting headache. He blamed his condition on an overdose of his host's sherry, but I knew for a certainty that he had been well enough before his dramatic demonstration of the previous evening. Of that demonstration, the medium said he could remember nothing; and yet he seemed distinctly uneasy and kept casting about the room and starting at the slightest unexpected movement, so that I believed his nerves had suffered a severe jolt.

It struck me that he, surely, must have been my assistant through the night; that he had spent some of the dark hours tending the fire in the great hearth. In any case, shortly after lunch and before the shadows of afternoon began to creep, he made his excuses and took his departure. I had somehow known that he would. And so three of us remained . . . three of the original five.

But if Danford's unexplained departure of the previous evening had disheartened Lord Marriot, and while Lavery's rather premature desertion had also struck a discordant note, at least Turnbull stood straight and strong on the side of our host. Despite Old Danford's absence, Turnbull would still go ahead with his part in the plan; an exorcist could always be found at some later date, if such were truly necessary. And certainly Lavery's presence was not prerequisite to Turnbull's forthcoming performance. Indeed, he wanted no one at all in attendance, desiring to be left entirely alone in the house. This was the only way he could possibly work, he assured us, and he had no fear at all about being on his own in the old place. After all, what was there to fear? This was only another experiment, wasn't it?

Looking back now I feel a little guilty that I did not argue the point further with Turnbull – about his staying alone in the old house overnight to sketch his automatic portrait of the unwanted tenant – but the man was so damned arrogant to my way of thinking, so sure of his theories and principles, that I offered not the slightest opposition. So we three all spent the evening reading and smoking before the log fire, and as night drew on Lord Marriot and I prepared to take our leave.

Then, too, as darkness fell over the oaks crowding dense and still beyond the gardens, I once again felt that unnatural oppressiveness creeping in upon me, that weight of unseen energies hovering in the suddenly sullen air.

Perhaps, for the first time, Lord Marriot felt it too, for he did not seem at all ill-disposed to leaving the house; indeed, there was an uncharacteristic quickness about him, and as we drove away in his car in the direction of the local village inn, I noticed that he involuntarily shuddered once or twice. I made no mention of it; the night was chill, after all . . .

At The Traveller's Rest, where business was only moderate, we inspected our rooms before making ourselves comfortable in the snug. There we played cards until about ten o'clock, but our minds were not on the game. Shortly after 10.30 Marriot called Turnbull to ask if all was going well. He returned from the telephone grumbling that Turnbull was totally ungrateful. He had not thanked Lord Marriot for his concern at all. The man demanded absolute isolation, no contact with the outside world whatever, and he complained that it would now take him well over an hour to go into his trance. After that he might begin to sketch almost immediately, or he might not start until well into the night, or there again the experiment could prove to be completely fruitless. It was all a matter of circumstance, and his chances would not be improved by useless interruptions.

We had left him seated in his shirt-sleeves before a

roaring fire. Close at hand were a bottle of wine, a plate of cold beef sandwiches, a sketch pad and pencils. These lay upon an occasional table which he would pull into a position directly in front of himself before sleeping, or, as he would have it, before 'going into trance'. There he sat, alone in that ominous old house.

Before retiring we made a light meal of chicken sandwiches, though neither one of us had any appreciable appetite. I cannot speak for Marriot, but as for me, it took me until well into the 'wee small hours' to get to sleep . . .

In the morning my titled friend was at my door while I was still half-way through washing. His outward appearance was ostensibly bright and breezy, but I sensed that his eagerness to get back to the old house and Turnbull was more than simply a desire to know the outcome of the latter's experiment; he was more interested in the man's welfare than anything else. Like my own, his misgivings with regard to his plan to learn something of the mysterious and alien entity at the house had grown through the night; now he would be more than satisfied simply to discover the medium well and unharmed.

And yet what could there possibly be at the place to harm him? Again, that question.

The night had brought a heavy frost, the first of the season, and hedgerows and verges were white as from a fall of snow. Half-way through the woods, on the long gravel drive winding in towards the house, there the horror struck! Manoeuvring a slight bend, Lord Marriot cursed, applied his brakes and brought the car skidding to a jarring halt. A shape, white and grey – and hideously red – lay huddled in the middle of the drive.

It was Turnbull, frozen, lying in a crystallized pool of his own blood, limbs contorted in the agony of death, his eyes glazed orbs that stared in blind and eternal horror at a sight Lord Marriot and I could hardly imagine. A thousand circular holes of about half an inch in diameter penetrated deep into his body, his face, all of his limbs; as if he had been the victim of some maniac with a brace and bit! Identical holes formed a track along the frosted grass verge from the house to this spot, as did Turnbull's flying footprints.

Against all my protests – weakened by nausea, white and trembling with shock as he was – still Lord Marriot raced his car the remainder of the way to the house. There we dismounted and he entered through the door which hung mutely ajar. I would not go in with him but stood dumbly wringing my hands, numb with horror, before the leering entrance.

A minute or so later he came staggering to the door. In his hand he carried a leaf from Turnbull's sketch pad. Before I could think to avert my eyes he thrust the almost completed sketch toward me, crying, 'Look! Look!'

I caught a glimpse of something bulbous and black, hairy and red-eyed – a tarantula, a bat, a dragon – whose joined legs were tipped with sharp, chitinous darts. A mere glimpse, without any real or lasting impression of detail, and yet –

'No!' I cried, throwing up my hands before my face, turning and rushing wildly back down the long drive. 'No, you fool, don't let me see it! I don't want to know! *I don't want to know!*'

THE THIEF IMMORTAL

Klaus August Scharme was born in a tiny village called Paradise close to Köln in the middle of the year 1940. The name of his birthplace has nothing to do with Scharme's story; the village was anything but paradisiacal, being a collection or huddle of farm buildings, some middling private dwellings and a grubby gasthaus, all reached along unmetalled roads, which, for at least four months of the year were little more than ruts around the perimeters of boggy fields.

Therefore, neither the date nor location of his origin was especially auspicious. The best we can say of them is that they were uninspired . . . drab beginnings for a man whose longevity would make him a legend of godlike proportions, not only in his own lifetime but also in every one of the countless *millions* of lives which would come and be lived and go – often in unseemly haste – before Scharme himself was yet fifty years old.

But here the paradox: he achieved that age not as might be expected in 1990, but in the summer of 2097. And the following story includes the facts of how that came about.

Aged sixteen years and three months, Scharme left Paradise and became an apprentice signwriter. He took up lodgings in Köln at the house of his master, where for the next five years he learned how to paint those intricate *Kreise* signs which signify with heraldic sigils the boundaries of the many and various districts of Germany. At that time such signs could be found on all major roads where they approached any specific district, and where for many years they had been the prey of avid 'art collectors' from England, France, the USA – the troops of NATO in general – energetically manoeuvring and war-gaming across the long-since conquered German countryside. But this too is a mere detail and should not be allowed to detract . . . except that it also served as Scharme's launching point on his trajectory of four hundred years' duration.

It started as a dream: Scharme dreamed that he was growing old at an unprecedented rate. He aged a day for every hour, then a week for every minute, finally a year for every second, at which point he collapsed in upon himself, died, crumbled into dust and blew away.

He woke up screaming, and it was the morning of his twenty-first birthday. Perhaps the dream had come about through a subconscious awareness of his proximity to the age of manhood; perhaps it had dawned on him that the first part of his life was done, ended like a chapter closed. But that same day, as Scharme replaced a purloined sign upon its post, he saw speeding by him a military Land Rover . . . and reclining in the open back of the vehicle a good half-dozen of these very signs over which he laboured so long and hard! The driver of this vehicle, a young Corporal in British uniform, laughed and waved as he sped into the distance; Scharme, wide-eyed in anger where he gazed after him, thought: '*Damn you . . . you should age a year for every sign you've stolen!*'

At which he was horrified to see the Land Rover swerve violently from the road to strike a tree!

Leaping onto his bicycle, Scharme raced to the scene of the accident. The Corporal, alas, was dead; also, he was old; moreover (and as Scharme would later work it out) it was probably the instantaneous aging which had caused him to swerve – making Klaus August Scharme a murderer! And he knew it was so, for at the moment of his wish – that the

Corporal should age commensurate with his thieving – he had felt *himself* the beneficiary of those years, some thirty-five in number. The Corporal had been twenty-five years of age; he was now sixty. Scharme had been twenty-one and still looked it, but some strange temporal instinct within told him that he would be fifty-six before he began to age again. Somehow – in some monstrous and inexplicable fashion – he had stolen all the young soldier's years!

And so for the next thirty-five years Scharme aged not at all but remained twenty-one; *but* – and most monstrously – in the twelve-month after that he aged altogether too many years, so that while by rights (?) he should only be twenty-two, his internal hourglass told him that in fact he had spilled the sands of ten whole years! It was the summer of 1997; K. A. Scharme had lived for fifty-seven years, should have aged by only twenty-two of them, and yet knew that physically he had aged *thirty*-two of them. In short, he knew that he was now getting old at ten times the normal rate, and that therefore he had started to pay the world back for the time he owed it. In just two and a half more years he'd be pushing sixty, and all the pleasures of an apparently eternal youth would be behind him and senility just around the corner. It was all grossly unfair and Scharme was very bitter about it.

So bitter, indeed, that the guilt he had felt over the past thirty-five years quite melted away. He determined to do something about his predicament, and of course it must be done quickly; when one is aging an entire year for every five weeks, time grows very short. But still Scharme was not a cruel man, and so chose his next victim (the very word left an unpleasant echo in his mind) with a deal of care and attention.

He chose, in fact, a crippled greypate who suffered incessant arthritic pains, stealing his last four years with the merest glance. The old man never knew what hit him but simply crumpled up in the street on his way to collect his pension. And Scharme was pleased that (a) the old boy would know no more pain, and (b) that the state was plainly a benefactor, likewise every taxpayer, and (c) that he himself, K. A. Scharme, would now live for a further four years at the constant age of only thirty-two and some few months. Which would surely be sufficient time to work out some sort of humane strategy.

Except . . . no sooner had his mental meter clocked up the defunct dodderer's four years, than it inexplicably halved them, alloting Scharme only two! Alarmed, he returned home and collapsed before his TV, where at that very moment they were showing an interview with a prisoner on Death Row. It was reckoned that this one could stave off his execution by a maximum of only two years, and that only at great expense. Scharme decided to save him and the state both money and trouble, and snatched his two remaining years right through the screen! The prisoner died right there in full view of many millions (good riddance, the majority said) but Scharme only gasped as the stolen time registered within him at a mere fraction of the time perceived: namely, six months!

It didn't take much of a mathematician to work out the implications. Complete this sequence: If thirty-five equals thirty-five, and four equals two, and two equals one-half . . .

Patently Scharme was only going to get one-eighth of his next victim's span of years; and after that one-sixteenth; then only one small thirty-second part, *und so weiter*. Which was precisely the way it was to work out.

But . . . let's not leap ahead. Scharme now had two and a half years of other people's time in which to think about it and plan for his vastly extended future. Which, diligently, he now set about to do. Nor did it take him thirty months by any means but only one day. You'll see why if you apply yourself to his problem:

His seventh victim would yield only one sixty-fourth of his remaining span, his eighth perhaps four or five months . . . *good God!* . . . By the time the vampire Scharme had taken his tenth victim – and even were that tenth a newborn infant – he would only be gaining a matter of weeks! Twenty victims later and he'd be down to seconds! Then half-seconds, microseconds, nanoseconds! By which time, quite obviously, he'd have arrived at the point where he was taking multiples of lives, perhaps even entire races at a gulp. Was that his destiny, then: to be a mass murderer? To be guilty of invisible genocide? To be the man who murdered an entire planet just to save his own miserable life?

Well, miserable it might be, but it was the only one he had. And life was cheap, as he above all other men was only too well aware. And so now he must use his two and a half year advantage to its fullest, and work out the *real* way it was going to be.

Scharme's grandfather had once told him: 'It takes hard work to earn a sum of money, but after that all it takes is time. Money in the bank doubles every ten years or so. That's something you should remember, Klaus August Scharme . . .' And Scharme had remembered.

And so for now he lived as frugally as possible, saved every *pfennig* he could get his hands on, banked his wages and watched the interest grow month by month, year by year. And while his money was growing, so he experimented.

For instance: he knew he could steal the lives of men, but what about animals? Scharme had read somewhere that no man knows the true age of sharks; so little is known about them that their span of years is beyond our scope. And he'd also read that barring accidents or the intervention of man, a shark *might* live for as long as two or three hundred years! Likewise certain species of tortoise, lizard, crocodile. Testing out the sharks, crocs and such, Scharme gained himself a good many years. But at the same time he lost some, too. The problem was that he couldn't know in advance how long these creatures were destined to live! A hammerhead off the Great Barrier Reef earned him three whole years (miraculous!), but another, taken the same day, was worth only an hour or two. Obviously that one had been set to meet its fate anyway. As for crocodiles: he ensured that several of those would never make it to the handbag stage!

And so eventually, without for the moment doing any further damage (to the *human* race, anyway) Scharme clocked up one hundred years on his mental chronometer and was able to give it a rest. He was more or less happy now that he could take it easy for a full century and still come out the other end only thirty-two years and some few months old. But rich? Oh, be certain he'd come out rich!

Except . . . what then, he wondered? What if – in the summer of 2097 when he'd used up all his stolen time – what if he then began to age too fast again? And just how fast *would* he age? Would it be ten years for every ordinary year, as before – or a hundred – or . . . a thousand? Or would he simply wither and die before he even knew it, before he had time to steal any more life? Obviously he should not allow that to happen. But at least with an entire century to give it a deal of considered thought, he wasn't going to let the knowledge of it spoil what he already had. Or what he was going to have . . .

The spring of 2097 eventually came around, and Scharme was a multi-millionaire. Back in the Year 2000 he had had only 23,300 Deutsch Marks in his Köln bank; in 2010 it had been 75,000; in 2050 the sum was 3,000,100; and now he was worth close to one hundred million. (Not in any bank in Köln, no, but in several numbered accounts in Switzerland.) And Scharme was still only thirty-two years old.

But as the spring of that year turned to summer the thief immortal was prepared and waiting, and he sat in his

Hamburg mansion and listened to the clocks in his head and in his very atoms ticking off the seconds to his fate. And he knew he was taking a great chance but took it anyway, simply because *he had to know!*

And so the time narrowed down to zero and Scharme's internal time clock – the register of his years – recommenced the sweep which he had temporarily stilled back in 1997. And so horrified was Scharme, so petrified at what transpired, that he let the thing run for a full three seconds before he was able to do anything about it. And then, on the count of three and when he was capable again, he pointed a trembling but deadly finger at a picture of Japan in his Atlas and absorbed the lives of all its millions – yes, every one of them – at a stroke! *And saw that he had only clocked up five extra years!*

He killed off Indonesia for another ten before his panic subsided – and then took half the fish in the Mediterranean just to be absolutely sure. Then, when he saw that he'd clocked up thirty-eight and a half years, he was satisfied – for a brief moment. Until as an afterthought (perhaps on a point of simple economy or ecology), he also took half of the *fishermen* in the Med and so evened up the balance.

And he knew that he must *never* let time creep up on him again, because if he did then it were certainly the end. For during the span of those three monstrous, uncontrolled seconds Klaus August Scharme had aged almost a *half-billion* such units and was now fifty years old!

Ah, but he would never get any older . . . not until the very last second, anyway.

There had been no one left to bury the dead in the Japanese and Indonesian Islands; for fifty years they were pestholes; mercifully, being islands, their plagues were contained. That lesser ravage (men called it The Ravage) which had slain so many in and around the Mediterranean was guessed to have had the same origin as the Japan/Indonesian Plagues, but science had never tracked it to its source. It was generally assumed that Mother Nature had simply bridled at one of Man's nuclear, ecological or chemical indiscretions. No one ever had cause to relate the horror to the being of Klaus August Scharme. No, not even when his strange longevity finally became known.

That was the fault of his doctor; rather, it came about through that doctor's diligence. Scharme had gone through a phase of worrying about diseases. He had reasoned that if, in a normal lifetime, a man will suffer several afflictions of mind and body, how then a man with many lifetimes? What fatal cancers were blossoming in him even now? What tumours? What micro-biological mutations, even as he was a mutation, were killing him? And when he had submitted himself for the most minute examination, he'd also submitted his medical records . . .

The news broke: the world had taken unto its bosom, or created, what appeared to be an immortal! The Second Coming? It could be! A miracle to bring lasting peace and tranquillity? Possibly. And Klaus August Scharme became the most fêted man in the history of the world. Church men, at first sceptical, eventually applauded; world leaders looked to him for his friendship and favours; wealth as great and even greater than his own billions was heaped at his feet.

And when the Maltese Plague struck in the Year 2163, Klaus August Scharme bought that island and sent in a million men to burn the bodies, cleanse the streets and build him his palace there. And still no one suspected that the Great Benefactor Scharme was in fact the Great Monster Scharme, a vampire thief drinking up the lives of men. But why should they?

Scharme gave work to the millions; he lavished billions of dollars, pounds, yen, lire, on charities across the face of the world; countless fortunes were spent in the search for the ultimate secret – that of eternal youth – which Scharme declared was fitting for all mankind and not just himself. He built hospitals, laboratories, schools, houses. He opened up the potential of the poorer countries; dug wells in the Sahara, repopulated ravaged islands (such as Japan, Indonesia), built dams and barriers to stem the floods in the Nile and Ganges; wiped out the locust (at a stroke, and without ever hinting at the miracle he employed); deliberately and systematically did all he could to provide the monies and the science requisite to prolonging the lives of men. Ah, of course he did! The longer men lived, the longer he would live. It was a question of careful culling, that was all . . .

In 2247, the whales died . . . but of no discernible disorder. Those largest of all Earth's creatures – protected, revered and preserved by man since the turn of the twenty-first Century – switched off like a light, wasted, erased to provide Scharme with life. And the thief immortal gaining only a moment or two from each huge, placid creature. Not all of them died; perhaps a dozen of each species were left to repopulate the oceans – naturally. Scharme was not an unreasonable man, and he was learning.

In the North Sea and the waters around England, across the Atlantic to the American coastline, there came the sudden and inexplicable decline of the cod; that was in 2287. But in the ensuing four years the rest of the food fishes surged and man did not go short. At the end of that period, in the spring of 2292, all the world's longest lived trees became firewood overnight. It was Nature, the Top Men said; it was Evolution, an ecological balancing act; it was the Survival of the Fittest. And in that last, at least, they were right; the survival of Klaus August Scharme.

But there were no more wars. World President Scharme

in his impregnable Malta fortress, rearing two miles high from the sea, would not allow wars; they were destructive and cost him too many lives. Nor would he allow pollution or disease, and wherever possible he took all steps to avoid natural disasters. The world had become a very wonderful place in which to live – if one could live long enough and avoid those unpredictable places wherein an apparently outraged Nature was wont to strike so pitilessly and without warning.

Scharme had long ago discovered that it was not the number of lives he took which determined the ever-shortening half-life of his obscene talent but the number of times he used that talent. Whether he took the life of a single man or an entire species of toad made no difference: always the sum of the span of stolen time was halved. And by the year 2309 he was already well down into the micro-seconds. Patently it was wasteful – what? It was sheer madness! – to take single lives and he would never do that again; indeed he had not done so since the late twentieth century.

Towards the end of 2309 he took seven-eighths of all the world's corals and earned himself only nine weeks! And that same night, after worriedly pacing the floors of his incredible palace fortress, Scharme eventually retired to dream his second inspirational dream. An inspiration, and a warning:

He saw a word: NECROMETER.

That single word above an instrument with one hundred little glass windows all in a row. Behind each window, on a black background, the same white digital number (or negative) gleamed like a long line of open mouths: one hundred 'O's, a century of zeroes.

Scharme was in a dark room, seated at some sort of console. He was strapped into a sturdy metal chair-like frame, held upright and immobile as a man in an electric chair. Behind the NECROMETER a massive wall reached away out of sight both vertically and horizontally. The wall was made up of trillions of tiny lights no bigger than pinheads, each one like a minuscule firefly, lending the wall a soft haze of light.

Scharme looked at the word again: NECROMETER. And at the digital counter beneath it. Even as he watched, the number I clicked into place in the window on the far right, in the next moment became a 2, a 3, 4, 5 . . .

The numbers began to flutter, reaching 1,000 in a moment, 10,000 in seconds. On the wall the tiny lights, singly, in small clusters, in masses, were blinking out, whole sections snuffing themselves before his eyes. On the NECROMETER the figure was into millions, tens of millions, billions; and a hideous fear, a soul-shrinking terror descended upon Scharme as he watched, strapped in his sturdy metal chair. If only he could break these straps he knew he could smash the counter, stop the lights from winking out, put an end to the wanton destruction of life, the death.

The death, yes. NECROMETER.

An instrument for measuring death!

But whose instrument? Obviously it belonged to Death himself. The entire – control room? – *was* Death!

Now the number on the counter was into the trillions, tens of trillions, hundreds of trillions, and entire sections of the wall were darkening like lights switched off in a sky-scraper. In as little time as it takes to tell the quintillions were breached, the counter whirring and blurring and humming now in a mechanical frenzy of death-dealing activity. The wall was going out. Life itself was being extinguished.

Scharme struggled frantically, uselessly with his straps, straining against them, clawing at them with trapped, spastic hands. The counters were slowing down, the wall dimming, the NECROMETER had almost completed its task. The world – perhaps even the Universe – was almost empty of life.

Only two tiny lights remained on the dark wall: two faintly glowing pinheads. Close together, almost touching, they seemed to swell enormous in the eye of Scharme's mind, blooming into beacons that riveted his attention.

Two lights. He – his life – must be one of them. And the other?

The Conqueror Worm!

The Old Man!

The Grim Reaper!

The Nine of Spades!

The black lumpish machine bank atop the console above the NECROMETER split open like a hatching egg, its metal casing cracking and flaking away in chunks.

An eye, crimson with blood, stared out; a mouth, dripping the blood of nameless, numberless lives, smiled a monstrous smile, opening up into an awesome, gaping maw.

Scharme's straps snapped open. His chair tilted forward and flexed itself, ejecting him screaming down Death's endlessly echoing throat . . .

In the Year 2310, Scharme built the NECROMETER into a new wing of his massive Malta stronghold, and not a man of the thousands of technicians and scientists and builders who constructed it could ever have guessed at its purpose. Nor would they have thought of trying to do so. It was sufficient that the Immortal Man-god Master and Benefactor of the World Klaus August Scharme desired it, and so it was done. And Scharme's Computer of Life – and more surely of Death – was fashioned almost exactly as his dream had prescribed.

Within its electrical memory were housed details of every known species of animal, insect and vegetable, the approximate spans of life of each, their locations upon a vast world globe which turned endlessly above the console. This last was lit from within, taking the place of the wall of lights; and this was Scharme's single improvement over his dream.

The computer contained details of every species that flew in the sky, walked or grew upon the ground, crawled beneath it or swam in the deeps of the seas. It kept as accurate as possible a record of births (and deaths, of course) and updated Scharme's precious seconds of vampiric life in a never-ending cycle of self-appointed self-serving sacrifice. It specified the region of the planet to be exploited, told Scharme whom or what to kill and when to do it, programmed his culling of life until it was the finest (and foulest) of fine arts.

And suddenly, with all the weight and worry of calculation and of decision-making taken from his shoulders, and with all of his long years of existence stretching out behind him and apparently before him, Scharme began to feel the inevitable *ennui* of his immortality. And until now, he had not once thought of taking a wife.

There were three main reasons for this.

First, despite all the years he had stolen, there had never seemed to be enough time for it. Second, he had feared to father children who might carry forward and spread his own mutation throughout the world, so robbing him of his future. Last, he knew how great was his power and mighty his position, and so would never be certain that a woman – any woman – would love him for himself and not for the glory of knowing him. All of which seemed valid arguments indeed . . . until the day he met Oryss.

Oryss was young, innocent and very beautiful: long-legged, firm-bodied, green-eyed and lightly tanned. And courting her, Scharme also discovered her to be without greed. Indeed, he was astonished that she turned him down on those very grounds: she could not marry him because people would say it was only his power and position which she loved. But while she visited him in his Maltese redoubt there occurred one of those unimaginable disasters with which, paradoxically, the world was now all too well acquainted. Her island, the island of Crete, was stricken with plague!

There were no survivors save Oryss; she could not go home to what was now a rotting pesthole; she became Scharme's wife and thus Queen of the World . . .

The years passed. She wanted children and he refused. Soon she was thirty-five and he was still fifty. But in three more years, when he saw how time was creeping up on her, Scharme began to despair. So that one day he called her to his most private place, the hall of the NECROMETER, and explained to her that machine's purpose. Except it had no purpose unless he also explained his talent, which he did. At first she was astonished, awed, frightened. And then she was quiet. Very quiet.

'What are you thinking?' he eventually asked her.

'Only of Crete,' she told him.

'The great whales have proliferated during the last hundred years,' he told her then. 'I would like to experiment, see if I can give you some of their time. I can't bear to see another wrinkle come into your face.'

'They were only laughter lines,' she said, sadly, as if she thought she might never laugh again.

'Here, hold my hands,' said Scharme. And there in the hall of the NECROMETER he willed half the whales dead and their time transferred to Oryss. And here the most astonishing thing of all: he discovered that his internal chronometer worked not only for him but also for his wife – *and that she had gained several millions of years!*

And he saw that because she was new to his art, it was for her as it had been at first for him: just as he had gained all of that almost forgotten Corporal's years, so had Oryss gained all of the years of the many whales. 'It could have been me!' he told himself then. 'If I had known at the beginning . . . it could have been me . . .' And while he clapped a hand to his forehead and reeled, and thought these things – things which he had always known, but which never before had been brought home so forcefully – so Oryss fainted at his feet.

He at once carried her to her bed, called his physicians, sat stroking her hand until the medical men were finished with their examination. And: 'What is it?' he whispered to them then, afraid that they would tell him the worst.

'Nothing, merely a faint,' they shrugged. But Scharme suspected it was much more than that. He felt it in his bones, a cold such as he had never known before, not even as a barefoot boy in Paradise in the winter. And mazed and mortally afraid he once more turned his eyes inwards and gazed upon the life-clock ticking in his being. Ah, and he saw how quickly the pendulum swung, how fast his time was running down! Too fast; the weight of Oryss's myriad years had tipped the scales; he had a month and then must take life again. Oh, a great many lives . . .

It was too much for him. Even for the Great Vampire Klaus August Scharme. To extend his life a single hour beyond the twenty-eight days remaining to him he must devour a hundred lifetimes, and for the next hour ten thousand, and for the next one hundred million! The figure would simply multiply itself each time he used his talent. Quickly he returned to the hall of the NECROMETER, fed the computer with these new figures, impatiently waited out the few seconds the machine stole from him to perform its task. And while he stood there trembling and waiting, so the NECROMETER balanced all the planet's teeming life against the single life of Klaus August Scharme, and finally delivered its verdict. He had only twenty-eight days, six hours, three minutes and forty-three seconds left – and not a second longer. Neither Scharme, nor any other living thing upon the face of the planet!

Gasping his horror, he fed new figures into the computer. What if he took *all* the Earth's life at a single stroke – with the exception, of course, of life in the air and on the land and in the waters around Malta? And the computer gave him back exactly the same result, for it had assumed that this was his question in the first instance!

At which, Scharme too fainted away . . .

But before he woke up he dreamed his third inspirational dream, whose essence was simplicity itself. He saw gigantic scales weighted on the one side with Oryss, and on the other with the planet Earth and all it contained. But for all that she was a single creature, still those cosmic scales were tilted in her favour. And between the pans of the scales, holding them aloft on arms which formed the pivot, stood Klaus August Scharme himself.

He awoke, and Oryss stood there close by, looking at the NECROMETER. Upon its screen were those terrible calculations which had caused her husband's faint. And from the look on her face Scharme supposed she understood them. And from the look on *his* face, she also understood that he had reached a decision.

'So,' she said then, 'it is ended.'

He climbed tiredly to his feet, burst into tears. 'It is the only way,' he said, folding her to his heart. 'But not yet, my love, not yet. I can wait . . . a day? Perhaps even a day and a night. But you must understand that what was mine to give, is also mine to take away.'

'Not so,' she clasped him coldly. 'For when you gave me my millions of years, you also gave me your talent. I feel it within me, ticking like a clock.'

He gasped and thrust her away, but she was pointing at him and had already commenced to say: 'You should age one second for every man, woman and child, every beast, fish, fowl and creeping thing which you destroyed in the island of Crete!' Which was the end of him, for he had something a deal less than two and a half millions of seconds left, and of creeping things alone, that would have sufficed to kill him. But Oryss had loved her island dearly.

Long ago, Scharme had conceived of a time when someone might see his NECROMETER, understand its purpose and meaning and attempt to kill him. And he had determined that if that time should ever come, then that his executioner must die with him. Now, even as he crumbled to dust, he fell upon a certain lever.

The console of the NECROMETER cracked open into a gaping mouth and the floor of the hall lashed like a crippled snake. A convulsion which hurled the beautiful Oryss and the vile vampiric debris of Klaus August Scharme into eternity within the clashing cogs and wheels and electrical daggers of the great machine. Scharme's fortress blew apart from its roots upwards, and the island of Malta collapsed inwards, and great tidal waves washed outwards to the furthest corners of the world.

And Time Itself felt a wrenching and a reckoning, and Inviolable Life – so long held upon Scharme's monstrous leash – rebelled and added to the space-time confusion. So that for a split second all was chaos until the vast Engine which is the Universe backfired . . . !

Laughing and waving, the Corporal sped away in his Land Rover. Scharme's short ladder shuddered for a moment beneath the post to which he'd nailed his *Kreise* sign, then stood still and empty. The *Kreise* sign swung all askew upon a single nail, the job unfinished. And at the foot of the ladder lay a small pile of rags and a handful of grey dust, which the winds of time quickly blew away . . .

NECROS

I

An old woman in a faded blue frock and black head-square
paused in the shade of Mario's awning and nodded good-
day. She smiled a gap-toothed smile. A bulky, slouch-
shouldered youth in jeans and a stained yellow T-shirt –
a slope-headed idiot, probably her grandson – held her
hand, drooling vacantly and fidgeting beside her.

Mario nodded good-naturedly, smiled, wrapped a piece
of stale *focaccia* in greaseproof paper and came from behind
the bar to give it to her. She clasped his hand, thanked him,
turned to go.

Her attention was suddenly arrested by something she
saw across the road. She started, cursed vividly, harshly,
and despite my meagre knowledge of Italian, I picked up
something of the hatred in her tone. 'Devil's spawn!' She
said it again. 'Dog! Swine!' She pointed a shaking hand and
finger, said yet again: 'Devil's spawn!' before making the
two-fingered, double-handed stabbing sign with which the
Italians ward off evil. To do this it was first necessary that
she drop her salted bread, which the idiot youth at once
snatched up.

Then, still mouthing low, guttural imprecations, dragging
the shuffling, *focaccia*-munching cretin behind her, she
hurried off along the street and disappeared into an
alley. One word that she had repeated over and over again
stayed in my mind: '*Necros! Necros!*' Though the word was

new to me, I took it for a curse-word. The accent she put on it had been poisonous.

I sipped at my Negroni, remained seated at the small circular table beneath Mario's awning and stared at the object of the crone's distaste. It was a motor car, a white convertible Rover and this year's model, inching slowly forward in a stream of holiday traffic. And it was worth looking at if only for the girl behind the wheel. The little man in the floppy white hat beside her – well, he was something else too. But *she* was – just something else.

I caught just a glimpse, sufficient to feel stunned. That was good. I had thought it was something I could never know again: that feeling a man gets looking at a beautiful girl. Not after Linda. And yet—

She was young, say twenty-four or -five, some three or four years my junior. She sat tall at the wheel, slim, raven-haired under a white, wide-brimmed summer hat which just missed matching that of her companion, with a complexion cool and creamy enough to pour over peaches. I stood up – yes, to get a better look – and right then the traffic came to a momentary standstill. At that moment, too, she turned her head and looked at me. And if the profile had stunned me . . . well, the full-frontal knocked me dead. The girl was simply, classically beautiful.

Her eyes were of a dark green but very bright, slightly tilted and perfectly oval under straight, thin brows. Her cheekbones were high, her lips a red Cupid's bow, her neck long and white against the glowing yellow of her blouse. And her smile—

—Oh, yes, she smiled.

Her glance, at first cool, became curious in a moment, then a little angry, until finally, seeing my confusion – that smile. And as she turned her attention back to the road and followed the stream of traffic out of sight, I saw a blush of colour spreading on the creamy surface of her cheek. Then she was gone.

Then, too, I remembered the little man who sat beside her. Actually, I hadn't seen a great deal of him, but what I had seen had given me the creeps. He too had turned his head to stare at me, leaving in my mind's eye an impression of beady bird eyes, sharp and intelligent in the shade of his hat. He had stared at me for only a moment, and then his head had slowly turned away; but even when he no longer looked at me, when he stared straight ahead, it seemed to me I could feel those raven's eyes upon me, and that a query had been written in them.

I believed I could understand it, that look. He must have seen a good many young men staring at him like that – or rather, at the girl. His look had been a threat in answer to my threat – and because he was practised in it, I had certainly felt the more threatened!

I turned to Mario, whose English was excellent. 'She has something against expensive cars and rich people?'

'Who?' he busied himself behind his bar.

'The old lady, the woman with the idiot boy.'

'Ah!' he nodded. 'Mainly against the little man, I suspect.'

'Oh?'

'You want another Negroni?'

'OK – and one for yourself – but tell me about this other thing, won't you?'

'If you like – but you're only interested in the girl, yes?' He grinned.

I shrugged. 'She's a good-looker . . .'

'Yes, I saw her.' Now he shrugged. 'That other thing – just old myths and legends, that's all. Like your English Dracula, eh?'

'Transylvanian Dracula,' I corrected him.

'Whatever you like. And Necros: that's the name of the spook, see?'

'Necros is the name of a vampire?'

'A spook, yes.'

'And this is a real legend? I mean, historical?'

He made a fifty-fifty face, his hands palms up. 'Local, I guess. Ligurian. I remember it from when I was a kid. If I was bad, old Necros sure to come and get me. Today,' again the shrug, 'it's forgotten.'

'Like the bogeyman.' I nodded.

'Eh?'

'Nothing. But why did the old girl go on like that?'

Again he shrugged. 'Maybe she think that old man Necros, eh? She crazy, you know? Very backward. The whole family.'

I was still interested. 'How does the legend go?'

'The spook takes the life out of you. You grow old, spook grows young. It's a bargain you make: he gives you something you want, gets what he wants. What he wants is your youth. Except he uses it up quick and needs more. All the time, more youth.'

'What kind of bargain is that?' I asked. 'What does the victim get out of it?'

'Gets what he wants,' said Mario, his brown face cracking into another grin. 'In your case the girl, eh? *If* the little man was Necros . . .'

He got on with his work and I sat there sipping my Negroni. End of conversation. I thought no more about it – until later.

II

Of course, I should have been in Italy with Linda, but . . . I had kept her 'Dear John' for a fortnight before shredding it, getting mindlessly drunk and starting in on the process of forgetting. That had been a month ago. The holiday had already been booked and I wasn't about to miss out on my trip to the sun. And so I had come out on my own. It was hot, the swimming was good, life was easy and the food superb. With just two days left to enjoy it, I told myself it hadn't been bad. But it would have been better with Linda.

Linda . . . She was still on my mind – at the back of it, anyway – later that night as I sat in the bar of my hotel beside an open bougainvillaea-decked balcony that looked down on the bay and the seafront lights of the town. And maybe she wasn't all that far back in my mind – maybe she was right there in front – or else I was just plain day-dreaming. Whichever, I missed the entry of the lovely lady and her shrivelled companion, failing to spot and recognise them until they were taking their seats at a little table just the other side of the balcony's sweep.

This was the closest I'd been to her, and—

Well, first impressions hadn't lied. This girl *was* beautiful. She didn't look quite as young as she'd first seemed – my own age, maybe – but beautiful she certainly was. And the old boy? He must be, could only be, her father. Maybe it sounds like I was a little naïve, but with her looks this lady really didn't need an old man. And if she did need one it didn't have to be *this* one.

By now she'd seen me and my fascination with her must have been obvious. Seeing it, she smiled and blushed at one and the same time, and for a moment turned her eyes away – but only for a moment. Fortunately her companion had his back to me or he must have known my feelings at once; for as she looked at me again – fully upon me this time – I could have sworn I read an invitation in her eyes, and in that same moment any bitter vows I may have made melted away completely and were forgotten. God, *please* let him be her father!

For an hour I sat there, drinking a few too many cocktails, eating olives and potato crisps from little bowls on the bar, keeping my eyes off the girl as best I could, if only for common decency's sake. But . . . all the time I worried frantically at the problem of how to introduce myself, and as the minutes ticked by it seemed to me that the most obvious way must also be the best.

But how obvious would it be to the old boy?

And the damnable thing was that the girl hadn't given me another glance since her original – invitation? Had I mistaken that look of hers – or was she simply waiting for me to make the first move? *God, let him be her father!*

She was sipping Martinis, slowly; he drank a rich red wine, in some quantity. I asked a waiter to replenish their glasses and charge it to me. I had already spoken to the bar steward, a swarthy, friendly little chap from the South called Francesco, but he hadn't been able to enlighten me. The pair were not resident, he assured me; but being resident myself I was already pretty sure of that.

Anyway, my drinks were delivered to their table; they looked surprised; the girl put on a perfectly innocent expression, questioned the waiter, nodded in my direction and gave me a cautious smile, and the old boy turned his head to stare at me. I found myself smiling in return but avoiding his eyes, which were like coals now, sunken deep in his brown, wrinkled face. Time seemed suspended – if only for a second – then the girl spoke again to the waiter and he came across to me.

'Mr Collins, sir, the gentleman and the young lady thank you and request that you join them.' Which was everything I had dared hope for – for the moment.

Standing up, I suddenly realized how much I'd had to drink. I willed sobriety on myself and walked across to their table. They didn't stand up but the little chap said, 'Please sit.' His voice was a rustle of dried grass. The waiter was behind me with a chair. I sat.

'Peter Collins,' I said. 'How do you do, Mr – er?—'

'Karpethes,' he answered. 'Nichos Karpethes. And this is my wife, Adrienne.' Neither one of them had made the effort to extend their hands, but that didn't dismay me. Only the fact that they were married dismayed me. He must be very, very rich, this Nichos Karpethes.

'I'm delighted you invited me over,' I said, forcing a smile, 'but I see that I was mistaken. You see, I thought I heard you speaking English, and I—'

'Thought we were English?' she finished it for me. 'A natural error. Originally I am Armenian, Nichos is Greek, of course. We do not speak each other's tongue, but we do both speak English. Are you staying here, Mr Collins?'

'Er, yes – for one more day and night. Then – 'I shrugged and put on a sad look, '– back to England, I'm afraid.'

'Afraid?' the old boy whispered. 'There is something to fear in a return to your homeland?'

'Just an expression,' I answered. 'I meant, I'm afraid that my holiday is coming to an end.'

He smiled. It was a strange, wistful sort of smile, wrinkling his face up like a little walnut. 'But your friends will be glad to see you again. Your loved ones—?'

I shook my head. 'Only a handful of friends – none of them really close – and no loved ones. I'm a loner, Mr Karpethes.'

'A loner?' His eyes glowed deep in their sockets and his hands began to tremble where they gripped the table's rim. 'Mr Collins, you don't—'

'We understand,' she cut him off. 'For although we are together, we too, in our way, are loners. Money has made Nichos lonely, you see? Also, he is not a well man, and time is short. He will not waste what time he has on frivolous friendships. As for myself – people do not understand our being together, Nichos and I. They pry, and I withdraw. And so, I too, am a loner.'

There was no accusation in her voice, but still I felt obliged to say: 'I certainly didn't intend to pry, Mrs—'

'Adrienne,' she smiled. 'Please. No, of course you didn't. I would not want you to think we thought that of you. Anyway I will *tell* you why we are together, and then it will be put aside.'

Her husband coughed, seemed to choke, struggled to his feet. I stood up and took his arm. He at once shook me off – with some distaste, I thought – but Adrienne had already signalled to a waiter. 'Assist Mr Karpethes to the gentleman's room,' she quickly instructed in very good Italian. 'And please help him back to the table when he has recovered.'

As he went, Karpethes gesticulated, probably tried to say something to me by way of an apology, choked again and reeled as he allowed the waiter to help him from the room.

'I'm . . . sorry,' I said, not knowing what else to say.

'He has attacks.' She was cool. 'Do not concern yourself. I am used to it.'

We sat in silence for a moment. Finally I began: 'You were going to tell me—'

'Ah, yes! I had forgotten. It is a symbiosis.'

'Oh?'

'Yes. I need the good life he can give me, and he needs . . . my youth. We supply each other's needs.' And so, in a way, the old woman with the idiot boy hadn't been wrong after all. A sort of bargain had indeed been struck. Between Karpethes and his wife. As that thought crossed my mind I felt the short hairs at the back of my neck stiffen for a moment. Goose-flesh crawled on my arms. After all, 'Nichos' was pretty close to 'Necros,' and now this youth thing again. Coincidence, of course. And after all, aren't all relationships bargains of sorts? Bargains struck for better or for worse.

'But for how long?' I asked. 'I mean, how long will it work for you?'

She shrugged. 'I have been provided for. And he will have me all the days of his life.'

I coughed, cleared my throat, gave a strained, self-conscious laugh. 'And here's me, the non-pryer!'

'No, not at all, I wanted you to know.'

'Well,' I shrugged, '– but it's been a pretty deep first conversation.'

'First? Did you believe that buying me a drink would entitle you to more than one conversation?'

I almost winced. 'Actually, I—'

But then she smiled and my world lit up. 'You did not need to buy the drinks,' she said. 'There would have been some other way.'

I looked at her inquiringly. 'Some other way to—?'

'To find out if we were English or not.'

'Oh!'

'Here comes Nichos now,' she smiled across the room. 'And we must be leaving. He's not well. Tell me, will you be on the beach tomorrow?'

'Oh – yes!' I answered after a moment's hesitation. 'I like to swim.'

'So do I. Perhaps we can swim out to the raft . . . ?'

'I'd like that very much.'

Her husband arrived back at the table under his own steam. He looked a little stronger now, not quite so shrivelled somehow. He did not sit but gripped the back of his chair with parchment fingers, knuckles white where the skin stretched over old bones. 'Mr Collins,' he rustled, '– Adrienne, I'm sorry . . .'

'There's really no need,' I said, rising.

'We really must be going.' She also stood. 'No, you stay here, er, Peter? It's kind of you, but we can manage. Perhaps we'll see you on the beach.' And she helped him to the door of the bar and through it without once looking back.

III

They weren't staying at my hotel, had simply dropped in for a drink. That was understandable (though I would have preferred to think that she had been looking for me) for *my* hotel was middling tourist-class while theirs was something else. They were up on the hill, high on the crest of a Ligurian spur where a smaller, much more exclusive place nestled in Mediterranean pines. A place whose lights spelled money when they shone up there at night, whose music came floating down from a tiny open-air disco like the laughter of high-living elementals of the air. If I was poetic it was because of her. I mean, that beautiful girl and that weary, wrinkled dried-up walnut of an old man. If anything, I was sorry for him. And yet in another way I wasn't.

And let's make no pretence about it – if I haven't said it already, let me say it right now – I wanted her. Moreover, there had been that about our conversation, her beach invitation, which told me that she was available.

The thought of it kept me awake half the night . . .

I was on the beach at 9.00 a.m. – they didn't show until 11.00. When they did, and when she came out of her tiny changing cubicle—

There wasn't a male head on the beach that didn't turn at least twice. Who could blame them? That girl, in *that* costume, would have turned the head of a sphinx. But – there was something, some little nagging thing, different about her. A maturity beyond her years? She held herself like a model, a princess. But who was it for? Karpethes or me?

As for the old man: he was in a crumpled lightweight summer suit and sunshade hat as usual, but he seemed a bit more perky this morning. Unlike myself he'd doubtless had a good night's sleep. While his wife had been changing he had made his way unsteadily across the pebbly beach to my table and sun umbrella, taking the seat directly opposite me; and before his wife could appear he had opened with: 'Good morning, Mr Collins.'

'Good morning,' I answered. 'Please call me Peter.'

'Peter, then,' he nodded. He seemed out of breath, either from his stumbling walk over the beach or a certain urgency which I could detect in his movements, his hurried, almost rude 'let's get down to it' manner.

'Peter, you said you would be here for one more day?'

'That's right,' I answered, for the first time studying him closely where he sat like some strange garden gnome half in the shade of the beach umbrella. 'This is my last day.'

He was a bundle of dry wood, a desiccated prune, a small, umber scarecrow. And his voice, too, was of straw, or autumn leaves blown across a shady path. Only his eyes were alive. 'And you said you have no family, few friends, no one to miss you back in England?'

Warning bells rang in my head. Maybe it wasn't so much urgency in him – which usually implies a goal or ambition still to be realized – but eagerness in that the goal was in sight. 'That's correct. I am, was, a student doctor. When I get home I shall seek a position. Other than that there's nothing, no one, no ties.'

He leaned forward, bird eyes very bright, claw hand reaching across the table, trembling, and—

Her shadow suddenly fell across us as she stood there in that costume. Karpethes jerked back in his chair. His face was working, strange emotions twisting the folds and wrinkles of his flesh into stranger contours. I could feel my heart thumping against my ribs . . . why, I couldn't say. I calmed myself, looked up at her and smiled.

She stood with her back to the sun, which made a dark silhouette of her head and face. But in that blot of darkness her oval eyes were green jewels. 'Shall we swim, Peter?'

She turned and ran down the beach, and of course I ran after her. She had a head start and beat me to the water, beat me to the raft, too. It wasn't until I hauled myself up beside her that I thought of Karpethes: how I hadn't even excused myself before plunging after her. But at least the water had cleared my head, bringing me completely awake and aware.

Aware of her incredible body where it stretched, almost touching mine, on the fibre deck of the gently bobbing raft.

I mentioned her husband's line of inquiry, gasping a little for breath as I recovered from the frantic exercise of our race. She, on the other hand, already seemed completely recovered. She carefully arranged her hair about her shoulders like a fan, to dry in the sunlight, before answering.

'Nichos is not really my husband,' she finally said, not looking at me. 'I am his companion, that's all. I could have told you last night, but . . . there was the chance that you really were curious only about our nationality. As for any 'veiled threats' he might have issued: that is not unusual. He might not have the vitality of younger men, but jealousy is ageless.'

'No,' I answered, 'he didn't threaten – not that I noticed. But jealousy? Knowing I have only one more day to spend here, what has he to fear from me?'

Her shoulders twitched a little, a shrug. She turned her face to me, her lips inches away. Her eyelashes were like silken shutters over green pools, hiding whatever swam in the deeps. 'I am young, Peter, and so are you. And you are very attractive, very . . . eager? Holiday romances are not uncommon.'

My blood was on fire. 'I have very little money,' I said. 'We are staying at different hotels. He already suspects me. It is impossible.'

'What is?' she innocently asked, leaving me at a complete loss.

But then she laughed, tossed back her hair, already dry, dangled her hands and arms in the water. 'Where there's a will . . .' she said.

'You know that I want you—' The words spilled out before I could control or change them.

'Oh, yes. And I want you.' She said it so simply, and yet suddenly I felt seared. A moth brushing the magnet candle's flame.

I lifted my head, looked towards the beach. Across seventy-five yards of sparkling water the beach umbrellas looked very large and close. Karpethes sat in the shade just as I had last seen him, his face hidden in shadow. But I knew that he watched.

'You can do nothing here,' she said, her voice languid – but I noticed now that she, too, seemed short of breath.

'This,' I told her with a groan, 'is going to kill me!'

She laughed, laughter that sparkled more than the sun on the sea. 'I'm sorry,' she said more soberly. 'It's unfair of me to laugh. But – your case is not hopeless.'

'Oh?'

'Tomorrow morning, early, Nichos has an appointment with a specialist in Genova. I am to drive him into the city tonight. We'll stay at a hotel overnight.'

I groaned my misery. 'Then my case is quite hopeless. I fly tomorrow.'

'But if I sprained my wrist,' she said, 'and so could not drive . . . and if he went into Genova by taxi while I stayed behind with a headache – because of the pain from my wrist –' Like a flash she was on her feet, the raft tilting, her body diving, striking the water into a spray of diamonds.

Seconds for it all to sink in – and then I was following her, labouring through the water in her churning wake. And as she splashed from the sea, seeing her stumble, go to her hands and knees in Ligurian shingle – and the pained look on her face, the way she held her wrist as she came to her feet. As easy as that!

Karpethes, struggling to rise from his seat, stared at her with his mouth agape. Her face screwed up now as I followed her up the beach. And Adrienne holding her 'sprained' wrist and shaking it, her mouth forming an elongated 'O'. The sinuous motion of her body and limbs, mobile marble with dew of ocean clinging saltily . . .

If the tiny man had said to me: 'I am Necros. I want ten years of your life for one night with her,' at that moment I might have sealed the bargain. Gladly. But legends are legends and he wasn't Necros, and he didn't, and I didn't. After all, there was no need . . .

IV

I suppose my greatest fear was that she might be 'having me on', amusing herself at my expense. She was, of course, 'safe' with me – in so far as I would be gone tomorrow and the 'romance' forgotten, for her, anyway – and I could also see how she was starved for young companionship, a fact she had brought right out in the open from the word go.

But why me? Why should I be so lucky?

Attractive? Was I? I had never thought so. Perhaps it was because I *was* so safe: here today and gone tomorrow, with little or no chance of complications. Yes, that must be it. *If* she wasn't simply making a fool of me. She might be just a tease—

But she wasn't.

At 8.30 that evening I was in the bar of my hotel – had been there for an hour, careful not to drink too much, unable to eat – when the waiter came to me and said there was a call for me on the reception telephone. I hurried out to reception where the clerk discreetly excused himself and left me alone.

'Peter?' Her voice was a deep well of promise. 'He's gone. I've booked us a table, to dine at 9.00. Is that all right for you?'

'A table? Where?' my own voice breathless.

'Why, up here, of course! Oh, don't worry, it's perfectly safe. And anyway, Nichos knows.'

'Knows?' I was taken aback, a little panicked. 'What does he know?'

'That we're dining together. In fact he suggested it. He didn't want me to eat alone – and since this is your last night . . .'

'I'll get a taxi right away,' I told her.

'Good. I look forward to . . . seeing you. I shall be in the bar.'

I replaced the telephone in its cradle, wondering if she always took an aperitif before the main course . . .

I had smartened myself up. That is to say, I was immaculate. Black bow-tie, white evening jacket (courtesy of C & A), black trousers and a lightly frilled white shirt, the only one I had ever owned. But I might have known that my appearance would never match up to hers. It seemed that everything she did was just perfectly right. I could only hope that that meant literally everything.

But in her black lace evening gown with its plunging neckline, short wide sleeves and delicate silver embroidery, she was stunning. Sitting with her in the bar, sipping our drinks – for me a large whisky and for her a tall Cinzano – I couldn't take my eyes off her. Twice I reached out for her hand and twice she drew back from me.

'Discreet they may well be,' she said, letting her oval green eyes flicker towards the bar, where guests stood and chatted, and back to me, 'but there's really no need to give them occasion to gossip.'

'I'm sorry. Adrienne,' I told her, my voice husky and close to trembling, 'but—'

'How is it,' she demurely cut me off, 'that a good-looking man like you is – how do you say it? – "going short?" '

I sat back, chuckled. 'That's a rather unladylike expression,' I told her.

'Oh? And what I've planned for tonight is ladylike?'

My voice went huskier still. 'Just what is your plan?'

'While we eat,' she answered, her voice low, 'I shall tell you.' At which point a waiter loomed, napkin over his arm, inviting us to accompany him to the dining room.

Adrienne's portions were tiny, mine huge. She sipped a slender, light white wine, I gulped blocky rich red from a glass the waiter couldn't seem to leave alone. Mercifully I was hungry – I hadn't eaten all day – else that meal must surely have bloated me out. And all of it ordered in advance, the very best in quality cuisine.

'This,' she eventually said, handing me her key, 'fits the door of our suite.' We were sitting back, enjoying liqueurs and cigarettes. 'The rooms are on the ground floor. Tonight you enter through the door, tomorrow morning you leave via the window. A slow walk down to the seafront will refresh you. How is that for a plan?'

'Unbelievable!'

'You don't believe it?'

'Not my good fortune, no.'

'Shall we say that we both have our needs?'

'I think,' I said, 'that I may be falling in love with you. What if I don't wish to leave in the morning?'

She shrugged, smiled, said: 'Who knows what tomorrow may bring?'

*   *   *

How could I ever have thought of her simply as another girl? Or even an ordinary young woman? Girl she certainly was, woman, too, but so . . . *knowing!* Beautiful as a princess and knowing as a whore.

If Mario's old myths and legends were reality, and if Nichos Karpethes were really Necros, then he'd surely picked the right companion. No man born could ever have resisted Adrienne, of that I was quite certain. These thoughts were in my mind – but dimly, at the back of my mind – as I left her smoking in the dining-room and followed her directions to the suite of rooms at the rear of the hotel. In the front of my mind were other thoughts, much more vivid and completely erotic.

I found the suite, entered, left the door slightly ajar behind me.

The thing about an Italian room is its size. An entire suite of rooms is vast. As it happened, I was only interested in one room, and Adrienne had obligingly left the door to that one open.

I was sweating. And yet . . . I shivered.

Adrienne had said fifteen minutes, time enough for her to smoke another cigarette and finish her drink. Then she would come to me. By now the entire staff of the hotel probably knew I was in here, but this was Italy.

V

I shivered again. Excitement? Probably.

I threw off my clothes, found my way to the bathroom, took the quickest shower of my life. Drying myself off, I padded back to the bedroom.

Between the main bedroom and the bathroom a smaller door stood ajar. I froze as I reached it, my senses suddenly alert, my ears seeming to stretch themselves into vast receivers to pick up any slightest sound. For there had been a sound. I was sure of it, from that room . . .

A scratching? A rustle? A whisper? I couldn't say. But a sound, anyway.

Adrienne would be coming soon. Standing outside that door I slowly recommenced towelling myself dry. My naked feet were still firmly rooted, but my hands automatically worked with the towel. It was nerves, only nerves. There had been no sound, or at most only the night breeze off the sea, whispering in through an open window.

I stopped towelling, took another step towards the main bedroom, heard the sound again. A small, choking rasp. A tiny gasping for air.

Karpethes? What the hell was going on?

I shivered violently, my suddenly chill flesh shuddering in an uncontrollable spasm. But . . . I forced myself to action, returned to the main bedroom, quickly dressed (with the exception of my tie and jacket) and crept back to the small room.

Adrienne must be on her way to me even now. She mustn't find me poking my nose into things, like a suspicious kid. I must kill off this silly feeling that had my skin crawling. Not that an attack of nerves was unnatural in the circumstances, on the contrary, but I wasn't about to let it spoil the night. I pushed open the door of the room, entered into darkness, found the light switch. Then—

I held my breath, flipped the switch.

The room was only half as big as the others. It contained a small single bed, a bedside table, a wardrobe. Nothing more, or at least nothing immediately apparent to my wildly darting eyes. My heart, which was racing, slowed and began to settle towards a steadier beat. The window was open, external shutters closed – but small night sounds were finding their way in through the louvres. The distant sounds of traffic, the toot of horns – holiday sounds from below.

I breathed deeply and gratefully, and saw something projecting from beneath the pillow on the bed. A corner of card or of dark leather, like a wallet or—

Or a passport!

A Greek passport, Karpethes', when I opened it. But how could it be? The man in the photograph was young, no older than me. His birth date proved it. But there was his name: Nichos Karpethes. Printed in Greek, of course, but still plain enough. His son?

Puzzling over the passport had served to distract me. My nerves had steadied up. I tossed the passport down, frowned at it where it lay upon the bed, breathed deeply once more . . . then froze solid!

A scratching, a hissing, a dry grunting – from the wardrobe.

Mice? Or did I in fact smell a rat?

Even as the short hairs bristled on the back of my neck I knew anger. There were too many unexplained things here. Too much I didn't understand. And what was it I feared? Old Mario's myths and legends? No, for in my experience the Italians are notorious for getting things wrong. Oh, yes, notorious . . .

I reached out, turned the wardrobe's doorknob, yanked the doors open.

At first I saw nothing of any importance or significance. My eyes didn't know what they sought. Shoes, patent leather, two pairs, stood side by side below. Tiny suits, no bigger than boys' sizes, hung above on steel hangers. And – my God, my God – a waistcoat!

I backed out of that little room on rubber legs, with the silence of the suite shrieking all about me, my eyes bulging, my jaw hanging slack—

'Peter?'

She came in through the suite's main door, came floating towards, me, eager, smiling, her green eyes blazing. Then blazing their suspicion, their anger, as they saw my condition. 'Peter!'

I lurched away as her hands reached for me, those hands I had never yet touched, which had never touched me. Then I was into the main bedroom, snatching my tie and jacket from the bed, (don't ask me why?) and out of the window, yelling some inarticulate, choking thing at her and lashing out frenziedly with my foot as she reached after me. Her eyes were bubbling green hells. '*Peter!*'

Her fingers closed on my forearm, bands of steel containing a fierce, hungry heat. And strong as two men, she began to lift me back into her lair!

I put my feet against the wall, kicked, came free and crashed backwards into shrubbery. Then up on my feet, gasping for air, running, tumbling, crashing into the night. Down madly tilting slopes, through black chasms of mountain pine with the Mediterranean stars winking overhead, and the beckoning, friendly lights of the village seen occasionally below . . .

In the morning, looking up at the way I had descended and remembering the nightmare of my panic-flight, I counted myself lucky to have survived it. The place was precipitous. In the end I *had* fallen, but only for a short distance. All in utter darkness, and my head striking something hard. But . . .

I did survive. Survived both Adrienne and my flight from her.

Waking with the dawn, stiff and bruised and with a massive bump on my forehead, I staggered back to my hotel, locked the door behind me – then sat there trembling and moaning until it was time for the coach.

Weak? Maybe I was, maybe I am.

But on my way into Genova, with people round me and

the sun hot through the coach's windows. I could think again. I could roll up my sleeve and examine that claw mark of four slim fingers and a thumb, branded white into my suntanned flesh, where hair would never grow again on skin sere and wrinkled.

And seeing those marks I could also remember the wardrobe and the waistcoat – and what the waistcoat contained.

That tiny puppet of a man, alive still but barely, his stick-arms dangling through the waistcoat's arm holes, his baby's head projecting, its chin supported by the tightly buttoned waistcoat's breast. And the large bulldog clip over the hanger's bar, its teeth fastened in the loose, wrinkled skin of his walnut head, holding it up. And his skinny little legs dangling, twig-things twitching there; and his pleading, pleading eyes!

But eyes are something I mustn't dwell upon.

And green is a colour I can no longer bear . . .

THE THING FROM THE
BLASTED HEATH

That, which I once boasted of as being the finest collection of morbid and macabre curiosities outside of the British Museum, is no more – and *still* I am unable to sleep. When night's furtive shadow steals over the moors, I lock and bolt my door to peer fearfully through my window at that spot in the garden which glows faintly, with its own inexplicable light, and about which the freshly grown grass is yellow and withered. Though I constantly put down seeds and crumbs no bird ever ventures into my garden, and without even the bees to visit them my fruit trees are barren and dying. No more will Old Cartwright come to my house of an evening to chat in the drowsy firelight or to share with me his home-pressed wines; for Old Cartwright is dead.

I have written of it to my friend in New England, he who sent me the shrub from the blasted heath, warning him never to venture again where once he went, for me lest he share a similar fate.

From the moment I first read of the blasted heath I knew I could never rest until I had something of it in my collection. I found myself a pen-friend in New England, developed a strong friendship with him and then, when by various means I had made him beholden to me, I sent him to do my bidding at the blasted heath. The area is a reservoir now, in a valley west of witch-haunted Arkham, but before men flooded that grey desolation the heath lay like a great diseased sore in the woods and fields. It had not always been so. Before the coming of the fine grey dust the place had been a fertile valley, with orchards and wildlife in plenty –

but that was all before the strange meteorite. Disease had followed the meteorite and after that had come the dust. Many and varied are the weird tales to come filtering out of that area, and fiction or superstition though they may or may not be the fact remains that men will not drink the water of that reservoir. It is tainted by a poison unknown to science which brings madness, delirium and a lingering, crumbling death. The entire valley has been closed off with barbed-wire fences and warning notices stand thick around its perimeter.

Nonetheless, my friend climbed those fences and ventured deep into the haunted heart of the place, to the very water's edge, where he dug in the rotting earth before leaving with my prize. Within twenty-four hours the thing was on its way to me, and after seeing it I could readily understand his haste in getting rid of it. I could not even give the thing a name. I doubt if anyone could have named that shrub for it was the child of strange radiation, not of this world, and therefore unknown to man. Its leaves were awful, hybrid things – thick, flacid and white like a sick child's hands – and its slender trunk and branches were terribly twisted and strangely veined. It was in such a poor state when I planted it in my garden that I did not think it would live. Unfortunately I was wrong; it soon began its luxuriant growth and Old Cartwright often used to warily prod it with his cane when he came visiting.

'What was you burnin' t'other night?' he asked me one morning in the garden. 'I seen t'glow from me winder. Looked like you was burnin' old films or summat! Funny, silver lookin' flames they was.'

I was puzzled by his remarks. 'Burning? Why, nothing! Where did you see this fire, Harry?'

' 'Ere in t'garden, or so I tho't! P'raps it were just t'glow from your fire reflected in you winder.' He nodded towards the house and spat expertly at the shrub. 'Seemed to be just about there where you thing is.' He moved a pace closer to the shrub and prodded it with his cane. 'Gettin' right fat, aint 'e?' Then he turned and looked at me curiously. 'Can't rightly say as I like yon.'

'It's just a plant, Harry, like any other,' I answered. Then, on afterthought: 'Well, perhaps not *quite* like any other. It looks ugly, I'll admit – but it's perfectly harmless. Surprises me you don't like it! You don't seem to mind my Death-Masks or the other things I've got.'

' 'Armless, *they* be,' he said. 'Interestin' toys and nowt else – but you wouldn't catch me plantin' yon in *my* garden!' He grinned at me in that way of his which meant 'I-know-something-you-don't-know,' and said: 'Anyhow, can you answer me this, Mr. Bell? What kind o' bush is it what t'birds don't settle on, eh?' He glanced sharply at the plant and then at me. 'Never seen a sparrer on it yet, I aint . . .' He spat again. 'Not as I blames 'em, mind you. I shouldn't fancy sittin' on *that* thing myself. Just look at them leaves what never seem to move in t'wind; and that lepry-white colour of the trunk and branches. Why! Yon looks more like a queer, leafy octypus than a shrub.'

At the time I thought very little of our conversation. Old Cartwright was always full of strange fancies and had said more or less the same things about my coaches when he first saw them. Yet a few weeks later, when I noticed the first *really* odd thing about the tree from the heath, I thought of his words again.

Oh, yes! It was a tree by then. It had nearly trebled its size since I planted it and was almost three feet tall. It had put out lots of new, greyly-mottled branches, and because its trunk and lower branches had thickened, the weirdly-knotted dark veins stood out clearly against the drowned-flesh texture of the tree's limbs. It was that day that I had to stop Old Cartwright from pestering it. I had thought he was going just a bit heavy with his cane, for after all, the tree *was* the show-piece of my collection and I did not want it damaged.

'It's you, ain't it, what glows at night?' he had asked of the thing, prodding away. 'It's you what shines like them yeller toadstools do! I come over 'ere last night, Mr. Bell, but you was already in bed. Tho't I seen a fire in your garden again, but it weren't a fire –*'twas 'im!*' He prodded the tree harder, actually shaking it. 'What kind o' tree is it?' he asked, 'what t'birds don't sit on and what glows at night, eh?' That was when I got angry and told him to leave the tree alone.

He could be petulant at times, Old Harry, and off he went in a huff in the direction of his cottage. I walked back towards the house and then, thinking I had been perhaps a bit too gruff with the old boy, I turned to call him back for a drink. Before I could open my mouth to shout I noticed the tree. *As God is my witness the thing was straining after Old Cartwright like a leashed dog strains after a cat. Its white leaves were all stretched out straight like horrid hands, pointing in his direction, and the trunk had literally bent towards his retreating figure . . .*

He was right. That night I stayed up purposely and saw it for myself. The tree *did* glow in the night, with a strange, silvery St. Elmo's Fire of its own. It was then that I decided to get rid of it, and what I found in the garden the next morning really clinched the matter.

I do not think that at the time the glowing really bothered me. As Old Harry himself had remarked, certain toadstools are luminous in the dark and I knew that the same thing holds true of one or two species of moss. Even higher life-forms – for instance many fishes of the great deeps – are known to carry their own peculiar lighting systems, and plankton lies luminous even upon the ocean's surface. No, I was sure that the glowing was not important; but that which

I found in the morning was something else! For none of the aforementioned life-forms are capable of doing that which I was ready to believe the tree had somehow done that night.

I noticed the thing's horrid new luxuriance the moment I stepped into the garden. It looked altogether . . . *stronger*, and the leaves and veins seemed somehow to be of a darker tint than before. I was so taken up by the change in the plant that I did not see the cat until I almost stepped on it. The body was lying in the grass at the foot of the tree and when I turned it over with my boot I was surprised that it was not stiff. The animal was obviously dead, being merely skin and bone, and . . .

I kneeled to examine the small, furry corpse – and felt the hackles suddenly rise at the back of my neck! *The body of the cat was not stiff – because there was nothing to stiffen!*

There were only bones inside that unnatural carcass; and looking closer I saw that the small mouth, nostrils and the anal exit were terribly mutilated. Of course, a car could have gone over the poor creature's body and forced its innards (I shuddered) outwards; but then who would have thrown the body into my garden?

And then I noticed something else: there were funny little molehills all about the foot of the tree! Now, I asked myself, since when are moles flesh-eaters? Or had they perhaps been attracted by the smell of the corpse? Funny, because I was damned if *I* could smell it! No, this was a freshly dead cat.

I had studied the tree before, of course, but now I gave it a really thorough going over. I suppose, in the back of my mind, that I was thinking of my *Dionaea Muscipulas* – my Venus-Flytraps – but for the life of me I could in no way match the two species. The leaves of *this* tree were not sticky, as I knew the leaves of some flesh-eaters to be, and their edges were not spiked or hinged. Nor did the plant seem to have the necessary *drainage* apparatus to do that which I feared had been done. There were no spines or thorns on the thing at all, and so far as I could tell there was nothing physically poisonous about it.

What then had *happened* to the cat? My own cat, a good companion of many years, had died of old age long before I ever heard of the blasted heath. I had always intended to get another. Now I was glad I had not done so. I did not know how this animal had died but one thing I was sure of – I could no longer abide the blasphemy from the heath in my garden. Collection or not, it had to go.

That same day I walked into Marske and put through a telephone call to a botanist friend in London. It was he who had sold me my fly-traps. I told him all about my tree and after I had assured him I was not 'pulling his leg' he said he would come up over the weekend to have a look at it. He told me that if the specimen was anything like my description he would be only too pleased to have it and would see that I did not lose on the deal.

That was on Thursday, and I went home from the village happy in the belief that by Sunday I would be rid of the thing from the blasted heath and the birds would be singing in my garden once again. I could not have even dreamt it then, but things were to happen before Sunday which would make it impossible for me ever to be happy again, or for that matter, ever again to have a good night's sleep.

That evening I developed an awful headache. I had a good double brandy and went to bed earlier than usual. The last thing to catch my attention before I dozed off was the silvery glow in the garden. It was so plain out there that I was surprised I had not noticed it before Old Harry Cartwright brought it to my attention.

My awakening was totally inexplicable. I found myself stretched flat on my face on the garden path just outside my front door. My headache had worsened until the pounding inside my skull was like a trip hammer.

'What in hell . . . ?' I said aloud as I looked dazedly

about. I had obviously tripped over the draft-strip on the doorstep; *but how had I come to be there in the first place?*

From my prone position I looked down the garden toward the tree. The clatter of my fall onto the gravel of the path must have disturbed the thing. It was straining in my direction with the same horrible eagerness it had displayed towards Old Cartwright. I got painfully to my feet and, as I turned to go into the house, saw that the tree was already swaying *away* from me to point up the road in the direction of Old Cartwright's place.

'What's bothering the thing now?' I wondered, going inside and locking the door again. I sat on my bed and tried to work it all out. Thank God for the draft-strip! I had been threatening all summer to remove it because hardly a day went by that I did not trip over it. 'Just as well I didn't,' I muttered to myself, unknowingly understating the fact. My meaning was simply that if people had seen me walking down the country road in the middle of the night, dressed only in my pyjama bottom – well, it just did not bear thinking about. The Marske villagers probably already thought me a bit queer because of my collection – Old Harry was a real gossip at times.

The night was perfectly calm and hardly a breeze disturbed the warm air. It was when this stillness was broken that I awoke once more. I had heard the iron gate to the garden slam shut. Thoroughly disgruntled by the night's disturbances I leapt out of bed and threw open the window. Old Cartwright was in the garden beside the tree. His eyes were wide open and staring at the thing, which was leaning toward him in that horribly familiar fashion.

Though I was surprised that the old boy was out there I was doubly astonished to note that he was attired only in his nightshirt. Could it be that he also was walking in his sleep? It seemed so. I opened my mouth to call out to him – but even as I did so I saw something which caused the breath to whoosh out of my lungs as my body constricted in a sudden agony of horror.

Something was happening to the ground around the plant's base! My first thought was molehills sprouting up about the trunk of the freak from the heath and around Old Harry's feet.

But the things coming up out of those little mounds of soil were not moles!

Roots!

My mind went numb with dreadful terror, a gibbering evil gripped my brain as I stumbled from the window to reel away across the room. I tried to cry out, to scream, but my throat seemed completely paralysed. The weirdness of the tree's mobility and the queer nocturnal gropings of its roots aside – *I had finally recognized in Old Cartwright's actions an exact replica of my own earlier that night!*

I lurched drunkenly down the hall to the door and unlocked it with fumbling, dead fingers. I tottered out into the night knowing that something monstrously un-natural was happening, aware that but for pure good fortune I might have been in the old man's place. As the night air hit me I regained control and ran down the garden yelling to the old man to get away – to get well away from the tree, the glowing horror . . .

But I was too late!

His naked feet stuck out from under the bright monster's branches – branches which were all folded downwards, covering his body. Then, as I went down on my knees in shock and disbelief, I saw that which twisted my mind and blasted my nerves into these useless knots that they have been ever since.

I had had the right idea about the tree – but I had looked at the problem in the wrong way! The thing was a freak, a mutation caused by radiations from another world. It had no parallel on Earth; and I, like a fool, had tried to compare it with the flytraps. True, the thing from the blasted heath *did* draw its nourishment from living things, *but the manner of its feeding was nonetheless the same as for most other soil-sprouted plants – it fed through its roots!*

Those slender roots, hidden from above by the way in which the branches had folded down, were all sharply-throned – and for each thorn there was a tiny sucker. Even as I watched, hypnotized, those vile roots were pulsing down into Cartwright's open mouth . . . until his lips began to split under the strain of their loathsome contents!

I began to scream as I saw the veins in the trunk and branches start their scarlet pulsing, and, as the entire plant commenced throbbing with a pale, pinkish suffusion, I passed into a merciful oblivion. *For Old Cartwright's entire body was jerking and twitching with a nauseating internal action which was not its own – and all the time his dead eyes stared and stared . . .*

There is not much more to tell. When I recovered consciousness I was still half insane. In a gibbering delirium I staggered to the woodshed and returned with the axe. Moaning in morbid loathing I cut the tree – once, twice – deeply across the trunk, and in a fit of uncontrollable twitching I watched the horror literally *bleed* to death!

The end had to be seen to be believed. Slowly the evil roots withdrew from Cartwright's body, shuddering and sluggishly pulling back underground, releasing their grisly internal hold on his bloodless form. The branches and leaves writhed and twined in a morbid dance of death; the horrible veins – *real* veins – pulsed to a standstill and the whole tree started to slope sideways as a terribble disintegration took hold on it. The unnatural glow surrounding the thing dimmed as it began visibly to rot where it stood. The smell of utter corruption which soon started to exude from the compost the hell-plant was rapidly becoming forced me to back away, dragging Old Cartwright's corpse after me.

I was brought up short by the garden fence and that was where I stayed, shivering and staring at the rapidly blackening mass in the garden.

When at last the glow had died away completely and all that remained of the tree was an odorous, sticky, reddish-black puddle, I noticed that the first light of dawn was already brightening the sky. It was then that I formed my plan. I had had more than my fill of horror – all I wanted to do was forget – and I knew the authorities would never believe my story; not that I intended trying to tell it.

I made a bonfire over the stinking spot where the plant had been, and as the first cock crowed in the distance I set fire to the pile of leaves and sticks and stood there until there was only a blackened patch on the grass to show that the horror from the heath had ever stood there. Then I dressed and walked into Marske to the police station.

No one could quite understand the absence of Old Cartwright's blood or the damage to his mouth and the other – internal – injuries which the post mortem later showed; but it was undeniable that he had been 'queer' for a long time and lately had been heard to talk openly about things that 'glowed at night' and trees with hands instead of leaves. Everyone had known, it appeared, that he would end up 'in a funny way.'

After I made my statement to the police – about how I had found Old Cartwright's body at dawn, in my garden – I put through another call to London and told my botanist friend that the tree had been destroyed in a garden fire. He said that it was unfortunate but did not really matter. He had to catch an evening 'plane to South America anyway and would be away for many months.

He asked me to see if I could get another specimen in the meantime.

*   *   *

But that is not quite the end of the story. All that I have related happened last summer. It is already spring. The birds have still not returned to my garden and though each night I take a sleeping pill before locking my door, I cannot rest.

I thought that in ridding myself of the remainder of my collection I might also kill the memory of that which once stood in my garden. I was wrong.

It makes no difference that I have given away my conches from the islands of Polynesia and have shattered into fragments the skull I dug from beneath the ground where once stood a Roman ruin. Letting my *Dionaea Muscipulas* die from lack of their singular nourishment has not helped me at all! My devil-drums and death-masks from Africa now rest beneath glass in Wharby Museum along with the sacrificial gown from Mua-Aphos. My collection of ten nightmare paintings by Pickman, Chandler Davies and Clark Ashton Smith now belong to an avid American collector, to whom I have also sold my complete set of Poe's works. I have melted down my Iceland meteorite and parted forever with the horribly inscribed silver figurine from India. The silvery fragments of unknown crystal from dead G'harne rest untended in their box and I have sold in auction all my books of Earth's elder madness.

Yes, that which I once boasted of as being the finest collection of morbid and macabre curiosities outside of the British Museum is no more; yet still I am unable to sleep. There is something – some fear that keeps me awake – which has caused me of late to chain myself to the bed when I lie down.

You see, I know that my doctor's assurance that it is 'all in my mind' is at fault, and I know that if ever I wake up in the garden again it will mean permanent insanity – or worse!

For the spot where the spring grass is twisted and yellow continues to glow feebly at night. Only a week ago I decided to clear the very soil from that area but as soon as I drove my spade into the ground I was sure I saw something black and wriggly – *like a looped off root* – squirm quickly down out of sight! Perhaps it is my imagination but I have also noticed, in the dead of night, that the floorboards sometimes creak beneath my room – and then, of course, there is that *other* thing.

I get the most dreadful headaches.

UZZI

Powell. Refer it to Powell.

That could well be the answer. Geoffrey Powell, who cribbed all my work at Oxford where we studied together, and stole my girl, too, and lives with her in that big house which should really be mine, making mine look like a kennel. Yes, I shall refer the matter to him. Big-headed, pompous bastard that he is, in his Harley Street consultancy, still he might be the only one to come up with the right answer. And if he does, certainly it will have been worth his exorbitant fee.

None of which would be necessary if Miles Clayton had gone to Powell in the first place; but he didn't, he came to me. He was overdue for a shave, bleary-eyed, and the smell on his breath was probably whisky. He didn't reek of drink, no, but he'd had a few. On the other hand his clothes were of an expensive cut, his car was new and rather superior to mine, and his wallet when he gave me his card was certainly well-stuffed.

A large, florid man, Miles Clayton smoked fat cigars and dealt in fancy liqueur chocolates which he imported. If this rather brief description of him makes him seem disagreeable or unpleasant, that is not the impression I wish to convey; on the contrary, he was a very 'nice' man. One cannot help one's looks. And of course, in his condition, which was other than usual . . .

Anyway, this is the story he told me: I was in Germany on business. The Teutoberger Wald. Been over there for five days, driving myself from venue to venue, and was up in the

159

mountains around Holzminden to visit a small family firm specializing in dark chocolate brandies. I had just got used to driving on the right-hand side of the road – or at least I thought I had – when it happened.

On the outskirts of a tiny village, where the road swept out of miles of pine forest and down into the harbour of a valley saddled between three hills, suddenly I found myself back on the left again! It must have been the absence of other vehicles, the repetitious twisting and twining of the road where it followed the contours through the trees, which was almost hypnotic, the sheer loveliness of the scenery all about. Anyway, I started to correct my error immediately; but in the next moment, coming around a bend into a built-up area—

I mean, she was just there! Now, I *believe* that by then I was on the right side of the road again – my side, I mean – but having just the moment before corrected myself . . . maybe I was a bit confused, d'you see? Whichever, I didn't react fast enough: even as I slammed my brakes on I was into her. *Bump!* She went up in the air, banged about on the roof-rack, plopped down on the road behind me. By which time I'd just about slewed to a halt.

I'd been well inside the limit – well, just inside it; it hadn't been my fault at all; she'd just appeared there, right the hell in my way! And it had happened right outside the local police station, where as luck would have it an 'Offizier' had just come out of the door. He'd seen the whole thing.

After that things happened very quickly. I suppose I was very nearly in a state of shock. I got out of the car, fell down – I was shaken, d'you see? – got up again and went to where the officer was kneeling beside her. On my way I'd seen the dent in my bonnet, the way the mascot was bent right back, a little blood on the roof-rack. But oh my God, there was a great deal more blood on the road, around the crumpled form of the girl!

Her dress at the front was torn, red and wet under her left breast, and blood was pumping from a great laceration in her neck. I thought about her being torn by the roof-rack and it made me grind my teeth. She was conscious, but only just.

The officer was a good 'un: cool as a cucumber, efficient as only the Germans can be. 'Go inside,' he told me. 'Hold the doors open for me. I have to move her.' And he very gently picked her up. I held the doors for him while he carried her inside the police station, into a room where he laid her down on a bed. Then he did what he could to staunch her wounds. Where her dress was torn I saw a wound which I couldn't believe I – my car – was responsible for. It was round and black in its middle, as if a bite had been taken out of her. I could see ribs in there. Then the officer put a thickly wadded dressing over it.

'Wait,' he told me, 'and I'll call an ambulance.' Of course he called it a 'Krankenwagen', but I'm quite fluent with German; I'll simply tell it all in English.

Anyway, he left the room and I heard him using a telephone. The girl caught at my hand. I sat there sweating, looking at her, and I saw how young she was, and how pretty. 'Oh, my God!' I said. 'My *God*!'

She patted my hand. I mean, she *patted* it! 'It wasn't your fault,' she said. 'An accident.'

'But . . . but . . .' It was all I could say.

'An accident,' she repeated. Her blood had seeped right through the mattress where she lay and was dripping on the floor. The young policeman was still on the phone.

'For God's sake hurry up!' I called out to him.

The girl was in a great deal of pain. Her face had twisted up and the dressing had come away from her side again. I pressed it home, gritted my teeth when I saw her grit hers. 'God! – if there's *anything* I can do—' I said.

'The devil,' she answered me, looking me straight in the

eye. 'Don't ask it of God. This isn't His work.' She was sinking into delirium.

'Listen,' I gasped, wringing my hands. 'I have money. A great deal. Only hang on, and—'

'No,' she said, her voice a whisper. 'I can't. This is punishment. I had forsaken . . .'

'Yes?'

'Oh, it doesn't matter. It's the end of me, and the end of Uzzi.'

Uzzi? Her child? A pet cat or dog? 'Listen,' I gabbled desperately. 'While you're recovering, I'll look after Uzzi. I'll—'

She shook her head, but oh so weakly. 'No,' she forced something of a smile, more a grimace, on to her face. 'I'll not recover. And don't . . . don't worry about . . . about Uzzi.'

'God!' I cried again. 'Don't die, please don't die. I'll look after Uzzi. I *swear* it!' I hardly knew what I was saying.

'*Swear it?*' Her eyes had shot wide open. She reached out a bloody, trembling hand towards my lips, as if to seal them . . . and fell back. Her eyes stayed open. When the policeman came back into the room he closed them and covered her body with a blanket. Covered her face, too . . .

That was the end of it – or should have been.

The ambulance came and took her away. I gave a written statement of what had happened. The policeman had seen the entire thing and corroborated my statement: it hadn't been my fault, no blame at all attached to me. There might be an inquest but I wouldn't be required to attend; the evidence of a police witness would suffice. I found it all too easy, too . . . simple! A girl was dead, and I was being told – quite literally – to drive on, not to concern myself.

'But her family . . .'

'No family. She lived alone. Here, in the village.'

'Relations, friends . . .'

He shook his head. 'None.'

'What? A pretty girl like that? I can't believe—'

'Wait,' he said, cutting me short. 'Look, she wasn't . . . an innocent. She wasn't . . . a good person.'

'What? Do you mean she was a whore? A criminal, perhaps? But what does that matter? I mean—'

'Please!' he said. 'I know what you mean. Very well: yes, she was a criminal. And I agree, that doesn't matter at all. But you are not to blame. I doubt if you'll ever hear anything about this again.'

It wasn't until I reached my destination later that night that I remembered Uzzi. I'd sworn to take care of him/her, whatever Uzzi was. A pet, I supposed. Ah, well – the Germans are a pretty humane lot, in their way. Doubtless Uzzi would find a new home. In any case, it was out of my hands now. If I didn't feel so guilty, maybe I'd even be a little relieved that I was out of the affair so light.

But I did recall seeing something in that police station that struck me as strange. Well, perhaps not then, but more recently it has taken on a certain significance. It was while I was waiting for the ambulance men to take the girl's body away that I noticed a stack of old, browning occurrence books on a shelf behind the duty desk: those great, ledger-like diary things in which the officer on duty at the desk keeps his daily log or record. The books were old, as I've said, and the dates on some of their spines went back as far as the mid-1930s, before the war.

The spines read: *Polizei Hohenstadt*, followed by the specific dates when the books were first taken into use, and the dates when they'd been completed and closed. These particulars were written in capitals, in heavy black ink, on labels glued to the spines. Several of the labels had fallen off, however, and the unfaded spines where they'd been bore a uniform legend: *Polizei Hexenstadt*, and then the dates as before. So that it seemed fairly obvious to me that at some time in the not too distant past the town had been renamed.

The reason I make mention of this is very simple to explain: *Hexenstadt* means 'Witch Town'. This is a fairly trivial fact which, in the circumstances, I might reasonably be expected to forget. But I haven't been allowed to forget it . . .

The morning after the accident I woke up bathed in stinking sweat – I thought it was sweat – following a night of hideous dreams. I couldn't remember what those nightmares were for sure, except I believe they went over, time and time again, the details of the accident and that look on the girl's face as she died, when I swore I'd take care of her Uzzi.

My hosts were the manufacturers of those chocolates I mentioned. God only knows what they'd think of me when I left and they came to tidy up my room! It stank as if a pig had spent the night there – or something worse than a pig. I thought that *I* had made the room smell like that.

I threw open the windows, let in the sweet mountain air, and dumped my bedsheets into a dirty linen basket. Pillowcases, too. Then I found fresh linen in a drawer and decked the bed, set the room to rights again.

After a shower I felt better, but I must have struggled in the night or been lying in an awkward position or something. My left side ached just under the armpit, causing me to favour that arm and hold it a little tenderly away from my side. But about what I've said with regard to the condition of my bedding:

Please understand, I have always been the most scrupulous of men personally. It's been a habit of mine as long as I can remember to bathe or at least shower every night, and often in the mornings, too. It was quite beyond me to fathom what sort of nightmare could squeeze juices like *those* from a man's pores!

Two days later I was on the car ferry out of Bremerhaven and so returned home. And no repetition of those terrible dreams until I found myself back at work here in London. Then, just a week ago—

The same thing again, but this time in earnest! And it has steadily progressed, worsened, until finally I've found myself driven to come and see you. Not that I've told you all of it – not yet – nor even the half of it. But God it's so weird, so utterly horrible that—

—That the fact is, I think I'm losing my mind!

I've told you about the 'sweat', which I thought was mine. Well, and at first I *did* think it – what else was I supposed to think? But as it got worse I knew it couldn't be mine. No man – nor any living, breathing, healthy creature of God's sweet earth – could possibly exist and have poison like that in him! Well, perhaps there are creatures that could: the octopus, maybe. Slugs and snails. But nothing remotely human.

My dreams began to change, take on a new and more desperately frightening form. So simple, and yet so terrifying. Part of it was the sensation of having somebody or something else in bed with me, a living person or being that snuggled to me as if for warmth and fastened to my flesh like a suckling child. With a child's greed, yes – but without its love or vulnerability. And most certainly far larger and stronger than any child. That was part of it.

The other part was . . .

You know how a cat purrs? Well, something in those nightmares of mine purred. But not like a cat. It did express a sort of satisfaction, contentedness, but that was where the similarity ended. Nor was it truly a purring, no, it was more the wet, frothy, huskily breathed repetition of a single word, spoken slaveringly over and over again: *Uzzi* – Uzzi – Uzzi!

Finally, Monday morning just four days ago, the thing

reached its peak. Or perhaps I should say it reached *a* peak. The dream was the same as before: a sort of lulling, warm embrace, a hypnotic drifting on some slimy ocean whose tides were irresistible. And deep inside a gnawing horror of some monstrous, impossible thing, which drifted with me and sang to me its hypnotic lullaby. Sang to me to numb my mind, anaesthetise me to the pain of its damned, leech-like sucking!

But when I woke up . . . the nightmare hadn't gone away. And it was no longer any use kidding myself that this . . . this slime was sweat! No, for it was in fact slime: a sticky film of the filthy stuff that clung like clear, stinking jelly to my bedsheets – *and to me*, all down my left side! What's more, there was a deep slimy depression in the bed to the left of where I'd slept: a wet, oval-shaped indentation as if a great cracked egg had lain there all through the night, seeping its fluids into my bed. And worse than any of this, I could no longer fool myself but had to admit that I was in pain; the left-hand side of my ribcage hurt like hell and felt . . . totally wrong.

I showered, carefully examined myself in a full-length mirror – and went immediately to see my doctor. Oh, yes, for I'd seen something like this before, except that then I'd thought my car was to blame. I also knew that it could get much worse, and I certainly wasn't going to wait around until it – whatever 'it' was – had eaten right through to my ribs!

The doctor took samples – blood, urine, tissue – and said he'd send them for testing. But he couldn't tell me what was wrong with me, not right there and then. In fact I got the impression he was baffled. He thought it was a purely physical thing, do you see? And I wasn't about to tell him what I *thought* was wrong with me. How could I? How could I explain to him what I made of the large, darkly indented weeping sore under my armpit? If I'd told him that, he'd think it was my mind that needed mending. And perhaps it is, which is why I've come to see you . . .

So that was four days ago. Since when—

It seemed to me that I must sort out my priorities, take some positive course of action. The first thing I must do was catch this beast 'in the act', as it were. At the doctor's (on the pretext that I had a lot of night studying to do) I'd got hold of some tablets to help me keep awake. That night I drank a lot of strong, black coffee, put a powerful electric torch under my pillow, finally took two of the tablets before going to bed. I tried to look at a book but after reading the same paragraph five or six times gave it up as a bad job. And at last, at about 1:30, I turned out the light. I wanted it to come, d'you see?

I tried to stay awake, but . . .

. . . The luminous hands on my alarm clock stood at 2:55 . . . I was adrift on that alien sea again, but striving against the lure of its tides . . . and at the same time I was in pain . . . and I knew that something bulky, clammy-cold and evil was glued to my side, droning its hideous song to keep me asleep:

Uzzi – Uzzi – Uzzi!

Don't ask me how I kept from crying out. Have you *tried* to cry out, when you're only half awake? Maybe I couldn't. It was like a dream when you want to run but don't seem to have any legs, when you want to scream and haven't got a voice. But as I struggled up from sleeping, so my sense of reality got stronger, and with it my feeling of freezing horror!

I was lying on my back and my left arm was draped loosely over the – torso? – of some slimy, oozing, corrugated oval shape which was pressing itself to me like a limpet. Its stench was that of the tomb, or perhaps some long-dead seabed heaved up to the surface, or a combination of the two with the thick, cloying reek of crushed toadstools thrown in for good measure. And in another moment I was conscious and my mind had switched itself on, and I knew that this was one hundred per cent reality. No longer a dream but the real, the *very* real thing. This was Uzzi!

Paralysed? Very nearly. But somehow I managed to work my hand up under my pillow, find my torch and drag it out – and press its rubber stud. And I shone the beam full on the sick-gleaming unnatural *thing* that lay there in the bed with me, sucking on my side!

Should I say it was a monstrous slug? A huge octopus which was all body-sac, with short feelers or tentacles fringed about its suctorial mouth? How to describe a thing which is indescribable, except to a madman? But I do recall that it had eyes. Where placed? Don't ask me, it's something I mustn't dwell on. It's difficult to tell it without picturing it, which is what I mustn't do. If I say they tipped *three* of its stubby tentacles . . . but, God! . . . they were very nearly *human* eyes. And evil leered out of them like the devil himself through the gates of hell!

It was Uzzi, the dead German witch's familiar, and it *was* something that the devil had sent to her out of hell. Except that now Uzzi was mine. And I was Uzzi's!

All of these thoughts, this knowledge, coming to me in a single instant, from one brief glimpse – the merest blaze of light from my torch – for in the next moment the horror was gone. Just like that: gone! Disappeared from my bed, the room, the house. But not gone far, never gone far; and as usual, it had left its stink and its slime behind . . .

I staggered through the house putting on all the lights, sobbing, holding my side, loathing Uzzi, myself, this whole nightmare existence in a universe we so wrongly imagine to be neat and tidy and ordered. And then I turned my fire up and sat there before it all through the rest of the night, drinking whisky, burning in my fever of terror and at the same time shuddering right through to my soul.

Since then I haven't slept at all, and I suppose it's starting to show.

Well, that's my story – it's why I've come to see you, Dr Charles. Now tell me: am I mad?

I had been so wrapped up in Miles Clayton's story that it took a little time to sink in that he was finished. I shook myself, asked if I might see his wound.

He took off his jacket, opened his shirt and showed me, explaining:

'Of course, it's had three nights to heal a little. I haven't slept, haven't let myself be alone in the dark for a minute.'

I looked at it: the bruising, the central, sore area itself. I simply looked at it, didn't touch it, and I came to my conclusions. As Clayton did up his shirt and put his jacket on again, I said: 'Do you follow your stars, Miles?'

'Eh?' I'd taken him by surprise. 'Astrology, d'you mean? Oh, yes – I'm a Pisces.' He frowned. 'A good year ahead, allegedly.'

I shrugged. 'Maybe, and maybe not. First I should get that cleared up, if I were you. And then I'd say you probably have a good many good years ahead.'

'Oh?' He looked doubtful, but interested.

I nodded. 'Tell me, have you ever had any psychic experiences?'

'Ghosts?' he shook his head. 'I'm not saying I don't believe, mind you. No, for I'm open-minded on such things. But Uzzi is the first time anything like this has —' He paused, looked puzzled. 'You changed the subject. I thought you were going to give me your opinion on my wound?'

'It might very well add up to the same thing', I told him. 'In fact I'd be willing to bet you don't walk under ladders, either.'

'You'd win your bet', he answered, looking tiredly

mystified. 'Why tempt fate? But what are you getting at?'

'Three possibilities with that trouble of yours,' I told him. 'Two of them purely physical. But first tell me something: did you ever have anything like this bruise – this damage, let's call it – before the accident in Germany?'

'Never so much as a pimple,' he answered. 'Now tell me what's on your mind.'

'Ah!' I smiled. 'But it's more what's on *your* mind, Miles. Three things, I said – three possibilities. But first let me say this: I for one *don't* believe in ghosts. I don't read my star forecasts and I'm not especially careful about ladders, or black cats crossing my path. In other words, I don't let that sort of thing influence me. But they do influence you. For all that you're a hard-headed businessman, you're susceptible to extramundane suggestions.

He inclined his head. 'Extramundane?'

'Not of this world,' I told him. 'You're a believer . . . in things. Do you believe in God, too?'

He looked a little indignant. 'Don't you?'

'Frankly, no. Nor do I believe in the Devil. Good and evil are real, certainly: evidence of both is all around. But their *origin* lies in the mind. In the minds of men!'

We both sat down. 'Go on,' he said.

I looked into his hollow, red-rimmed eyes and smiled. 'Right! First the wound in your side. While you're waiting for that doctor of yours to spark, I'd get a second opinion. Go to a specialist – you can afford it. Now, I'm obviously not that sort of doctor, but having looked at this damage of yours three things spring immediately to mind. One: it's a cancer. A skin cancer, nasty but not fatal, and you should get it seen to at once. Two: it's a nest of rodent ulcers, which—'

'What?' He leaned forward. 'What sort of ulcers?'

'Rodent,' I repeated. 'Burrowing. Gradually working their way under the skin and destroying tissue. I've an old friend who gets them, and he also gets treatment for them. Radiation, laser – there are several types of treatment. Every now and then he breaks out, but in a matter of weeks they have it under control. That wound of yours has precisely the same sort of dark indentations around its circumference, and—'

'Teeth marks,' he cut me off. 'That's where Uzzi clamps himself on to me – if it is a "he"!' He sighed wearily. 'All right, you've made two guesses – wrong ones, I'm afraid – so what's the third?'

I shrugged, said: 'It's psychosomatic – and that *is* something I know about. And if all else fails, it's the only possible diagnosis.'

'Psychosomatic?' He curled his lip, then immediately apologized. 'I'm sorry. But does that mean what I think it means?'

'A mental illness,' I answered. 'Of a sort.'

'Go on.'

'Mind and body are linked, Miles,' I continued. 'It's not just a one-way deal – each controls the other. The problem is your guilt. You're doing this to yourself!'

His interest at once turned to anger. Which was what I'd more than half expected. 'Am I really paying you for this?' he said. 'You mean you think I'm eating my own side away? That everything that's happening to me is generated up here?' He tapped his head. 'And does that explain why my bed's a swamp every time I sleep in it, after Uzzi's visited me? I mean, are you really telling me that I'm—'

'Insane? But that's what you came to find out, isn't it?'

He closed his grimacing mouth, slumped down in his chair. 'And am I?'

'No,' I shook my head. 'You just feel guilty, that's all, and you feel you have a great debt to pay.'

His eyes opened wide and I knew he was hooked. And I

believed I knew how to cure him. 'A debt?' he said. 'To the girl, d'you mean?'

I nodded. 'To her, and to Uzzi.'

He shrank down again. 'You're forgetting something,' he said. 'I've *seen* Uzzi!'

'But only in the night, in the dark, when you're half asleep and your conscience is most vulnerable. Only wake up, turn on the light, and – no Uzzi. It's a figment of darkness, of the night, *of your mind!*'

'Guilt . . .' he said. But there was hope in his eyes.

'Oh, yes!' I drove my point home. 'Guilty, because you can't be sure even now that you were driving on the correct side of the road. Guilty – because you'd let your attention wander. Guilty, of course, for you drove your car into that poor girl and broke her body. Guilty, because there was nothing you could do to save her – and more especially guilty, in your own mind, because you got off scot-free. But worst of all: guilty because you couldn't even honour her last request, that you look after Uzzi! And so your mind's paying your debt for you, and in so doing is slowly destroying your body – and must soon destroy itself, too. Except we won't allow that. Psychosomatic, as I said.'

He put his face in his hands and sobbed, real tears that dripped from between his fingers. 'God, yes!' his muffled, racked voice came to me. 'God, I *am* guilty!'

'But you're not,' I told him, 'and there is a cure.'

He looked up and his face was pink jelly. 'A . . . a cure?'

'Of course. To begin with, you weren't to blame for the accident. Now, I know you've *said* you weren't to blame, but you have to really believe it. After all, that young German policeman saw the whole thing, didn't he? So that's all it was, an accident. There are thousands just like it, all over the world, every day. As for Uzzi: you were probably right. A pet kitten, or maybe a dog. But Germany's a civilized country. Uzzi will be taken care of.'

He stood up, stumbled to my desk, almost fell across it to grasp my hand. 'Lord, if only I could be sure of that!'

'Listen,' I said. 'You can be sure. It was that promise you made, that's all, when you swore you'd look after him. That's what made the connection in your mind. A wrong connection. And now all we have to do is break it.'

'And you can do that?' He was crushing my hand. I gently freed myself, said:

'Of course. For I have no belief in such things. Now, Miles, I want you to try very hard and remember everything we've talked about. You'll very soon see how it all makes sense. And I want you to believe that you're going to be OK. As for Uzzi: you can forget all about that. You see, I'll take care of Uzzi. I swear I will!'

That was a week ago. I've tried to contact Clayton but he's in Switzerland. I understand they make fabulous chocolates there. My God, chocolates!

My bedroom's a mess and there's this horrible sore in the middle of my chest and my wife has run away, where I don't know.

I woke up this morning at 4:00, and Uzzi was lying on me like some obscene nightmare lover, with those . . . *appendages* sliming on my face.

That's why I've made up a story – similar to Clayton's, except mine is a false one, about a gypsy curse – which I plan to tell to that fat greasy bastard Powell. Yes, I'll refer my case to him, and then I'll take a nice long trip abroad somewhere. No guilt will attach to me, for I don't believe in such. And I know that Powell doesn't either. After all, he has my office, the girl I should have, the house I should rightly occupy. So why shouldn't he have this, too?

It couldn't happen to a nicer fellow.

Uzzi . . . Uzzi . . . Uzzi . . .

HAGGOPIAN

1

Richard Haggopian, perhaps the world's greatest authority on ichthyology and oceanography, to say nothing of the many allied sciences and subjects, was at last willing to permit himself to be interviewed. I was jubilant, elated – I could not believe my luck! At least a dozen journalists before me, some of them so high up in literary circles as to be actually offended by so mundane an occupational description, had made the futile journey to Kletnos in the Aegean to seek Haggopian the Armenian out; but only my application had been accepted. Three months earlier, in early June, Hartog of *Time* had been refused, and before him Mannhausen of *Weltzukunft*, and therefore my own superiors had seen little hope for me. And yet the name of Jeremy Belton was not unknown in journalism; I had been lucky on a number of so-called 'hopeless' cases before. Now, it seemed, this luck of mine was holding. Richard Haggopian was away on yet another ocean trip, but I had been asked to wait for him.

It is not hard to say why Haggopian excited such interest among the ranks of the world's foremost journalists; any man with his scientific and literary talents, with a beautiful young wife, with an island-in-the-sun, and (perhaps most important of all), with a blatantly negative attitude toward even the most beneficial publicity, would certainly have attracted the same interest. And to top all this Haggopian was a millionaire!

Myself, I had recently finished a job in the desert – the latest Arab-Israeli confrontation – to find myself with time and a little money to spare, and so my superiors had asked me to have a bash at Haggopian. That had been a fortnight ago, and since then I had done my best towards procuring an interview. Where others had failed miserably I had been successful.

For eight days I had waited on the Armenian's return to Haggopiana – his tiny island hideaway two miles east of Kletnos and midway between Athens and Iraklion, purchased by and named after himself in the early forties – and just when it seemed that my strictly limited funds must surely run out, then Haggopian's great silver hydrofoil, the *Echinoidea*, cut a thin scar on the incredible blue of the sea to the south-west as it sped in to a mid-morning mooring. With binoculars from the flat white roof of my Kletnos – hotel? – I watched the hydrofoil circle the island until, in a blinding flash of reflected sunlight, it disappeared beyond Haggopiana's wedge of white rock. Two hours later the Armenian's man came across in a sleek motorboat to bring me (I hoped) news of my appointment. My luck was indeed holding! I was to attend Haggopian at three in the afternoon; a boat would be sent for me.

At three I was ready, dressed in sandals, cool grey slacks and a white T-shirt – the recommended civilized attire for a sunny afternoon in the Aegean – and when the sleek motorboat came back for me I was waiting for it at the natural rock wharf. On the way out to Haggopiana, as I gazed over the prow of the craft down through the crystal-clear water at the gliding, shadowy groupers and the clusters of black sea-urchins (the Armenian had named his hydrofoil after the latter), I did a mental check-up on what I knew of the elusive owner of the island ahead:

Richard Hemeral Angelos Haggopian, born in 1919 of an illicit union between his penniless but beautiful half-breed

Polynesian mother and millionaire Armenian-Cypriot father – author of three of the most fascinating books. I had ever read, books for the layman, telling of the world's seas and all their multiform denizens in simple, uncomplicated language – discoverer of the Taumotu Trench, a previously unsuspected hole in the bed of the South Pacific almost seven thousand fathoms deep; into which, with the celebrated Hans Geisler, he descended in 1955 to a depth of twenty-four thousand feet – benefactor of the world's greatest aquariums and museums in that he had presented at least two hundred and forty rare, often freshly discovered specimens to such authorities in the last fifteen years, etc., etc.

Haggopian the much married – three times, in fact, and all since the age of thirty – apparently an unfortunate man where brides were concerned. His first wife (British) died at sea after nine years' wedded life, mysteriously disappearing overboard from her husband's yacht in calm seas on the shark-ridden Barrier Reef in 1958; number two (Greek-Cypriot) died in 1964 of some exotic wasting disease and was buried at sea; and number three – one Cleanthis Leonides, an Athenian model of note, wed on her eighteenth birthday – had apparently turned recluse in that she had not been seen publicly since her union with Haggopian two years previously.

Cleanthis Haggopian – yes! Expecting to meet her, should I ever be lucky enough to get to see her husband, I had checked through dozens of old fashion magazines for photographs of her. That had been a few days ago in Athens, and now I recalled her face as I had seen it in those pictures – young, naturally, and beautiful in the Classic Greek tradition. She had been a 'honey'; would, of course, still be; and again, despite rumours that she was no longer living with her husband, I found myself anticipating our meeting.

In no time at all the flat white rocky ramparts of the island loomed to some thirty feet out of the sea, and my navigator swung his fast craft over to the left, passing between two jagged points of salt-incrusted rock standing twenty yards or so out from Haggopiana's most northern point. As we rounded the point I saw that the east face of the island looked far less inhospitable; there was a white sand beach, with a pier at which the *Echinoidea* was moored, and, set back from the beach in a cluster of pomegranate, almond, locust and olive trees, an immensely vast and sprawling flat-roofed bungalow.

So this was Haggopiana! Hardly, I thought, the 'island paradise' of Weber's article in *Neu Welt*! It looked as though Weber's story, seven years old now, had been written no closer to Haggopiana than Kletnos; I had always been dubious about the German's exotic superlatives.

At the dry end of the pier my quarry waited. I saw him as, with the slightest of bumps, the motorboat pulled in to mooring. He wore grey flannels and a white shirt with the sleeves rolled down. His thin nose supported heavy, opaquely-lensed sunglasses. This was Haggopian – tall, bald, extremely intelligent and very, very rich – his hand already outstretched in greeting.

Haggopian was a shock. I had seen photographs of him of course, quite a few, and had often wondered at the odd sheen such pictures had seemed to give his features. In fact the only decent pictures I had seen of him had been pre-1958 and I had taken later shots as being simply the result of poor photography; his rare appearances in public had always been very short ones and unannounced, so that by the time cameras were clicking he was usually making an exit. Now, however, I could see that I had short-changed the photographers. He *did* have a sheen to his skin – a peculiar phosphorescence almost – that highlighted his features and even partially reflected something of the glare of the sun. There must, too, be something wrong with the man's eyes. Tears glistened on his cheeks, rolling thinly down from behind the dark lenses. He carried in his left hand a square of silk with which, every now and then, he would dab at this tell-tale dampness; all this I saw as I approached him along the pier, and right from the start I found him strangely – yes, repulsive.

'How do you do, Mr. Belton?' his voice was a thick, heavily accented rasp that jarred with his polite inquiry and manner of expression. 'I am sorry you have had to wait so long. I got your message in Famagusta, right at the start of my trip, but I am afraid I could not put my work off.'

'Not at all, sir, I'm sure that this meeting will more than amply repay my patience.'

His handshake was no less a shock, though I tried my best to keep him from seeing it, and after he turned to lead me up to the house I unobtrusively wiped my hand on the side of my T-shirt. It was not that Haggopian's hand had been damp with sweat, which might be expected – rather, or so it seemed to me, I felt as though I had taken hold of a handful of garden snails!

I had noticed from the boat a complex of pipes and valves between the sea and the house, and now, approaching that sprawling yellow building in Haggopian's wake (his stride was clumsy, lolling), I could hear the muffled throb of pumps and the gush of water. Once inside the huge, refreshingly cool bungalow, it became apparent just what the sounds meant. I might have known that this man, so in love with the sea, would surround himself with his life's work. The place was nothing less than a gigantic aquarium!

Massive glass tanks, in some cases room length and ceiling high, made up the walls, so that the sunlight filtering through from exterior, porthole-like windows entered the room in greenish shades that dappled the marble floor and gave the place an eerie, submarine aspect.

There were no printed cards or boards to describe the finny dwellers in the huge tanks, and as he led me from room to room it became clear why such labels were unnecessary. Haggopian knew each specimen intimately, his rasplike voice making a running commentary as we visited in turn the bungalow's many wings:

'An unusual coelenterate, this one, from three thousand feet. Difficult to keep alive – pressure and all that. I call it *Physalia haggopia* – quite deadly. If one of those tentacles should even brush you . . . *phttt*! Makes a water-baby of the Portuguese Man-o'-War' (this of a great purplish mass with trailing, wispy-green tentacles, undulating horribly through the water of a tank of huge proportions). Haggopian, as he spoke, deftly plucked a small fish from an open tank on a nearby table, throwing it up over the lip of the greater tank to his 'unusual coelenterate'. The fish hit the water with a splash, swam down and straight into one of the green wisps – and instantly stiffened! In a matter of seconds the hideous jelly-fish had settled on its prey to commence a languid ingestion.

'Given time,' Haggopian gratingly commented, 'it would do the same to you!'

In the largest room of all – more a hall than a room proper – I paused, literally astonished at the size of the tanks and the expertise which had obviously gone into their construction. Here, where sharks swam through brain and other coral formations, the glass of these miniature oceans must have been tremendously thick, and backdrops had been arranged to give the impression of vast distances and sprawling submarine vistas.

In one of these tanks hammerheads of over two metres in length were cruising slowly from side to side, ugly as hell and looking twice as dangerous. Metal steps led up to this tank's rim, down the other side and into the water itself. Haggopian must have seen the puzzled expression on my face for he said: 'This is where I used to feed my lampreys – they had to be handled carefully. I have none now; I returned the last of my specimens to the sea three years ago.'

Three years ago? I peered closer into the tank as one of the hammerheads slid his belly along the glass. There on the white and silver underside of the fish, between the gill-slits and down the belly, numerous patches of raw red showed, many of them forming clearly defined circles where the close-packed scales had been removed and the suckerlike mouths of the lampreys had been at work. No, Haggopian's 'three years' had no doubt been a slip of the tongue – three days, more like it! Many of the wounds were clearly of recent origin, and before the Armenian ushered me on I was able to see that at least another two of the hammer-heads were similarly marked.

I stopped pondering my host's mistake when we passed into yet another room whose specimens must surely have caused any conchologist to cry out in delight. Again tanks lined the walls, smaller than many of the others I had so far seen, but marvellously laid out to duplicate perfectly the natural environs of their inhabitants. These inhabitants were the living gems of almost every ocean on earth; great conches and clams from the South Pacific; the small, beautiful *Haliotis excavata* and *Murex monodon* from the Great Barrier Reef; the amphora-like *Delphinula formosa* from China, and weird uni- and bi-valves of every shape and size in their hundreds. Even the windows were of shell – great, translucent, pinkly-glowing fan-shells, porcelain thin yet immensely strong, from very deep waters – suffusing the room in blood tints as weird as the submarine dappling of the previous rooms. The aisles, too, were crammed with trays and show-cases full of dry shells, none of them indexed in any way, and again Haggopian showed off his expertise by casually naming any specimens I paused to study and by briefly describing their habits and the foreign deeps in which they were indigenous.

My tour was interrupted here when Costas, the Greek who had brought me from Kletnos, entered this fascinating room of shells to murmur something of obvious importance to his employer. Haggopian nodded his head in agreement and Costas left, returning a few moments later with half-a-dozen other Greeks who each, in their turn, had a few words with Haggopian before departing. Eventually we were alone again.

'They were my men,' he told me, 'some of them for almost twenty years, but now I have no further need for them. I have paid them their last wages, they have said their farewells, and now they are going away. Costas will take them to Kletnos and return later for you. By then I should have finished my story.'

'I don't quite follow you, Mr. Haggopian. You mean you're going into seclusion here? What you said just then sounded ominously final.'

'Seclusion? Here? No, Mr. Belton – but final, yes! I have learned as much of the sea as I can from here, and in any case only one phase in my education remains. For that phase I need no . . . *tuition*! You will see.'

He saw the puzzled look on my face and smiled a wry smile. 'You find difficulty in understanding me, and that is hardly surprising. Few men, if any, have known my circumstances before, of that I am reasonably certain; and that is why I have chosen to speak now. You are fortunate in that you caught me at the right time; I would never have taken it upon myself to tell my story had I not been so persistently pursued – there are horrors best unknown – but perhaps the telling will serve as a warning. It gives me pause, the number of students devoted to the lore of the sea that would emulate my works and discoveries. But in any case, what you no doubt believed would be a simple interview will in fact be my swan-song. Tomorrow, when the island is deserted, Costas will return and set all the living specimens loose. There are means here by which even the largest fishes might be returned to the sea. Then Haggopiana will be truly empty.'

'But why? To what end – and where do you intend to go?' I asked. 'Surely this island is your base, your home and stronghold? It was here that you wrote your wonderful books, and—'

'My base and stronghold, as you put it, yes!' he harshly cut me off. 'The island has been these things to me, Mr Belton, but my home? No more! That – is my home!' He shot a slightly trembling hand abruptly out in the general direction of the Cretean Sea and the Mediterranean beyond. 'When your interview is over, I shall walk to the top of the rocks and look once more at Kletnos, the closest landmass of any reasonable size. Then I will take my *Echinoidea* and guide her out through the Kasos Straits on a direct and deliberate course until her fuel runs out. There can be no turning back. There is a place unsuspected in the Mediterranean – where the sea is so deep and cool, and where—'

He broke off and turned his strangely shining face to me: 'But there – at this rate the tale will never be told. Suffice to say that the last trip of the *Echinoidea* will be to the bottom – and that I shall be with her!'

'Suicide?' I gasped, barely able to keep up with Haggopian's rapid revelations. 'You intend to – drown yourself?'

At that Haggopian laughed, a rasping cough of a laugh that somehow reminded me of a seal's bark. 'Drown myself? Can you drown these?' he opened his arms to encompass a miniature ocean of strange conches; 'or these?' he waved through a door at a crystal tank of exotic fish.

For a few moments I stared at him in dumb amazement

and concern, uncertain as to whether I stood in the presence of a sane man or—?

He gazed at me intently through the dark lenses of his glasses, and under the scrutiny of those unseen eyes I slowly shook my head, backing off a step.

'I'm sorry, Mr Haggopian – I just . . .'

'Unpardonable,' he rasped as I struggled for words, 'my behaviour is unpardonable! Come, Mr Belton, perhaps we can be comfortable out here.' He led me through a doorway and out on to a patio surrounded by lemon and pomegranate trees. A white garden table and two cane chairs stood in the shade. Haggopian clapped his hands together once, sharply, then offered me a chair before clumsily seating himself opposite. Once again I noticed how all the man's movements seemed oddly awkward.

An old woman, wrapped around Indian-fashion in white silk and with the lower half of her face veiled in a shawl that fell back over her shoulders, answered the Armenian's summons. He spoke a few guttural yet remarkably *gentle* words to her in Greek. She went, stumbling a little with her years, to return a short while later with a tray, two glasses, and (amazingly) an English beer with the chill still on the bottle.

I saw that Haggopian's glass was already filled, but with no drink I could readily recognize. The liquid was greenly cloudy – sediment literally swam in his glass – and yet the Armenian did not seem to notice. He touched glasses with me before lifting the stuff to his lips and drinking deeply. I too, took a deep draught, for I was very dry; but, when I had placed my glass back on the table, I saw that Haggopian was still drinking! He completely drained off the murky, unknown liquid, put down the glass and again clapped his hands in summons.

At this point I found myself wondering why the man did not remove his sunglasses. After all, we were in the shade, had been even more so during my tour of his wonderful aquarium. Glancing at the Armenian's face I was reminded of his eye trouble as I again saw those thin trickles of liquid flowing down from behind the enigmatic lenses. And with the re-appearance of this symptom of Haggopian's optical affliction, the peculiar shiny film on his face also returned. For some time that – diffusion? – had seemed to be clearing; I had thought it was simply that I was becoming used to his looks. Now I saw that I had been wrong, his appearance was as odd as ever. Against my will I found myself thinking back on the man's repulsive handshake . . .

'These interruptions may be frequent,' his rasp cut into my thoughts. 'I am afraid that in my present phase I require a very generous intake of liquids!'

I was about to ask just what 'phase' he referred to when the old woman came back with a further glass of murky fluid for her master. He spoke a few more words to her before she once more left us. I could not help but notice, though, as she bent over the table, how very dehydrated the woman's face looked; with pinched nostrils, deeply wrinkled skin, and dull eyes sunk deep beneath the bony ridges of her eyebrows. An island peasant-woman, obviously – and yet, in other circum-stances, the fine bone-structure of that face might almost have seemed aristocratic. She seemed, too, to find a peculiar magnetism in Haggopian; leaning forward towards him noticeably, visibly fighting to control an apparent desire to touch him whenever she came near him.

'She will leave with you when you go. Costas will take care of her.'

'Was I staring?' I guiltily started, freshly aware of an odd feeling of unreality and discontinuity. 'I'm sorry, I didn't intend to be rude!'

'No matter – what I have to tell you makes a nonsense of all matters of sensibility. You strike me as a man not easily . . . *frightened*, Mr Belton?'

'I can be surprised, Mr Haggopian, and shocked – but frightened? Well, among other things I have been a war correspondent for some time, and—'

'Of course, I understand – but there are worse things than the man-made horrors of war!'

'That may be, but I'm a journalist. It's my job. I'll take a chance on being – frightened.'

'Good! And please put aside any doubts you may by now have conceived regarding my sanity, or any you may yet conceive during the telling of my story. The proofs, at the end, will be ample.'

I started to protest but he quickly cut me off: 'No, no, Mr Belton! You would have to be totally insensible not to have perceived the – strangeness here.'

He fell silent as for the third time the old woman appeared, placing a pitcher before him on the table. This time she almost fawned on him and he jerked away from her, nearly upsetting his chair. He rasped a few harsh words in Greek and I heard the strange, shrivelled creature sob as she turned to stumble away.

'What on earth is *wrong* with the woman?'

'In good time, Mr Belton,' he held up his hand, 'all in good time.' Again he drained his glass, refilling it from the pitcher before commencing his tale proper; a tale through which I sat for the most part silent, later hypnotized, and eventually horrified to the end.

2

'My first ten years of life were spent in the Cook Islands, and the next five in Cyprus,' Haggopian began, 'always within shouting distance of the sea. My father died when I was sixteen, and though he had never acknowledged me in his lifetime he willed to me the equivalent of two-and-one-half millions of pounds sterling! When I was twenty-one I came into this money and found that I could now devote myself utterly to the ocean – my one real love in life. By that I mean *all* oceans. I love the warm Mediterranean and the South Pacific, but no less the chill Arctic Ocean and the teeming North Sea. Even now I love them – even now!

'At the end of the war I bought Haggopiana and began to build my collection here. I wrote about my work and was twenty-nine years old when I finished *The Cradle Sea*. Of course it was a labour of love. I paid for the publication of the first edition myself, and though money did not really matter, subsequent reprints repaid me more than adequately. It was my success with that book – I used to enjoy success – and with *The Sea: A New Frontier*, which prompted me to commence work upon *Denizens of the Deep*. I had been married to my first wife for five years by the time I had the first rough manuscript of my work ready, and I could have had the book published there and then but for the fact that I had become something of a perfectionist both in my writing and my studies. In short there were passages in the manuscript, whole chapters on certain species, with which I was not satisfied.

'One of these chapters was devoted to the sirenians. The dugong and the manatee, particularly the latter, had fascinated me for a long time in respect of their undeniable connections with the mermaid and siren legends of old renown; from which, of course, their order takes its name. However, it was more than merely this initially that took me off on my "Manatee Survey", as I called those voyages, though at that time I could never have guessed at the importance of my quest. As it happened, my inquiries were to lead me to the first real pointer to my future – a frightful hint of my ultimate destination, though of course I never recognized it as such.' He paused.

'Destination?' I felt obliged to fill the silence. 'Literary or scientific?'

'My *ultimate* destination!'

'Oh!'

I sat and waited, not quite knowing what to say, an odd position for a journalist! In a moment or two Haggopian continued, and as he spoke I could feel his eyes staring at me intently through the opaque lenses of his spectacles:

'You are aware perhaps of the theories of continental drift – those concepts outlined initially by Wegener and Lintz, modified by Vine, Matthews and others – which have it that the continents are gradually 'floating' apart and that they were once much closer to one another? Such theories are sound, I assure you; primal Pangaea did exist, and was trodden by feet other than than those of men. Indeed, that first great continent knew life before man first swung down from the trees and up from the apes!

'But at any rate, it was partly to further the work of Wegener and the others that I decided upon my "Manatee Survey" – a comparison of the manatees of Liberia, Senegal and the Gulf of Guinea with those of the Caribbean and the Gulf of Mexico. You see, Mr Belton, of all the shores of Earth these two are the only coastal stretches within which manatees occur in their natural state. Surely you would agree that this is excellent zoological evidence for continental drift?

'Well, with these scientific interests of mine very much at heart, I eventually found myself in Jacksonville on the East Coast of North America; which is just as far north as the manatee may be found in any numbers. In Jacksonville, by chance, I heard of certain strange stones taken out of the sea – stones bearing weathered hieroglyphs of fantastic antiquity, presumably washed ashore by the back-currents of the Gulf Stream. Such was my interest in these stones and their possible source – you may recall that Mu, Atlantis and other mythical sunken lands and cities have long been favourite themes of mine – that I quickly concluded my "Manatee Survey" to sail to Boston, Massachusetts, where I had heard that a collector of such oddities kept a private museum. He, too, it turned out, was a lover of oceans, and his collection was full of the lore of the sea; particularly the North Atlantic which was, as it were, on his doorstep. I found him most erudite in all aspects of the East Coast, and he told me many fantastic tales of the shores of New England. It was the same New England coastline, he assured me, whence hailed those ancient stones bearing evidence of primal intelligence – *an intelligence I had seen traces of in places as far apart as the Ivory Coast and the islands of Polynesia!'*

For some time Haggopian had been showing a strange and increasing agitation, and now he sat wringing his hands and moving restlessly in his chair. 'Ah, yes, Mr Belton – was it not a discovery? For as soon as I saw the American's basalt fragments I *recognized* them! They were small, those pieces, yes, but the inscriptions upon them were the same as I had seen cut in great black pillars in the coastal jungles of Liberia – pillars long cast up by the sea and about which, on moonlit nights, the natives cavorted and chanted ancient liturgies! I had known those liturgies, too, Belton, from my childhood in the Cook Island – *Iā-, R'lyeh! Cthulhu fhtagn!'*

With this last thoroughly alien gibberish fluting weirdly from his lips the Armenian had risen suddenly to his feet, his head aggressively forward, and his knuckles white as they pressed down on the table. Then, seeing the look on my face as I quickly leaned backwards away from him, he slowly relaxed and finally fell back into his seat as though exhausted. He let his hands hang limp and turned his face to one side.

For at least three minutes Haggopian sat like this before turning to me with the merest half-apologetic shrug of his shoulders. 'You – you must excuse me, sir. I find myself very easily given these days to over-excitement.'

He took up his glass and drank, then dabbed again at the rivulets of liquid from his eyes before continuing: 'But I digress, mainly I wished to point out that once, long ago, the Americas and Africa were Siamese twins, joined at their middle by a lowland strip which sank as the continental drift began. There were cities in those lowlands, do you see? And evidence of those prehistoric places still exists at the points where once the two masses co-joined. As for Polynesia, well, suffice to say that the beings who built the ancient cities – beings who seeped down from the stars over inchoate aeons – once held dominion over all the world. But they left other traces, those beings, queer gods and cults and even stranger – minions!

'However, quite apart from these vastly interesting geological discoveries, I had, too, something of a genealogical interest in New England. My mother was Polynesian, you know, but she had old New England blood in her too; my great-great-grandmother was taken from the islands to New England by a deck hand on one of the old East India sailing ships in the late 1820s, and two generations later my grandmother returned to Polynesia when her American husband died in a fire. Until then the line had lived in Innsmouth, a decaying New England seaport of ill repute, where Polynesian women were anything but rare. My grandmother was pregnant when she arrived in the islands, and the American blood came out strongly in my mother, accounting for her looks; but even now I recall that there was something not quite right with her face – something about the eyes.

'I mention all this because . . . because I cannot help but wonder if something in my genealogical background has to do with my present – *phase*.'

Again that word, this time with plain emphasis, and again

I felt inclined to inquire which *phase* Haggopian meant – but too late, for already he had resumed his narrative:

'You see, I heard many strange tales in Polynesia as a child, and I was told equally weird tales by my Boston collector friend – of *things* that come up out of the sea to mate with men, and of their terrible progeny!'

For the second time a feverish excitement made itself apparent in Haggopian's voice and attitude; and again his agitation showed as his whole body trembled, seemingly in the grip of massive, barely repressed emotions.

'Did you know,' he suddenly burst out, 'that in 1928 Innsmouth was purged by Federal agents? Purged of *what*, I ask you? And why were depth-charges dropped off Devil's Reef? It was after this blasting and following the storms of 1930 that many oddly fashioned articles of golden jewelry were washed up on the New England beaches; and at the same time those black, broken, horribly hieroglyphed stones began to be noticed and picked up by beachcombers!

'*Iā-R'lyeh!* What monstrous things lurk even now in the ocean depths, Belton, and what other things *return* to that cradle of Earthly life?'

Abruptly he stood up to begin pacing the patio in his swaying, clumsy lope, mumbling gutturally and incoherently to himself and casting occasional glances in my direction where I sat, very disturbed now by his obviously aberrant mental condition, at the table.

At that distinct moment of time, had there been any easy means of escape, I believe I might quite happily have given up all to be off Haggopiana. I could see no such avenue of egress, however, and so I nervously waited until the Armenian had calmed himself sufficiently to resume his seat. Again moisture was seeping in a slow trickle from beneath the dark lenses, and once more he drank of the unknown liquid in his glass before continuing:

'Once more I ask you to accept my apologies, Mr Belton,

and I crave your pardon for straying so wildly from the principal facts. I was speaking before of my book, *Denizens of the Deep*, and of my dissatisfaction with certain chapters. Well, when finally my interest in New England's shores and mysteries waned, I returned to that book, and especially to a chapter concerning ocean parasites. I wanted to compare this specific branch of the sea's creatures with its land-going counterpart, and to introduce, as I had in my other chapters, oceanic myths and legends that I might attempt to explain them away.

'Of course, I was limited by the fact that the sea cannot boast so large a number of parasitic creatures as the land. Why, almost every land-going animal – bird and insect included – has its own little familiar living in its hair or feathers or feeding upon it in some parasitic fashion or other.

'None the less I dealt with the hagfish and lamprey, with certain species of fish-leech and whale-lice, and I compared them with fresh-water leeches, types of tapeworm, fungi and so on. Now, you might be tempted to believe that there is too great a difference between sea- and land-dwellers, and of course in a way there is – but when one considers that all life as we know it sprang originally from the sea . . . ?'

'When I think now, Mr. Belton, of the vampire in legend, occult belief and supernatural fiction – how the monster brings about hideous changes and deteriorations in his victim until that victim dies, and then returns as a vampire himself – then I wonder what mad fates drove me on. And yet how was I to know, how could any man foresee . . . ?

'But there – I anticipate, and that will not do. My revelation must come in its own time, you must be prepared, despite your assurances that you are not easily frightened.

'In 1956 I was exploring the seas of the Solomon Islands in a yacht with a crew of seven. We had moored for the night on a beautiful uninhabited little island off San Cristobal, and the next morning, as my men were de-camping and preparing the yacht for sea, I walked along the beach looking for conches. Stranded in a pool by the tide I saw a great shark, its gills barely in the water and its rough back and dorsal actually breaking the surface. I was sorry for the creature, of course, and even more so when I saw that it had fastened to its belly one of those very bloodsuckers with which I was still concerned. Not only that, but the hagfish was a beauty! Four feet long if it was an inch and definitely of a type I had never seen before. By that time *Denizens of the Deep* was almost ready, and but for that chapter I have already mentioned the book would have been at the printer's long since.

'Well, I could not waste the time it would take to two the shark to deeper waters, but none the less I felt sorry for the great fish. I had one of my men put it out of its misery with a rifle. Goodness knows how long the parasite had fed on its juices, gradually weakening it until it had become merely a toy of the tides.

'As for the hagfish – he was to come with us! Aboard my yacht I had plenty of tanks to take bigger fish than him, and of course I wanted to study him and include a mention of him in my book.

'My men managed to net the strange fish without too much trouble and took it aboard, but they seemed to be having some difficulty getting it back out of the net and into the tank. You must understand, Mr Belton, that these tanks were sunk into the decks, with their tops level with the planking. I went over to give a hand before the fish expired, and just as it seemed we were sorting the tangle out the creature began thrashing about! It came out of the net with one great flexing of its body – and took me with it into the tank!

'My men laughed at first, of course, and I would have

laughed with them – *if that awful fish had not in an instant fastened itself on my body, its suction-pad mouth grinding high on my chest and its eyes boring horribly into mine!'*

3

After a short pause, during which pregnant interval his shining face worked horribly, the Armenian continued:

'I was delirious for three weeks after they dragged me out of the tank. Shock? – poison? – I did not know at the time. *Now* I know, but it is too late; possibly it was too late even then.

'My wife was with us as cook, and during my delirium, as I had feverishly tossed and turned in my cabin bed, she had tended me. Meanwhile my men had kept the hagfish – a previously unknown species of *Myxinoidea* – well supplied with small sharks and other fish. They never allowed the cyclostome to completely drain any of its hosts, you understand, but they knew enough to keep the creature healthy for me no matter its loathsome manner of taking nourishment.

'My recovery, I remember, was plagued by recurrent dreams of monolithic submarine cities, cyclopean structures of basaltic stone peopled by strange, hybrid beings part human, part fish and part batrachian; the amphibious Deep Ones, minions of Dagon and worshippers of sleeping Cthulhu. In those dreams, too, eerie voices called out to me and whispered things of my forebears – things which made me scream through my fever at the hearing!

'After I recovered the times were many I went below decks to study the hagfish through the glass sides of its tank. Have you ever seen a hagfish or lamprey close up, Mr Belton? No? Then consider yourself lucky. They are ugly creatures, with looks to match their natures, eel-like and primitive – and their mouths, Belton – their horrible, rasp-like, sucking mouths!

'Two months later, toward the end of the voyage, the horror really began. By then my wounds, the raw places on my chest where the thing had had me, were healed completely; but the memory of that first encounter was still terribly fresh in my mind, and—

'I see the question written on your face, Mr Belton, but indeed you heard me correctly – I did say my *first* encounter! Oh, yes! There were more encounters to come, plenty of them!'

At this point in his remarkable narrative Haggopian paused once more to dab at the rivulets of moisture seeping from behind his sun-glasses, and to drink yet again from the cloudy liquid in his glass. It gave me a chance to look about me; possibly I still thought an immediate escape route should such become necessary.

The Armenian was seated with his back to the great bungalow, and as I glanced nervously in that direction I saw a face move quickly out of sight in one of the smaller, porthole windows. Later, as my host's story progressed, I was able to see that the face in the windows belonged to the old servant woman, and that her eyes were fixed firmly upon him in a kind of hungry fascination. Whenever she caught me looking at her she withdrew.

'No,' Haggopian finally went on, 'the hagfish was far from finished with me – far from it. For as the weeks went by my interest in the creature grew into a sort of obsession, so that every spare moment found me staring into its tank or examining the curious marks and scars it left on the bodies of its unwilling hosts. And so it was that I discovered how those hosts were *not* unwilling! A peculiar fact, and yet—

'Yes, I found that having once played host to the

cyclostome, the fishes it fed upon were ever eager to resume such liaisons, even unto death! When I first discovered this odd circumstance I experimented, of course, and I was later able to establish quite definitely that following the initial violation the hosts of the hagfish submitted to subsequent attacks with a kind of soporofic pleasure!

'Apparently, Mr Belton, I had found in the sea the perfect parallel of the vampire of land-based legend. Just what this meant, the utter horror of my discovery, did not dawn on me until – until—

'We were moored off Limassol in Cyprus prior to starting on the very last leg of our trip, the voyage back to Haggopiana. I had allowed the crew – all but one man, Costas, who had no desire to leave the yacht – ashore for a night out. They had all worked very hard for a long time. My wife, too, had gone to visit friends in Limassol. I was happy enough to stay aboard, my wife's friends bored me; and besides, I had been feeling tired, a sort of lethargy, for a number of days.

'I went to bed early. From my cabin I could see the lights of the town and hear the gentle lap of water about the legs of the pier at which we were moored. Costas was drowsing aft with a fishing-line dangling in the water. Before I dropped off to sleep I called out to him. He answered, in a sleepy sort of way, to say that there was hardly a ripple on the sea and that already he had pulled in two fine mullets.

'When I regained consciousness it was three weeks later and I was back here on Haggopiana. The hagfish had had me again! They told me how Costas had heard the splash and found me in the cyclostome's tank. He had managed to get me out of the water before I drowned, but had needed to fight like the very devil to get the monster off me – or rather, to *get me off the monster!*

'Do the implications begin to show, Mr Belton?

'You see this?' He unbuttoned his shirt to show me the

marks on his chest – circular scars of about three inches in diameter, like those I had seen on the hammerheads in their tank – and I stiffened in my chair, my mouth falling open in shock as I saw their great number! Down to a silken cummerbund just below his rib-cage he unbuttoned his shirt, and barely an inch of his skin remained unblemished; some of the scars even overlapped!

'Good God!' I finally gasped.

'*Which God?*' Haggopian instantly rasped across the table, his fingers trembling again in that strange passion. 'Which God, Mr Belton? Jehovah or Oannes – the Man-Christ or the Toad-Thing – god of Earth or Water? *Iā-R'lyeh, Cthulhu fhtagn; Yibb-Tstll; Yot-Sothothl!* I know many gods, sir!'

Again, jerkily, he filled his glass from the pitcher, literally gulping at the sediment-loaded stuff until I thought he must choke. When finally he put down his empty glass I could see that he had himself once more under a semblance of control.

'That second time,' he continued, 'everyone believed I had fallen into the tank in my sleep, and this was by no means a wild stretch of the imagination; as a boy I had been something of a somnambulist. At first even I believed it was so, for at that time I was still blind to the creature's power over me. They say that the hagfish is blind, too, Mr Belton, and members of the better known species certainly are – but *my* hag was not blind. Indeed, primitive or not, I believed that after the first three or four times he was actually able to recognise me! I used to keep the creature in the tank where you saw the hammerheads, forbidding anyone else entry to that room. I would pay my visits at night, whenever the – *mood* – came on me; and he would be there, waiting for me, with his ugly mouth groping at the glass and his queer eyes peering out in awful anticipation. He would go straight to the steps as soon as I began to climb them, waiting for me restlessly in the water until I joined him there. I would wear a snorkel, so as to be able to breathe while he – while it . . .'

Haggopian was trembling all over now and dabbing angrily at his face with his silk handkerchief. Glad of the chance to take my eyes off the man's oddly glistening features, I finished off my drink and refilled my glass with the remainder of the beer in the bottle. The chill was long off the beer by then – the beer itself was almost stale – but in any case, understandably I believe, the edge had quite gone from my thirst for anything of Haggopian's. I drank solely to relieve my mouth of its clammy dryness.

'The worst of it was,' he went on after a while, 'that what was happening to me was not against my will. As with the sharks and other host-fish, so with me. I *enjoyed* each hideous liaison as the alcoholic enjoys the euphoria of his whisky; as the drug addict delights in his delusions; and the results of my addiction were no less destructive! I experienced no more periods of delirium, such as I had known following my first two "sessions" with the creature, but I could feel that my strength was slowly but surely being sapped. My assistants knew that I was ill, naturally – they would have had to be stupid not to notice the way my health was deteriorating or the rapidity with which I appeared to be ageing – but it was my wife who suffered the most.

'I could have little to do with her, do you see? If we had led any sort of normal life then she must surely have seen the marks on my body. That would have required an explanation, one I was not willing – indeed, unable – to give! Oh, but I waxed cunning in my addiction, and no one guessed the truth behind the strange "disease" which was slowly killing me, draining me of my life's blood.

'A little over a year later, in 1958, when I knew I was on death's very doorstep, I allowed myself to be talked into undertaking another voyage. My wife loved me deeply still and believed a prolonged trip might do me good. I think that Costas had begun to suspect the truth by then; I even caught him one day in the forbidden room staring curiously at the cyclostome in its tank. His suspicion became even more aroused when I told him that the creature was to go with us. He was against the idea from the start. I argued however that my studies were incomplete, that I was not finished with the hag and that eventually I intended to release the fish at sea. I intended no such thing. In fact, I did not believe I would last the voyage out. From sixteen stone in weight I was down to nine!

'We were anchored off the Great Barrier Reef the night my wife found me with the hagfish. The others were asleep after a birthday party aboard. I had insisted that they all drink and make merry so that I could be sure I would not be disturbed, but my wife had taken very little to drink and I had not noticed. The first thing I knew of it was when I saw her standing at the side of the tank, looking down at me and the . . . thing! I will always remember her face, the horror and awful *knowledge* written upon it, and her scream, the way it split the night!

'By the time I got out of the tank she was gone. She had fallen or thrown herself overboard. Her scream had roused the crew and Costas was the first to be up and about. He saw me before I could cover myself. I took three of the men and went out in a little boat to look for my wife. When we got back Costas had finished off the hagfish. He had taken a great hook and gaffed the thing to death. Its head was little more than a bloody pulp, but even in death its suctorial mouth continued to rasp away – at nothing!

'After that, for a whole month, I would have Costas nowhere near me. I do not think he *wanted* to be near me – I believe he knew that my grief was not solely for my wife!

'Well, that was the end of the first phase, Mr Belton. I rapidly regained my weight and health, the years fell off my face and body, until I was almost the same man I had been. I say "almost", for of course I could not be exactly the same. For one thing I had lost all my hair – as I have said, the creature had depleted me so thoroughly that I had been on death's very doorstep – and also, to remind me of the horror, there were the scars on my body and the greater scar on my mind which hurt me still whenever I thought of the look on my wife's face when last I had seen her.

'During the next year I finished my book, but mentioned nothing of my discoveries during the course of my "Manatee Survey", and nothing of my experiences with the awful fish. I dedicated the book, as you no doubt know, to the memory of my poor wife; but yet another year was to pass before I could get the episode with the hagfish completely out of my system. From then on I could not bear to think back on my terrible obsession.

'It was shortly after I married for the second time that phase two began . . .

'For some time I had been experiencing a strange pain in my abdomen, between my navel and the bottom of my ribcage, but had not troubled myself to report it to a doctor. I have an abhorrence of doctors. Within six months of the wedding the pain had disappeared – to be replaced by something far worse!

'Knowing my terror of medical men, my new wife kept my secret, and though we neither of us knew it, that was the worst thing we could have done. Perhaps if I had seen about the thing sooner—

'You see, Mr Belton, I had developed – yes, an organ! An *appendage*, a snout-like thing had grown out of my stomach, with a tiny hole at its end like a second navel! Eventually, of course, I was obliged to see a doctor, and after he examined me and told me the worst I swore him – or rather, I *paid* him – to secrecy. The organ could not be removed, he said, it was part of me. It had its own blood vessels, a major artery and connections with my lungs and stomach. It was not malignant in the sense of a morbid tumour. Other than this he was unable to explain the snout-like thing away. After an exhaustive series of tests, though, he was further able to say that my blood, too, had undergone a change. There seemed to be far too much salt in my system. The doctor told me then that by all rights I ought not to be alive!

'Nor did it stop there, Mr Belton, for soon other changes started to take place – this time in the snout-like organ itself when that tiny navel at its tip began to open up!

'And then . . . and then . . . my poor wife . . . *and my eyes*!'

Once more Haggopian had to stop. He sat there gulping like – *like a fish out of water!* – with his whole body trembling violently and the thin streams of moisture trickling down his face. Again he filled his glass and drank deeply of the filthy liquid, and yet again he wiped at his ghastly face with the square of silk. My own mouth had gone very dry, and even if I had had anything to say I do not believe I could have managed it. I reached for my glass, simply to give myself something to do while the Armenian fought to control himself, but of course the glass was empty.

'I – it seems – you –' mine host half gulped, half rasped, then gave a weird, harshly choking bark before finally settling himself to finishing his unholy narrative. Now his voice was less human than any voice I had ever heard before:

'You – have – more nerve than I thought, Mr Belton, and – you were right; you are not easily shocked or frightened. In the end it is I who am the coward, for I cannot tell the rest of the tale. I can only – *show* you, and then you must leave. You can wait for Costas at the pier . . .'

With that Haggopian slowly stood up and peeled off his open shirt. Hypnotized I watched as he began to unwind the silken cummerbund at his waist, watched as his – *organ* –

came into view, as it blindly groped in the light like the snout of a rooting pig! But the thing was not a snout!

Its end was an open, gasping mouth – red and loathsome, with rows of rasp-like teeth – and in its sides breathing gillslits showed, moving in and out as the thing sucked at thin air!

Even then the horror was not at an end, for as I lurched reelingly to my feet the Armenian took off those hellish sunglasses! For the first time I saw his eyes; *his bulging fisheyes – without whites, like jet marbles, oozing painful tears in the constant ache of an alien environment – eyes adapted for the murk of the deeps!*

I remember how, as I fled blindly down the beach to the pier, Haggopian's last words rang in my ears; the words he rasped as he threw down the cummerbund and removed the dark-lensed sunglasses from his face: 'Do not pity me, Mr Belton,' he had said. 'The sea was ever my first love, and there is much I do not know of her even now – but I will, I will. And I shall not be alone of my kind among the Deep Ones. There is one I know who awaits me even now, and one other yet to come!'

On the short trip back to Kletnos, numb though my mind ought to have been, the journalist in me took over and I thought back on Haggopian's hellish story and its equally hellish implications. I thought of his great love of the ocean, of the strangely cloudy liquid with which he so obviously sustained himself, and of the thin film of protective slime which glistened on his face and presumably covered the rest of his body. I thought of his weird forebears and of the exotic gods they had worshipped; of *things* that came up out of the sea to mate with men! I thought of the fresh marks I had seen on the undersides of the hammerhead sharks in the great tank, marks made by no parasite for Haggopian had returned his lampreys to the sea all of three years earlier; and I thought of that second wife the Armenian had mentioned who, rumour had it, had died of some 'exotic wasting disease'! Finally, I thought of those other rumours I had heard of his *third* wife: how she was no longer living with him – but of the latter it was not until we docked at Kletnos proper that I learned how those rumours, understandable though the mistake was, were in fact mistaken.

For it was then, as the faithful Costas helped the old woman from the boat, that she stepped on her trailing shawl. That shawl and her veil were one and the same garment, so that her clumsiness caused a momentary exposure of her face, neck and one shoulder to a point just above her left breast. In that same instant of inadvertent unveiling, I saw the woman's full face for the first time – and also the livid scars where they began just beneath her collar-bone!

At last I understood the strange magnetism Haggopian had held for her, that magnetism not unlike the unholy attraction between the morbid hagfish of his story and its all too willing hosts! I understood, too, my previous interest in her classic, almost aristocratic features – *for now I could see that they were those of a certain Athenian model lately of note! Haggopian's third wife, wed to him on her eighteenth birthday! And then, as my whirling thoughts flashed back yet again to that second wife, 'buried at sea', I knew finally, cataclysmically what the Armenian had meant when he said: 'There is one who awaits me even now, and one other yet to come!'*

THE PICNICKERS

This story comes from a long time ago. I was a boy, so that shows how long ago it was. Part of it is from memory, and the rest is a reconstruction built up over the years through times when I've given it a lot of thought, filling in the gaps; for I wasn't privy to everything that happened that time, which is perhaps as well. But I do know that I'm prone to nightmares, and I believe that this is where they have their roots, so maybe getting it down on paper is my rite of exorcism. I hope so.

The summers were good and hot in those days, and no use anyone telling me that that's just an old man speaking, who only remembers the good things; they *were* better summers! I could, and did, go down to the beach at Harden every day. I'd get burned black by the time school came around again at the end of the holidays. The only black you'd get on that beach these days would be from the coal dust. In fact there isn't a beach any more, just a sloping moonscape of slag from the pits, scarred by deep gulleys where polluted water gurgles down to a scummy, foaming black sea.

But at that time, men used to crab on the rocks when the tide was out, and cast for cod right off the sandbar where the small waves broke. And the receding sea would leave blue pools where we could swim in safety. Well, there's probably still sand down there, but it's ten foot deep under the strewn black guts of the mines, and the only pools now are pools of slurry.

It was summer when the gypsies came, the days were long

and hot, and the beach was still a great drift of aching white sand.

Gypsies. They've changed, too, over the years. Now they travel in packs, motorized, in vehicles that shouldn't even be on the roads: furtive and scruffy, long-haired thieves who nobody wants and who don't much try to be wanted. Or perhaps I'm prejudiced. Anyway, they're not the real thing any more. But in those days they were. Most of them, anyway . . .

Usually they'd come in packets of three or four families, small communities plodding the roads in their intricately painted, hand-carved horse-drawn caravans, some with canvas roofs and some wooden; all brass and black leather, varnished wood and lacquered chimney-stacks, wrinkled brown faces and shiny brown eyes; with clothes pegs and various gew-gaws, hammered trinkets and rings that would turn your fingers green, strange songs sung for halfpennies and fortunes told from the lines in your hand. And occasionally a curse if someone was bad to them and theirs.

My uncle was the local doctor. He'd lost his wife in the Great War and never remarried. She'd been a nurse and died somewhere on a battlefield in France. After the war he'd travelled a lot in Europe and beyond, spent years on the move, not wanting to settle. And when she was out of his system (not that she ever was, not really; her photographs were all over the house) then he had come home again to England, to the north-east where he'd been born. In the summers my parents would go down from Edinburgh to see him, and leave me there with him for company through the holidays.

This summer in question would be one of the last – of that sort, anyway – for the next war was already looming; of course, we didn't know that then.

'Gypsies, Sandy!' he said that day, just home from the

mine where there'd been an accident. He was smudged with coal dust, which turned his sweat black where it dripped off him, with a pale band across his eyes and a white dome to his balding head from the protection of a miner's helmet.

'Gypsies?' I said, all eager. 'Where?'

'Over in Slater's Copse. Seen 'em as I came over the viaduct. One caravan at least. Maybe there'll be more later.'

That was it: I was supposed to run now, over the fields to the copse, to see the gypsies. That way I wouldn't ask questions about the accident in the mine. Uncle Zachary didn't much like to talk about his work, especially if the details were unpleasant or the resolution an unhappy one. But I wanted to know anyway. 'Was it bad, down the mine?'

He nodded, the smile slipping from his grimy face as he saw that I'd seen through his ruse. 'A bad one, aye,' he said. 'A man's lost his legs and probably his life. I did what I could.' Following which he hadn't wanted to say any more. And so I went off to see the gypsies.

Before I actually left the house, though, I ran upstairs to my attic room. From there, through the binoculars Uncle Zachary had given me for my birthday, I could see a long, long way. And I could even see if he'd been telling the truth about the gypsies, or just pulling my leg as he sometimes did, a simple way of distracting my attention from the accident. I used to sit for hours up there, using those binoculars through my dormer window, scanning the land all about.

To the south lay the colliery: 'Harden Pit', as the locals called it. Its chimneys were like long, thin guns aimed at the sky; its skeletal towers with their huge spoked wheels turning, lifting or lowering the cages; and at night its angry red coke ovens roaring, discharging their yellow and white-blazing tonnage to be hosed down into mounds of foul-steaming coke.

Harden Pit lay beyond the viaduct with its twin lines of

tracks glinting in the sunlight, shimmering in a heat haze. From here, on the knoll where Uncle Zachary's house stood – especially from my attic window – I could actually look down on the viaduct a little, see the shining tracks receding toward the colliery. The massive brick structure that supported them had been built when the collieries first opened up, to provide transport for the black gold, one viaduct out of many spanning the becks and streams of the north-east where they ran to the sea. 'Black gold', they'd called coal even then, when it cost only a few shillings per hundredweight!

This side of the viaduct and towards the sea cliffs, there stood Slater's Copse, a close-grown stand of oaks, rowans, hawthorns and hazelnuts. Old Slater was a farmer who had sold up to the coal industry, but he'd kept back small pockets of land for his and his family's enjoyment, and for the enjoyment of everyone else in the colliery communities. Long after this whole area was laid to waste, Slater's patches of green would still be here, shady oases in the grey and black desert.

And in the trees of Slater's Copse . . . Uncle Zachary hadn't been telling stories after all! I could glimpse the varnished wood, the young shire horse between his shafts, the curve of a spoked wheel behind a fence.

And so I left the house, ran down the shrub-grown slope of the knoll and along the front of the cemetery wall, then straight through the graveyard itself and the gate on the far side, and so into the fields with their paths leading to the new coast road on the one side and the viaduct on the other. Forsaking the paths, I forged through long grasses laden with pollen, leaving a smoky trail in my wake as I made for Slater's Copse and the gypsies.

Now, you might wonder why I was so taken with gypsies and gypsy urchins. But the truth is that even old Zachary in his rambling house wasn't nearly so lonely as me. He had his work, calls to make every day, and his surgery in Essingham five nights a week. But I had no one. With my 'posh' Edinburgh accent, I didn't hit it off with the colliery boys. Them with their hard, swaggering ways, and their harsh north-eastern twang. They called themselves 'Geordies', though they weren't from Newcastle at all; and me, I was an outsider. Oh, I could look after myself. But why fight them when I could avoid them? And so the gypsies and I had something in common: we didn't belong here. I'd played with the gypsies before.

But not with this lot.

Approaching the copse, I saw a boy my own age and a woman, probably his mother, taking water from a spring. They heard me coming, even though the slight summer breeze off the sea favoured me, and looked up. I waved . . . but their faces were pale under their dark cloth hats, where their eyes were like blots on old parchment. They didn't seem like my kind of gypsies at all. Or maybe they'd had trouble recently, or were perhaps expecting trouble. There was only one caravan and so they were one family on its own.

Then, out of the trees at the edge of the copse, the head of the family appeared. He was tall and thin, wore the same wide-brimmed cloth hat, looked out at me from its shade with eyes like golden triangular lamps. It could only have been a sunbeam, catching him where he stood with the top half of his body shaded; paradoxically, at the same time the sun had seemed to fade a little in the sky. But it was strange and I stopped moving forward, and he stood motionless, just looking. Behind him stood a girl, a shadow in the trees; and in the dappled gloom her eyes, too, were like candle-lit turnip eyes in October.

'Hallo!' I called from only fifty feet away. But they made no answer, turned their backs on me and melted back into the copse. So much for 'playing' with the gypsies! With this bunch, anyway. But . . . I could always try again later. When they'd settled in down here.

I went to the viaduct instead.

The viaduct both fascinated and frightened me at one and the same time. Originally constructed solely to accommodate the railway, with the addition of a wooden walkway it also provided miners who lived in one village but worked in the other with a shortcut to their respective collieries. On this side, a mile to the north, stood Essingham; on the other, lying beyond the colliery itself and inland a half-mile or so toward the metalled so-called 'coast road', Harden. The viaduct fascinated me because of the trains, shuddering and rumbling over its three towering arches, and scared me because of its vertiginous walkway.

The walkway had been built on the ocean-facing side of the viaduct, level with the railway tracks but separated from them by the viaduct's wall. It was of wooden planks protected on the otherwise open side, by a fence of staves five feet high. Upward-curving iron arms fixed in brackets underneath held the walkway aloft, alone sustaining it against gravity's unending exertions. But they always looked dreadfully thin and rusty to me, those metal supports, and the vertical distance between them and the valley's floor seemed a terribly great one. In fact it was about one hundred and fifty feet. Not a *terrific* height, really, but it only takes a fifth of that to kill or maim a man if he falls.

I had an ambition: to walk across it from one end to the other. So far my best attempt had taken me a quarterway across before being forced back. The trouble was the trains. The whistle of a distant train was always sufficient to send me flying, heart hammering, racing to get off the walkway before the train got onto the viaduct! But this time I didn't even make it that far. A miner, hurrying towards me from the other side, recognised me and called: 'Here, lad! Are you the young 'un stayin' with Zach Gardner?'

'Yes, sir,' I answered as he stamped closer. He was in his 'pit black', streaked with sweat, his boots clattering on the wooden boards.

'Here,' he said again, groping in a grimy pocket. 'A threepenny bit!' He pressed the coin into my hand. 'Now *run*! God knows you can go faster than me! Tell your uncle he's to come at once to Joe Anderson's. The ambulance men won't move him. Joe won't let them! He's delirious but he's hangin' on. We diven't think for long, though.'

'The accident man?'

'Aye, that's him. Joe's at home. He says he can feel his legs but not the rest of his body. It'd be reet funny, that, if it wasn't so tragic. Bloody cages! He'll not be the last they trap! Now scramble, lad, d'you hear?'

I scrambled, glad of any excuse to turn away yet again from the challenge of the walkway.

Nowadays . . . a simple telephone call. And in those days, too, we had the phone; some of us. But Zachary Gardner hated them. Likewise cars, though he did keep a motorcycle and sidecar for making his rounds. Across the fields and by the copse I sped, aware of faces in the trees but not wasting time looking at them, and through the graveyard and up the cobbled track to the flat crest of the knoll, to where my uncle stood in the doorway in his shirtsleeves, all scrubbed clean again. And I gasped out my message.

Without a word, nodding, he went to the lean-to and started up the bike, and I climbed slowly and dizzily to my attic room, panting my lungs out. I took up my binoculars and watched the shining ribbon of road to the west, until Uncle Zachary's bike and sidecar came spurting into view, the banging of its pistons unheard at this distance; and I continued to watch him until he disappeared out of sight toward Harden, where a lone spire stood up, half-hidden by a low hill. He came home again at dusk, very quiet, and we heard the next day how Joe Anderson had died that night.

The funeral was five days later at two in the afternoon; I watched for a while, but the bowed heads and the slim, sagging frame of the miner's widow distressed me and made me feel like a voyeur. So I watched the gypsies picnicking instead.

They were in the field next to the graveyard, but separated from it by a high stone wall. The field had lain fallow for several years and was deep in grasses, thick with clovers and wild flowers. And up in my attic room, I was the only one who knew the gypsies were there at all. They had arrived as the ceremony was finishing and the first handful of dirt went into the new grave. They sat on their coloured blanket in the bright sunlight, faces shaded by their huge hats, and I thought: *how odd!* For while they had picnic baskets with them, they didn't appear to be eating. Maybe they were saying some sort of gypsy grace first. Long, silent prayers for the provision of their food. Their bowed heads told me that must be it. Anyway, their inactivity was such that I quickly grew bored and turned my attention elsewhere . . .

The shock came (not to me, you understand, for I was only on the periphery of the thing, a child, to be seen and not heard) only three days later. The first shock of several, it came first to Harden village, but like a pebble dropped in a still pond its ripples began spreading almost at once.

It was this: the recently widowed Muriel Anderson had committed suicide, drowning herself in the beck under the viaduct. Unable to bear the emptiness, still stunned by her husband's absence, she had thought to follow him. But she'd retained sufficient of her senses to leave a note: a simple plea that they lay her coffin next to his, in a single grave. There were no children, no relatives; the funeral should be simple, with as few people as possible. The sooner she could be with Joe again the better, and she didn't want their reunion complicated by crowds of mourners. Well, things were easier in those days. Her grief quickly became the grief of the entire village, which almost as quickly dispersed, but her wishes were respected.

From my attic room I watched the gravediggers at work on Joe Anderson's plot, shifting soil which hadn't quite settled yet, widening the hole to accommodate two coffins. And later that afternoon I watched them climb out of the hole, and saw the way they scratched their heads. Then they separated and went off, one towards Harden on a bicycle, heading for the viaduct shortcut, and the other coming my way, towards the knoll, coming no doubt to speak with my Uncle Zachary. Idly, I looked for the gypsies then, but they weren't picnicking that day and I couldn't find them around their caravan. And so, having heard the gravedigger's cautious knock at the door of the house, and my uncle letting him in, I went downstairs to the latter's study.

As I reached the study door I heard voices: my uncle's soft tones and the harsher, local dialect of the gravedigger, but both used so low that the conversation was little more than a series of whispers. I've worked out what was said since then, as indeed I've worked most things out, and so am able to reconstruct it here:

'*Holes*, you say?' That was my uncle.

'Aye!' said the other, with conviction. 'In the side of the box. Drilled there, like. Fower of them.' (Fower meaning four.)

'Wormholes?'

'Bloody big worms, gaffer!' (Worms sounding like 'warms'.) 'Big as half-crowns, man, those holes! And anyhow, he's only been doon a fortneet.'

There was a pause before: 'And Billy's gone for the undertaker, you say?'

'Gone for Mr Forster, aye. I told him, be as quick as you can.'

'Well, John,' (my uncle's sigh) 'while we're waiting, I suppose I'd better come and see what it is that's so worried you . . .'

I ducked back then, into the shadows of the stairwell. It wasn't that I was a snoop, and I certainly didn't feel like one, but it was as well to be discreet. They left the house and I followed on, at a respectful distance, to the graveyard. And I sat on the wall at the entrance, dangling my long skinny legs and waiting for them, sunbathing in the early evening glow. By the time they were finished in there, Mr Forster had arrived in his big, shiny hearse.

'Come and see this,' said my uncle quietly, his face quite pale, as Mr Forster and Billy got out of the car. Mr Forster was a thin man, which perhaps befitted his calling, but he was sweating anyway, and complaining that the car was like a furnace.

'That coffin,' his words were stiff, indignant, 'is of the finest oak. Holes? Ridiculous! I never heard anything like it! Damage, more like,' and he glowered at Billy and John. '*Spade* damage!' They all trooped back into the graveyard, and I went to follow them. But my uncle spotted me and waved me back.

'You'll be all right where you are, Sandy my lad,' he said. So I shrugged and went back to the house. But as I turned away I did hear him say to Mr Forster: 'Sam, it's not spade damage. And these lads are quite right. Holes they said, and holes they are – four of them – all very neat and tidy, drilled right through the side of the box and the chips still lying there in the soil. Well, you screwed the lid down, and though I'll admit I don't like it, still I reckon we'd be wise to have it open again. Just to see what's what. Joe wouldn't mind, I'm sure, and there's only the handful of us to know about it. I reckon it was clever of these two lads to think to come for you and me.'

'You because you're the doctor, and because you were

closest,' said Forster grudgingly, 'and me because they've damaged my coffin!'

'No,' John Lane spoke up, 'because you built it – your cousin, anyhow – and it's got holes in it!'

And off they went, beyond my range of hearing. But not beyond viewing. I ran as quickly as I could.

Back in my attic room I was in time to see Mr Forster climb out of the hole and scratch his head as the others had done before him. Then he went back to his car and returned with a toolkit. Back down into the hole he went, my uncle with him. The two gravediggers stood at the side, looking down, hands stuffed in their trouser pockets. From the way they crowded close, jostling for a better position, I assumed that the men in the hole wee opening the box. But then Billy and John seemed to stiffen a little. Their heads craned forward and down, and their hands slowly came out of their pockets.

They backed away from the open grave, well away until they came up against a row of leaning headstones, then stopped and looked at each other. My uncle and Mr Forster came out of the grave, hurriedly and a little undignified, I thought. They, too, backed away; and both of them were brushing the dirt from their clothes, sort of crouched down into themselves.

In a little while they straightened up, and then my uncle gave himself a shake. He moved forward again, got down once more into the grave. He left Mr Forster standing there wringing his hands, in company with Billy and John. My binoculars were good ones and I could actually see the sweat shiny on Mr Forster's thin face. None of the three took a pace forward until my uncle stood up and beckoned for assistance.

Then the two gravediggers went to him and hauled him out. And silent, they all piled into Mr Forster's car which he started up and headed for the house. And of course I would have liked to know what this was all about, though I guessed I wouldn't be told. Which meant I'd have to eavesdrop again.

This time in the study the voices weren't so hushed; agitated, fearful, even outraged, but not hushed. There were four of them and they knew each other well, and it was broad daylight. If you see what I mean.

'Creatures? Creatures?' My Forster was saying as I crept to the door. 'Something in the ground, you say?'

'Like rats, d'you mean?' (John, the senior gravedigger.)

'I really don't know,' said my uncle, but there was that in his voice which told me that he had his suspicions. 'No, not rats,' he finally said; and now he sounded determined, firm, as if he'd come to a decision. 'Now look, you two, you've done your job and done it well, but this thing mustn't go any further. There's a guinea for each of you – from me, my promise – but you can't say anything about what you've seen today. Do you hear?'

'Whatever you say, gaffer,' said John, gratefully. 'But what'll you do about arl this? I mean—'

'Leave it to me,' my uncle cut him off. 'And mum's the word, hear?'

I heard the scraping of chairs and ducked back out of sight. Uncle Zachary ushered the gravediggers out of the house and quickly returned to his study. 'Sam,' he said, his voice coming to me very clear now, for he'd left the door ajar, 'I don't think it's rats. I'm sure it isn't. Neither is it worms of any sort, nor anything else of that nature.'

'Well, it's certainly nothing to do with me!' the other was still indignant, but more shocked than outraged, I thought.

'It's something to do with all of us, Sam,' said my uncle. 'I mean, how long do you think your business will last if this gets out, eh? No, it has nothing to do with you or the quality of workmanship,' he continued, very quickly. 'There's nothing personal in it at all. Oh, people will still die here, of course they will – but you can bet your boots they'll not want to be *buried* here!'

'But what on earth *is* it?' Forster's indignation or shock had evaporated; his voice was now very quiet and awed.

'I was in Bulgaria once,' said my uncle. 'I was staying at a small village, very tranquil if a little backward, on the border. Which is to say, the Danube. There was a flood and the riverbank got washed away, and part of the local graveyard with it. Something like this came to light, and the local people went very quiet and sullen. At the place I was staying, they told me there must be an "Obour" in the village. What's more, they knew how to find it.'

'An Obour?' said Forster. 'Some kind of animal?'

My uncle's voice contained a shudder when he answered: 'The worst possible sort of animal, yes.' Then his chair scraped and he began pacing, and for a moment I lost track of his low-uttered words. But obviously Mr Forster heard them clearly enough.

'*What*? Man, that's madness! And you a doctor!'

My uncle was ever slow to take offence. But I suspected that by now he'd be simmering. 'They went looking for the Obour with lanterns in the dark – woke up everyone in the village, in the dead of night, to see what they looked like by lantern light. For the eyes of the Obour are yellow – and triangular!'

'Madness!' Forster gasped again.

And now my uncle *was* angry. 'Oh, and do you have a better suggestion? So you tell me, Sam Forster, what *you* think can tunnel through packed earth and do . . . that?'

'But I—'

'Look at this book,' my uncle snapped. And I heard him go to a bookshelf, then his footsteps crossing the room to his guest.

After a while: 'Russian?'

'Romanian – but don't concern yourself with the text, look at the pictures!'

Again a pause before: 'But . . . this is too . . .'

'Yes, I know it is,' said my uncle, before Forster could find the words he sought. 'And I certainly hope I'm wrong, and that it is something ordinary. But tell me, can *anything* of this sort be ordinary?'

'What will we do?' Forster was quieter now. 'The police?'

'What?' (my uncle's snort.) 'Sergeant Bert Coggins and his three flat-foot constables? A more down-to-earth lot you couldn't ask for! Good Lord, no! The point is, if this really is something of the sort I've mentioned, it mustn't be frightened off. I mean, we don't know how long it's been here, and we certainly can't allow it to go somewhere else. No, it must be dealt with here and now.'

'How?'

'I've an idea. It may be feasible, and it may not. But it certainly couldn't be considered outside the law, and it has to be worth a try. We have to work fast, though, for Muriel Anderson goes down the day after tomorrow, and it will have to be ready by then. Come on, let's go and speak to your cousin.'

Mr Forster's cousin, Jack Boulter, made his coffins for him; so I later discovered.

'Wait,' said Forster, as I once more began backing away from the door. 'Did they find this . . . this *creature*, these Bulgarian peasants of yours?'

'Oh, yes,' my uncle answered. 'They tied him in a net and drowned him in the river. And they burned his house down to the ground.'

When they left the house and drove away I went into the study. On my uncle's desk lay the book he'd shown to Mr Forster. It was open, lying face down. Curiosity isn't confined to cats: small girls and boys also suffer from it.

Or if they don't, then there's something wrong with them.

I turned the book over and looked at the pictures. They were woodcuts, going from top to bottom of the two pages in long, narrow panels two to a page. Four pictures in all, with accompanying legends printed underneath. The book was old, the ink faded and the pictures poorly impressed; the text, of course, was completely alien to me.

The first picture showed a man, naked, with his arms raised to form a cross. He had what looked to be a thick rope coiled about his waist. His eyes were three-cornered, with radiating lines simulating a shining effect. The second picture showed the man with the rope uncoiled, dangling down loosely from his waist and looped around his feet. The end of the rope seemed frayed and there was some detail, but obscured by age and poor reproduction. I studied this picture carefully but was unable to understand it; the rope appeared to be fastened to the man's body just above his left hip. The third picture showed the man in an attitude of prayer, hands steepled before him, with the rope dangling as before, but crossing over at knee height into the fourth frame. There it coiled upward and was connected to the loosely clad body of a skeletally thin woman, whose flesh was mostly sloughed away to show the bones sticking through.

Now, if I tell my reader that these pictures made little or no sense to me, I know that he will be at pains to understand my ignorance. Well, let me say that it was not ignorance but innocence. I was a boy. None of these things which I have described made any great impression on me *at that time*. They were all incidents – mainly unconnected in my mind, or only loosely connected – occurring during the days I spent at my uncle's house; and as such they were very small pieces in the much larger jigsaw of my world, which was far more occupied with beaches, rock pools, crabs and eels, bathing in the sea, the simple but satisfying meals my uncle prepared for us, etc. It is only in the years passed in between, and in certain dreams I have dreamed, that I have made the connections. In short, I was not investigative but merely curious.

Curious enough, at least, to scribble on a scrap of my uncle's notepaper the following words:

'Uncle Zachary,
  Is the man in these pictures a gypsy?'

For the one connection I *had* made was the thing about the eyes. And I inserted the note into the book and closed it, and left it where I had found it – and then promptly forgot all about it, for there were other, more important things to do.

It would be, I think, a little before seven in the evening when I left the house. There would be another two hours of daylight, then an hour when the dusk turned to darkness, but I would need only a third of that total time to complete my projected walk. For it was my intention to cross the fields to the viaduct, then to cross the viaduct itself (!) and so proceed into Harden. I would return by the coast road, and back down the half-metalled dene path to the knoll and so home.

I took my binoculars with me, and as I passed midway between Slater's Copse and the viaduct, trained them upon the trees and the gleams of varnished woodwork and black, tarred roof hidden in them. I could see no movement about the caravan, but even as I stared so a figure rose up into view and came into focus. It was the head of the family, and he was looking back at me. He must have been sitting in the grass by the fence, or perhaps upon a tree stump, and had stood up as I focused my glasses. But it was curious that he should be looking at me as I was looking at him.

His face was in the shade of his hat, but I remember thinking: *I wonder what is going on behind those queer, three-*

cornered eyes of his? And the thought also crossed my mind:
*I wonder what he must think of me, spying on him so rudely
like this*!

I immediately turned and ran, not out of any sort of fear
but more from shame, and soon came to the viaduct. Out on
to its walkway I proceeded, but at a slow walk now, not
looking down through the stave fence on my left but
straight ahead, and yet still aware that the side of the
valley was now descending steeply underfoot, and that
my physical height above solid ground was increasing with
each pace I took. Almost to the middle I went, before
thinking to hear in the still, warm evening air the haunt-
ing, as yet distant whistle of a train. A train! And I pictured
the clattering, shuddering, rumbling agitation it would
impart to the viaduct and its walkway!

I turned, made to fly back the way I had come . . . and
there was the gypsy. He stood motionless, at the far end of
the walkway, a tall, thin figure with his face in the shade of
his hat, looking in my direction – looking, I knew, at me.
Well, I wasn't going back *that* way! And now there *was*
something of fear in my flight, but mainly I suspect fear of
the approaching train. Whichever, the gypsy had supplied
all the inspiration I needed to see the job through to the end,
to answer the viaduct's challenge. And again I ran.

I reached the far side well in advance of the train, and
looked back to see if the gypsy was still there. But he wasn't.
Then, safe where the walkway met the rising slope once
more, I waited until the train had passed, and thrilled to the
thought that I had actually done it, crossed the viaduct's
walkway! It would never frighten me again. As to the gypsy:
I didn't give him another thought. It wasn't him I'd been
afraid of but the viaduct, obviously . . .

The next morning I was up early, knocked awake by my
uncle's banging at my door. 'Sandy?' he called. 'Are you up?

I'm off into Harden, to see Mr Boulter the joiner. Can you
see to your own breakfast?'

'Yes,' I called back, 'and I'll make some sandwiches to
take to the beach.'

'Good! Then I'll see you when I see you. Mind how you
go. You know where the key is.' And off he went.

I spent the entire day on the beach. I swam in the tidal
pools, caught small crabs for the fishermen to use as bait,
fell asleep on the white sand and woke up itchy, with my
sunburn already peeling. But it was only one more layer of
skin to join many gone the same way, and I wasn't much
concerned. It was late afternoon by then, my sandwiches
eaten long ago and the sun beginning to slip; I felt small
pangs of hunger starting up, changed out of my bathing
costume and headed for home again.

My uncle had left a note for me pinned to the door of his
study where it stood ajar:

Sandy,
   I'm going back to the village, to Mr Boulter's yard and
then to the Vicarage. I'll be in about 9.00 p.m. – maybe.
See you then, or if you're tired just tumble straight into
bed.

– Zach

P.S. There are fresh sandwiches in the kitchen!

I went to the kitchen and returned munching on a beef
sandwich, then ventured into the study. My uncle had
drawn the curtains (something I had never before known
him to do during daylight hours) and had left his reading
lamp on. Upon his desk stood a funny contraption that
caught my eye immediately. It was a small frame of rough,
half-inch timber off-cuts, nailed together to form an oblong
shape maybe eight inches long, five wide and three deep –
like a box without top or bottom. It was fitted where the top

would go with four small bolts at the corners; these held in position twin cutter blades (from some woodworking machine, I imagined), each seven inches long, which were slotted into grooves that ran down the corners from top edge to bottom edge. Small magnets were set central of the ends of the box, level with the top, and connected up to wires which passed through an entirely separate piece of electrical apparatus and then to a square three-pin plug. An extension cable lay on the study floor beside the desk, but it had been disconnected from the mains supply. My last observation was this: that a three-quarter-inch hole had been drilled through the wooden frame on one side.

Well, I looked at the whole set-up from various angles but could make neither head nor tail of it. It did strike me, however, that if a cigar were to be inserted through the hole in the side of the box, and the bolts on that side released, then the cigar's end would be neatly severed! But my uncle didn't smoke . . .

I experimented anyway, and when I drew back two of the tiny bolts toward the magnets, the cutter on that side at once slid down its grooves like a toy guillotine, thumping onto the top of the desk! For a moment I was alarmed that I had damaged the desk's finish . . . until I saw that it was already badly scored by a good many scratches and gouges, where apparently my uncle had amused himself doing much the same thing; except that he had probably drawn the bolts mechanically, by means of the electrical apparatus.

Anyway, I knew I shouldn't be in his study fooling about, and so I put the contraption back the way I had found it and returned to the kitchen for the rest of the sandwiches. I took them upstairs and ate them, then listened to my wireless until about 9.00 p.m. – and still Uncle Zachary wasn't home. So I washed and got into my pyjamas, which was when he chose to return – with Harden's vicar (the Reverend Fawcett) and Mr Forster, and Forster's cousin, the joiner Jack Boulter, all in tow. As they entered the house I hurried to show myself on the landing.

'Sandy,' my uncle called up to me, looking a little flustered. 'Look, I'm sorry, nephew, but I've been very, very busy today. It's not fair, I know, but—'

'It's all right,' I said. 'I had a smashing day! And I'm tired.' Which was the truth. 'I'm going to read for a while before I sleep.'

'Good lad!' he called up, obviously relieved that I didn't consider myself neglected. 'See you tomorrow.' And he ushered his guests into his study and so out of sight. But again he left the door ajar, and I left mine open, so that I could hear something of their voices in the otherwise still night; not everything they said, but some of it. I wasn't especially interested; I tried to read for a few minutes, until I felt drowsy, then turned off my light. And now their voices seemed to float up to me a little more clearly, and before I slept snatches of their conversation impressed themselves upon my mind, so that I've remembered them:

'I really can't say I like it very much,' (the vicar's piping voice, which invariably sounded like he was in the pulpit). 'But . . . I suppose we must know what this thing is.'

' "Who",' (my uncle, correcting him). 'Who it is, Paul. And not only know it but destroy it!'

'But . . . a person?'

'A sort of person, yes. An almost-human being.'

Then Mr Forster's voice, saying: 'What bothers me is that the dead are supposed to be laid to rest! How would Mrs Anderson feel if she knew that her coffin . . .' (fading out).

'But don't you see?' (My uncle's voice again, raised a little, perhaps in excitement or frustration.) 'She is the instrument of Joe's revenge!'

'Dreadful word!' (the vicar.) 'Most *dreadful*! Revenge, indeed! You seem to forget, Zachary, that God made all creatures, great, small, and—'

'And monstrous? No, Paul, these things have little or nothing to do with God. Now listen, I've no lack of respect for your calling, but tell me: if you were to die tomorrow – God forbid – then where would *you* want burying, eh?'

Then the conversation faded a little, or perhaps I was falling asleep. But I do remember Jack Boulter's voice saying: 'Me, Ah'll wark at it arl neet, if necessary. An' divven worry, it'll look no different from any other coffin. Just be sure you get them wires set up, that's arl, before two o'clock.'

And my uncle answering him: 'It will be done, Jack, no fear about that . . .'

The rest won't take long to tell.

I was up late, brought blindingly awake by the sun, already high in the sky, striking slantingly in through my window. Brushing the sleep from my eyes, I went and looked out. Down in the cemetery the gravediggers John and Billy were already at work, tidying the edges of the great hole and decorating it with flowers, but also filling in a small trench only inches deep, that led out of the graveyard and into the bracken at the foot of the knoll. John was mainly responsible for the latter, and I focused my glasses on him. There was something furtive about him: the way he kept looking this way and that, as if to be sure he wasn't observed, and whistling cheerily to himself as he filled in the small trench and disguised his work with chippings. It seemed to me that he was burying a cable of some sort.

I aimed my glasses at Slater's Copse next, but the curtains were drawn in the caravan's window and it seemed the gypsies weren't up and about yet. Well, no doubt they'd come picnicking later.

I washed and dressed, went downstairs and breakfasted on a cereal with milk, then sought out my uncle – or would have, except that for the first time in my life I found his study door locked. I could hear voices from inside, however, and so I knocked.

'That'll be Sandy,' came my uncle's voice, and a moment later the key turned in the lock. But instead of letting me in, he merely held the door open a crack. I could see Jack Boulter in there, working busily at some sort of apparatus on my uncle's desk – a device with a switch, and a small coloured light-bulb – but that was all.

'Sandy, Sandy!' my uncle sighed, throwing up his hands in despair.

'I know,' I smiled, 'you're busy. It's all right, Uncle, for I only came down to tell you I'll be staying up in my room.'

That caused him to smile the first smile I'd seen on his face for some time. 'Well, there's a bit of Irish for you,' he said. But then he quickly sobered. 'I'm sorry, nephew,' he told me, 'but what I'm about really, is most important.' He opened the door a little more. 'You see how busy we are?'

I looked in and Jack Boulter nodded at me, then continued to screw down his apparatus onto my uncle's desk. Wires led from it through the curtains and out of the window, where they were trapped and prevented from slipping or being disturbed by the lowered sash. I looked at my uncle to see if there was any explanation.

'The, er – the wiring!' he finally blurted. 'We're testing the wiring in the house, that's all. We shouldn't want the old place to burn down through faulty wiring, now should we?'

'No, indeed not,' I answered, and went back upstairs.

I read, listened to the wireless, observed the land all about through my binoculars. In fact I had intended to go to the beach again, but there was something in the air: a hidden excitement, a muted air of expectancy, a sort of quiet tension. And so I stayed in my room, just waiting for something to happen. Which eventually it did.

And it was summoned by the bells, Harden's old church bells, pealing out their slow, doleful toll for Muriel Anderson.

But those bells changed everything. I can hear them even now, see and *feel* the changes that occurred. Before, there had been couples out walking: just odd pairs here and there, on the old dene lane, in the fields and on the paths. And yet by the time those bells were only half-way done the people had gone, disappeared, don't ask me where. Down in the graveyard, John and Billy had been putting the finishing touches to their handiwork, preparing the place, as it were, for this latest increase in the Great Majority; but now they speeded up, ran to the tiled lean-to in one tree-shaded corner of the graveyard and changed into clothes a little more fitting, before hurrying to the gate and waiting there for Mr Forster's hearse. For the bells had told everyone that the ceremony at Harden church was over, and that the smallest possible cortège was now on its way. One and a half miles at fifteen miles per hour, which meant a journey of just six minutes.

Who else had been advised by the bells, I wondered?

I aimed my binoculars at Slater's Copse, and . . . they were there, all four, pale figures in the trees, their shaded faces turned toward the near-distant spire across the valley, half-hidden by the low hill. And as they left the cover of the trees and headed for the field adjacent to the cemetery, I saw that indeed they had their picnic baskets with them: a large one which the man and woman carried between them, and a smaller one shared by their children. As usual.

The hearse arrived, containing only the coffin and its occupant, a great many wreaths and garlands, and of course the Reverend Fawcett and Mr Forster, who with John and Billy formed the team of pallbearers. Precise and practised, they carried Muriel Anderson to her grave where the only additional mourner was Jack Boulter, who had gone down from the house to join them. He got down into the flower-decked hole (to assist in the lowering of the coffin, of course) and after the casket had gone down in its loops of silken rope finally climbed out again, assisted by John and Billy. There followed the final service, and the first handful of soil went into the grave.

Through all of this activity my attention had been riveted in the graveyard; now that things were proceeding towards and end, however, I once again turned my glasses on the picnickers. And there they sat cross-legged on their blanket in the long grass outside the cemetery wall, with their picnic baskets between them. But *motionless* as always, with their heads bowed in a sort of grace. They sat there – as they had sat for Joe Anderson, and Mrs Jones the greengrocer-lady, and old George Carter the retired miner, whose soot-clogged lungs had finally collapsed on him – offering up their silent prayers or doing whatever they did.

Meanwhile, in the graveyard:

At last the ceremony was over, and John and Billy set to with their spades while the Reverend Fawcett, Jack Boulter and Mr Forster climbed the knoll to the house, where my uncle met them at the door. I heard him greet them, and the Vicar's high-pitched, measured answer:

'Zach, Sam here tells me you have a certain book with pictures? I should like to see it, if you don't mind. And then of course there's the matter of a roster. For now that we've initiated this thing I suppose we must see it through, and certainly I can see a good many long, lonely nights stretching ahead.'

'Come in, come in,' my uncle answered. 'The book? It's in my study. By all means come through.'

I *heard* this conversation, as I say, but nothing registered – not for a minute or two, anyway. Until—

There came a gasping and a frantic clattering as my uncle, with the Reverend Fawcett hot on his heels, came flying up the stairs to the landing, then up the short stairs to my room. They burst in, quite literally hurling the door wide, and my uncle was upon me in three great strides.

'Sandy,' he gasped then, 'what's all this about gypsies?' I put my glasses aside and looked at him, and saw that he was holding the sheet of notepaper with my scribbled query. He gripped my shoulder. 'Why do you ask if the man in these pictures is a gypsy?'

Finally I knew what he was talking about. 'Why, because of their eyes!' I answered. 'Their three-cornered eyes.' And as I picked up my binoculars and again trained them on the picnickers, I added: 'But you can't see their faces from up here, because of their great hats . . .'

My uncle glanced out of the window and his jaw dropped. 'Good Lord!' he whispered, eyes bulging in his suddenly white face. He almost snatched the glasses from me, and his huge hands shook as he put them to his eyes. After a moment he said, 'My God, my God!' Simply that; and then he thrust the glasses at the Reverend Fawcett.

The Reverend was no less affected; he said, 'Dear Jesus! Oh my dear sweet Jesus! In broad daylight! Good heavens, Zach – *in broad daylight*!'

Then my uncle straightened up, towered huge, and his voice was steady again as he said: 'Their shirts – look at their shirts!'

The vicar looked, and grimly nodded. 'Their shirts, yes.'

From the foot of the stairs came Jack Boulter's sudden query: 'Zach, Reverend, are you up there? Zach, why man ar'm sorry, but there must be a fault. Damn the thing, but ar'm getna red light!'

'Fault?' cried my uncle, charging for the door and the stairs, with the vicar right behind him. 'There's no fault, Jack! Press the button, man – *press the button*!'

Left alone again and not a little astonished, I looked at the gypsies in the field. Their shirts? But they had simply pulled them out of their trousers, so that they fell like small, personal tents to the grass where they sat. Which I imagined must keep them quite cool in the heat of the afternoon. And anyway, they always wore their shirts like that, when they picnicked.

But what was this? To complement the sudden uproar in the house, now there came this additional confusion outside! What could have startled the gypsies like this? What on earth was wrong with them? I threw open the window and leaned out, and without knowing why, found my tongue cleaving to the roof of my mouth as once more, for the last time, I trained my glasses on the picnickers. And how to explain what I saw then? I saw it, but only briefly, in the moments before my uncle was there behind me, clapping his hand over my eyes, snatching the window and curtains shut, prising the glasses from my half-frozen fingers. Saw *and* heard it!

The gypsies straining to their feet and trying to run, overturning their picnic baskets in their sudden frenzy, seeming anchored to the ground by fat white ropes which lengthened behind them as they stumbled outward from their blanket. The agony of their dance there in the long grass, and the way they dragged on their ropes to haul them out of the ground, like strangely hopping blackbirds teasing worms; their terrified faces and shrieking mouths as their hats went flying; their shirts and dresses billowing, and their unbelievable screams. All four of them, screaming as one, but shrill as a keening wind, hissing like steam from a nest of kettles, or lobsters dropped live into boiling water, and yet cold and alien as the sweat on a dead fish!

And then the man's rope, incredibly long and taut as a bowstring, suddenly coming free of the ground – and likewise, one after another, the ropes of his family – and all of them *living things* that writhed like snakes and sprayed crimson from their raw red ends!

But all glimpsed so briefly, before my uncle intervened, and so little of it registering upon a mind which really couldn't accept it – not then. I had been aware, though, of the villagers where they advanced inexorably across the field, armed with the picks and shovels of their trade (what? Ask John and Billy to keep mum about such as this? Even for a guinea?). And of the gypsies spinning like dervishes, coiling up those awful appendages about their waists, then wheeling more slowly and gradually crumpling exhausted to the earth; and of their picnic baskets scattered on the grass, all tumbled and . . . empty.

I've since discovered that in certain foreign parts 'Obour' means 'night demon', or 'ghost', or 'vampire'. While in others it means simply 'ghoul'. As for the gypsies: I know their caravan was burned out that same night, and that their bones were discovered in the ashes. It hardly worried me then and it doesn't now, and I'm glad that you don't see nearly so many of them around these days; but of course I'm prejudiced.

As they say in the north-east, a burden shared is a burden halved. But really, my dreams have been a terrible burden, and I can't see why I should continue to bear it alone.

This then has been my rite of exorcism. At least I hope so . . .

ZACK PHALANX *IS* VLAD THE IMPALER

Harry S. Skatsman, Jr., was livid. He was a tiny, fat, cigar-chewing, fire-eating, primadonna-taming, scene-shooting ball of absolutely *livid* livid. Of all things: an accident! And on his birthday, too! Zack Phalanx, superstar, 'King of the Bad Guys', had been involved in some minor accident back in Beverly Hills; an accident which, however temporarily, had curtailed his appearance on location.

Skatsman groaned, his scarlet jowls drooping and much of the anger rushing out of him in one vast sigh. What if the accident was worse than he'd been told? What if Zack was out of the film (horrible thought) permanently? All that *so*-expensive advance publicity – all the bother over visas and work permits, and the trouble with the local villagers – all for nothing. Of course, they could always get someone to fill Zack's place (Kurt Douglash, perhaps?) but it wouldn't be the same. In his mind's eye Skatsman could see the head-lines in the film rags already: '*Zack Phalanx WAS Vlad the Impaler!*'

The little fat man groaned again at this mental picture, then leaned forward in his plush leather seat and snarled (he never spoke to anyone, always snarled) at his driver: 'Joe, you sure the message said Zack was only *slightly* hurt? He didn't *stick* himself on his steering wheel or something?'

'Yeah, slightly hurt,' Joe grunted. 'Minor accident.' Joe had been driving his boss now for so many years, on location in so many parts of the world, that Skatsman's snarls no longer fazed him—

—But they fazed most everyone else.

Even as the big car ploughed steadily through mid-afternoon mist as it rose up out of the valleys on old, winding roads that were often only just third class, high above in the village-sized huddle of caravans, huts and shacks, up in the glowering Carpathian Mountains, Harry S. Skatsman's colleagues prepared themselves for all hell let loose when the florid, fiery little director returned.

They all knew now that Zack Phalanx had been injured, that his arrival at Jlaskavya airport had been 'unavoidably delayed'. And they knew moreover just exactly what that meant where Skatsman was concerned. The little fat man would be utterly unapproachable, poisonous, raging one minute and sobbing the next in unashamed frustration, until 'Old Grim-Grin' (as Phalanx was fondly known in movie circles) showed up. Then they could shoot his all-important scenes.

This dread of the director in dire mood was shared by all and sundry, from the producer, Jerry Sollinger (a man of no mean status himself), right down to Sam 'Sugar' Sweeney, the coffee-boy – who was in fact a man of sixty-three – and including sloe-eyed Shani Silarno, the heroine of this, Skatsman's fourteenth epic.

Oh, there was going to be a fuss, all right, but what – they all asked among themselves – would the fuss really be all about? For in all truth Zack Phalanx's scenes were not to be many. His magic box-office name on the billboards, starred as Vlad the Impaler himself, was simply to be a draw, a 'name' to pull the crowds. For the same reason Shani Silarno was cheesecake, though certainly she had far more footage than the grim, scarfaced, sardonic, ugly, friendly 'star' of the picture.

And most of that picture, filmed already, had been dashed off to Hollywood for the usual pre-release publicity screenings – except for the Phalanx scenes, which, now that the star was known to be out of it, however temporarily,

Jerry Solinger had explained away in a hastily drummed-up, fabulously expensive telephone call as being simply too terrific, too fantastically *good* to be shown in any detail before the actual premier. Of course, the gossip columnists would know better, but hopefully before they got their wicked little claws into the story Phalanx would be out here in Romania and all would be well . . .

But meanwhile the important battle scenes, all ketchup and *zenf* though they were, would have to wait on the arrival of Old Grim-Grin, injured in some minor traffic accident.

Producer Jerry Sollinger was beginning to wish he'd never heard of Vlad the Impaler; or rather, that Harry S. Skatsman had never heard of him. Sollinger could still remember when first the fat little director had snarled into his office to slam down upon his desk a file composed of bits and pieces of collected facts and lore concerning one Vlad Dracula. This Vlad – Vlad being a title of some sort, possibly 'Prince' – had been a fifteenth-century warlord, a Wallach of incredible cruelty. Like his ancestors before him, he had led his people against wave after wave of invading Turks, Magyars, Bulgars, Lombards and others equally barbaric, to beat them back from his princedom aerie in the foreboding mountains of Carpathia.

He was, in short, the original Dracula; but whichever historian appended the words 'the Impaler' to his name had in mind a different sort of impaling than did Bram Stoker when he wrote his popular novel. Vlad V Tsepeth Dracula of Wallachia had earned his name by sticking the captured hundreds of his enemies vertically on rank after rank of upright stakes, where they might sit and scream out the mercifully short remainder of their lives in hideous agony while he and other nobles laughed and cantered their warhorses up and down amidst the blood and gore.

The vampire legend in connection with Vlad V probably

sprang up not only from this monstrous method of execution, but also from the fact that a Wallachian curse has it (despite his lying dead for over five hundred years) that Vlad the Impaler 'will return from the grave with his warriors of old to protect his lands if ever again invaders penetrate his boundaries.'

This, roughly, was the information Skatsman's file contained, and to its cover he had stapled a single sheet of paper bearing the following story-line, his synoptic 'plan' of the epic-to-be:

'Vlad Drac, (Zack Phalanx), scorned by his subjects and the sovereigns of neighbouring kingdoms and princedoms alike for his chicken, pacifist ways, finally loses his cool and takes up the sword against the invader (something like *Friendly Persuasion* but with mountains and battle-axes). This only after his castle has been burned right off the edge of its precipice by the advancing Turks, and after his niece, the young Princess Minerna, (Shani Silarno), has been raped by the Turk barbarian boss, (Tony Kwinn?). To conclude, we'll have Vlad V suicide after his boys mistakenly stick his mistress, (Glory Graeme?), who has dressed like a Turk camp-follower to escape the invaders, not realizing that Vlad has already whupped them? Robert Black can whip this up into something good.' To this brief, almost cryptic outline, Skatsman had appended his signature.

And from that simple seed, the idea had blossomed, mushrooming into a giant project, an epic; by which time it had been too late for Sollinger to back out. Truth of the matter was that the producer was a little fearful of these so-called 'epic' productions: just such a project had almost ruined him many years ago. But with such a story – with the awesome, disquieting grandeur of the Carpathian Mountains as background, with a list of stars literally type-cast into the very parts for which they were acclaimed and which they played best, with Skatsman as director (and he was a very *good* director, despite his tantrums) – well, what *could* go wrong?

Much could go wrong . . .

And yet at first it had seemed like plain sailing. The new peace-pact with the Eastern-bloc countries had helped them in the end to get the necessary visas; that and the promise of recruitment as extras of hundreds of the poor, local villagers into bit parts. And this latter of course had saved much on costumary, for the dress and costumes of these people had not much changed in five centuries. On the other hand, there had been little of the film-star in them. When they were used, each fragment of each and every scene had to be directed with the most minute attention to detail, always through an interpreter and invariably with the end result that Skatsman, before he could be satisfied, would have the set in uproar. The stars would be threatening to walk out, the local 'actors' themselves gibbering in fear of the little man's temper, as though the director were the great Vlad V himself resurrected!

Indeed, when finally those locals – all two hundred eighty of them – *had* walked off the set, flatly refusing to work any longer on the giant production, Skatsman had been blamed. Not to his face, of course not, but behind his back the cast and technicians had 'known' that he was the spanner in the works. This did not explain, though, the fact that when Philar Jontz the PR man went after the runaways, in fact to pay them their last wages, he discovered two empty villages! Not only had the rather primitive 'actors' deserted the film – not that it mattered greatly, for all of their important scenes were already in the can – but they had taken their families, friends, indeed the entire populations of their home villages with them. Stranger still, the quaint old town into which they had all moved *en masse* was only a mile or so further down the mountain road. Whatever they were running away from, well, they had not bothered to run very far!

Ever the PR man, Jontz had followed them, only to discover that in the now badly overcrowded town no one would have anything to do with him, neither refugees nor regular inhabitants. Mystified, he had returned to his colleagues.

Within a day or so, however, rumours had found their way back to the mobile town in the mountains. The whispers were vague and inconclusive and no one really bothered much to listen to them, but in essence they gave the lie to anyone who might try to attach the blame to Skatsman. No (the rumours said), the villagers had not been frightened off by the little boss; and no, they had not found the work distasteful – the money had been more than welcome and they were very grateful.

But did the rich American bosses not know that there had been strange rumblings in the mountains? And were they not aware that in Recjaviscjorska a priest had foretold queer horror in the highlands? Why! – wasn't it common knowledge that an ancient burial place in the grounds of certain crumbling and massive ruins high in the rocky passes was suddenly most – unquiet? No, better that the Americans be given a wide berth until, one way or the other, they were gone and the mountains were peaceful again.

Though of course he had his ear to the ground, still it was all far beyond Philar Jontz's understanding, and even had he thought or bothered himself to look at a map of the region (though there was no reason why he should) it is doubtful that he would have noticed anything at all out of the ordinary. Maps being what they are in that country, in all probability the ancient boundaries would not be marked, and so Jontz would not have seen that the two deserted villages lay within the perimeter of what once had been the princedom of Vlad V Tsepeth Dracula of Wallachia, or that

the now bulging town lower down the mountain slopes lay
outside the centuried prince's domain . . .

Now all this had happened before the latest crisis, but even
then Phalanx had been overdue on location, delayed for
first one reason and then another in Hollywood. And so a
number of restless, wasted days had gone by, until finally
came that great morning when the poisonous little director
received the telephone message everyone had been waiting
and praying for. Old Grim-Grin was on his way at last; he
would be on the mid-afternoon flight into Jlaskavya; could
someone meet him and his retinue at the airport to escort
them to location?

Could someone meet them, indeed! Skatsman *himself*
would meet them; and without further ado the delighted
director had set out in his huge car with Joe, his driver,
down the steep mountain roads to distant Jlaskavya.

For once in his life Skatsman had been truly happy. He
had known (he told Joe) that it was all going to be okay.
Nothing ever went wrong on his birthday – nothing *dared*
go wrong on his birthday! And thus he had snarled cheer-
fully to Joe all the way to the dismal airport . . . where
finally he had been informed of his superstar's latest and
most serious delay.

Having picked up a smattering of the local language, it
was Joe who first received the news, and when Skatsman
had recovered from his initial convulsions it was Joe who
phoned the facts through to Philar Jontz in the overcrowded town where the PR man had not yet given up
trying to solve the mystery of the runaway extras. Jontz, in
turn, had taken the dread message back to his film friends in
the mountains.

Later, it also fell to the PR man to spot the horde of
extras – all costumed for a battle scene, helmeted and
leather-sandaled, with a variety of shields, swords, maces

and lances – as they came creeping down out of the higher passes, flanked by riders astride great warhorses. The PR man had been astounded, but only for a moment, and then he had given a *whoop* of understanding.

Why, Skatsman, the old fraud! They might have expected something like this of him. Wasn't it his birthday? This explained everything. The runaway extras, the alleged 'accident' of Zack Phalanx: it had all been a build-up to the Big Surprise. And surely that great, grim-faced, leading rider *was* Zack Phalanx?

Dusk was settling over the mountains like a great grey mantle by that time, and the actors and technicians and all were already settling in their caravans and tents, preparing for the next day's work or bedding down for the night. Philar Jontz's cry went up for all of them to hear:

'Well, I'll be damned! Zack! Zack Phalanx! Where's that old rogue Skatsman hiding?' Then they heard his quavering, querying exclamation of disbelief, and finally his awful, rising scream, cut off by a thick sound not unlike a meat cleaver sinking into a side of beef . . .

Something less than an hour later, Harry S. Skatsman's big car came round the last bend in the winding mountain road and turned off onto the fringe of the flat, cleared area that housed the sprawling units of the vast, mobile film town. The headlights cut a swathe of light between the shadowed ranks of shacks, trailers, trucks, caravans and tents – illuminating a scene that caused Joe to slam on his brakes so hard that Skatsman almost shot headlong over into the front of the car. Twin rows of stakes stretched away towards a bleak background of dark and sullen mountains, and atop each stake sat the motionless form of a dressed dummy, head down and arms bound.

'What in hell –?' Skatsman snarled, leaping from the car with an agility all out of character with his shape and size. A hundred torches suddenly flared in the dark behind the shacks, trucks and tents, and their bearers came forward out of the shadows to form a circle about Skatsman and the car.

And suddenly the director knew, just as Philar Jontz had 'known', what it was all about. Why, this was one of Zack's scenes! The stakes, torches, the grimly-helmeted warriors . . .

'Where is he?' Skatsman roared, slapping his thigh and doing a little jig. 'Where's that bastard Zack Phalanx? I might have known he wouldn't forget my birthday!'

The silent torch-bearers closed in, tightening the circle. Down the path of stakes horses came clopping, the lead horse carrying a huge figure clad in the cape and apparel of a warrior prince.

'Zack! Zack!' cried Skatsman, pushing forward – to be grabbed and held tight between two of the encircling torch-bearers. And then he smelled a smell that was not grease-paint, and beneath the nearest helmet he saw—

'*Zack!*' he uselessly croaked once more.

At the same time Joe, too, noticed something very wrong – namely, the skeletal claw that held a torch close to his driver's window. He convulsively gunned the car's big motor, twisting the wheel, spinning the car on madly screaming tyres. A hurled lance crashed through the wind-screen and pinned him like a fly to the upholstery of his seat. His arms flew wide in a last spasm and the car turned on its side, splintering the nearest stake and flinging the grisly corpse it supported in a welter of entrails at the director's feet. No dummy this but a dumb blonde! – Shani Silarno, naked but for a torn and bloodstained dressing-gown, eyes glazed and bulging.

Skatsman swayed and would have fallen, but he was flanked now by two great horses. Their riders reached down to lift him bodily from the ground. He kicked feebly at thin air as they cantered with him down between the ranks of stakes to where the caped Vlad V now waited.

Before the director's unbelieving eyes there passed a bobbing procession of mutilated forms, some of them still writhing weakly on the cruel stakes. Jerry Sollinger, Glory Graeme, Sam 'Sugar' Sweeney, they were all there. Even Philar Jontz, though only his head decorated its stake.

As the horses drew level with the bony horror in the cape, Skatsman was lifted higher still and he saw the waiting, needle-sharp point of the last, empty stake. He might perhaps have screamed but only knew how to snarl. He did neither but threw back his head and laughed – albeit hysterically, insanely – laughed right into the fleshless, helmeted face whose black eye-sockets so keenly regarded him.

He was Harry S. Skatsman, wasn't he? And this was his epic, wasn't it? This was *his* big scene!

What else could he do?

'Action! Camera!' he snarled – as they rammed him down onto that last terrible fang of Vlad the Impaler.

THE HOUSE OF THE TEMPLE

1. The Summons

I suppose under the circumstances it is only natural that the police should require this belated written statement from me; and I further suppose it to be in recognition of my present highly nervous condition and my totally unwarranted confinement in this *place* that they are allowing me to draw the thing up without supervision. But while every kindness has been shown me, still I most strongly protest my continued detainment here. Knowing what I now know, I would voice the same protest in respect of detention in *any* prison or institute anywhere in Scotland . . . anywhere in the entire British Isles.

Before I begin, let me clearly make the point that, since no charges have been levelled against me, I make this statement of my own free will, fully knowing that in so doing I may well extend my stay in this detestable place. I can only hope that upon its reading, it will be seen that I had no alternative but to follow the action I describe.

You the reader must therefore judge. My actual sanity – if indeed I am still sane – my very *being*, may well depend upon your findings . . .

I was in New York when the letter from my uncle's solicitors reached me. Sent from an address in the Royal Mile, that great road which reaches steep and cobbled to the esplanade of Edinburgh Castle itself, the large, sealed manila envelope had all the hallmarks of officialdom, so that even before I opened it I feared the worst.

Not that I had been close to my uncle in recent years (my mother had brought me out of Scotland as a small child, on the death of my father, and I had never been back) but certainly I remembered Uncle Gavin. If anything I remembered him better than I did my father; for where Andrew McGilchrist had always been dry and introverted, Uncle Gavin had been just the opposite. Warm, outgoing and generous to a fault, he had spoilt me mercilessly.

Now, according to the letter, he was dead and I was named his sole heir and beneficiary; and the envelope contained a voucher which guaranteed me a flight to Edinburgh from anywhere in the world. And then of course there was the letter itself, the contents of which further guaranteed my use of that voucher; for only a fool could possibly refuse my uncle's bequest, or fail to be interested in its attendant, though at present unspecified, conditions.

Quite simply, by presenting myself at the offices of Macdonald, Asquith and Lee in Edinburgh, I would already have fulfilled the first condition toward inheriting my uncle's considerable fortune, his estate of over three hundred acres and his great house where it stood in wild and splendid solitude at the foot of the Pentlands in Lothian. All of which seemed a very far cry from New York . . .

As to what I was doing in New York in the first place:

Three months earlier, in mid-March of 1976 – when I was living alone in Philadelphia in the home where my mother had raised me – my fiancée of two years had given me back my ring, run off and married a banker from Baltimore. The novel I was writing had immediately metamorphosed from a light-hearted love story into a doom-laden tragedy, became meaningless somewhere in the transformation, and ended up in my waste-paper basket. That was that. I sold up and moved to New York, where an artist friend had been willing to share his apartment until I could find a decent place of my own.

I had left no forwarding address, however, which explained the delayed delivery of the letter from my uncle's solicitors; the letter itself was post-marked March 26th, and from the various marks, labels and redirections on the envelope, the US Mail had obviously gone to considerable trouble to find me. And they found me at a time when the lives of both myself and my artist friend, Carl Earlman, were at a very low ebb. I was not writing and Carl was not drawing, and despite the arrival of summer our spirits were on a rapid decline.

Which is probably why I jumped at the opportunity the letter presented, though, as I have said, certainly I would have been a fool to ignore or refuse the thing . . . Or so I thought at the time.

I invited Carl along if he so desired, and he too grasped at the chance with both hands. His funds were low and getting lower; he would soon be obliged to quit his apartment for something less ostentatious; and since he, too, had decided that he needed a change of locale – to put some life back into his artwork – the matter was soon decided and we packed our bags and headed for Edinburgh.

It was not until our journey was over, however – when we were settled in our hotel room in Princes Street – that I remembered my mother's warning, delivered to me deliriously but persistently from her deathbed, that I should never return to Scotland, certainly not to the old house. And as I vainly attempted to adjust to the jet-lag and the fact that it was late evening while all my instincts told me it should now be day, so my mind went back over what little I knew of my family roots, of the McGilchrist line itself, of that old and rambling house in the Pentlands where I had been born, and especially of the peculiar reticence of Messrs Macdonald, Asquith and Lee, the Scottish solicitors.

Reticence, yes, because I could almost feel the hesitancy in their letter. It seemed to me that they would have preferred *not* to find me; and yet, if I were asked what it was that gave me this impression, then I would be at a loss for an answer. Something in the way it was phrased, perhaps – in the dry, professional idiom of solicitors – which too often seems to me to put aside all matters of emotion or sensibility; so that I felt like a small boy offered a candy . . . and warned simultaneously that it would ruin my teeth. Yes, it seemed to me that Messrs Macdonald, Asquith and Lee might actually be *apprehensive* about my acceptance of their conditions – or rather, of my uncle's conditions – as if they were offering a cigar to an addict suffering from cancer of the lungs.

I fastened on that line of reasoning, seeing the conditions of the will as the root of the vague uneasiness which niggled at the back of my mind. The worst of it was that these conditions were not specified; other than to say that if I could not or would not meet them, still I would receive fifteen thousand pounds and my return ticket home, and that the residue of my uncle's fortune would then be used to carry out his will in respect of 'the property known as Temple House.'

Temple House, that rambling old seat of the McGilchrists where it stood locked in a steep re-entry; and the Pentland Hills a grey and green backdrop to its frowning, steep-gabled aspect; with something of the Gothic in its structure, something more of Renaissance Scotland, and an aura of antiquity all its own which, as a child, I could still remember loving dearly. But that had been almost twenty years ago and the place had been my home. A happy home, I had thought; at least until the death of my father, of which I could remember nothing at all.

But I did remember the pool – the deep, grey pool where it lapped at the raised, reinforced, east-facing garden wall – the pool and its ring of broken quartz pillars, the remains of the temple for which the house was named. Thinking back over the years to my infancy, I wondered if perhaps the pool had been the reason my mother had always hated the place. None of the McGilchrists had ever been swimmers, and yet water had always seemed to fascinate them. I would not have been the first of the line to be found floating face-down in that strange, pillar-encircled pool of deep and weedy water; and I had used to spend hours just sitting on the wall and staring across the breeze-rippled surface . . .

So my thoughts went, as tossing in my hotel bed late into the night, I turned matters over in my mind . . . And having retired late, so we rose late, Carl and I; and it was not until 2 p.m. that I presented myself at the office of Macdonald, Asquith and Lee on the Royal Mile.

2. The Will

Since Carl had climbed up to the esplanade to take in the view, I was alone when I reached my destination and entered M.A. and L.'s offices through a door of yellow-tinted bull's-eye panes, passing into the cool welcome of a dim and very *Olde Worlde* anteroom; and for all that this was the source of my enigmatic summons, still I found a reassuring air of charm and quiet sincerity about the place. A clerk led me into an inner chamber as much removed from my idea of a solicitor's office as is Edinburgh from New York, and having been introduced to the firm's Mr Asquith, I was offered a seat.

Asquith was tall, slender, high-browed and balding, with a mass of freckles which seemed oddly in contrast with his late middle years, and his handshake was firm and dry. While he busied himself getting various documents, I was given a minute or two to look about this large and bewilderingly cluttered room of shelves, filing cabinets, cupboards and three small desks. But for all that, the place seemed grossly disordered – still Mr Asquith quickly found what he was looking for and seated himself opposite me behind his desk. He was the only partner present and I the only client.

'Now, Mr McGilchrist,' he began. 'And so we managed to find you, did we? And doubtless you're wondering what it's all about, and you probably think there's something of a mystery here? Well, so there is, and for me and my partners no less than for yourself.'

'I don't quite follow,' I answered, searching his face for a clue.

'No, no of course you don't. Well now, perhaps this will explain it better. It's a copy of your uncle's will. As you'll see, he was rather short on words; hence the mystery. A more succinct document – which nevertheless hints at so much more – I've yet to see!'

'I, Gavin McGilchrist,' (the will began) 'of Temple House in Lothian, hereby revoke all Wills, Codicils or Testamentary Dispositions heretofore made by me, and I appoint my Nephew, John Hamish McGilchrist of Philadelphia in the United States of America, to be the Executor of this, my Last Will and direct that all my Debts, Testamentary and Funeral Expenses, shall be paid as soon as conveniently may be after my death.

'I give and bequeath unto the aforementioned John Hamish McGilchrist everything I possess, my Land and the Property standing thereon, with the following Condition: namely that he alone shall open and read the Deposition which shall accompany this Will into the hands of the

Solicitors; and that furthermore he, being the Owner, shall destroy Temple House to its last stone within a Three-month of accepting this Condition. In the event that he shall refuse this undertaking, then shall my Solicitors, Macdonald, Asquith and Lee of Edinburgh, become sole Executors of my Estate, who shall follow to the letter the Instructions simultaneously deposited with them.'

The will was dated and signed in my uncle's scratchy scrawl.

I read it through a second time and looked up to find Mr Asquith's gaze fixed intently upon me. 'Well,' he said, 'and didn't I say it was a mystery? Almost as strange as his death . . .' He saw the immediate change in my expression, the frown and the question my lips were beginning to frame, and held up his hands in apology. 'I'm sorry,' he said, 'so very sorry – for of course you know nothing of the circumstances of his death, do you? I had better explain:

'A year ago,' Asquith continued, 'your uncle was one of the most hale and hearty men you could wish to meet. He was a man of independent means, as you know, and for a good many years he had been collecting data for a book. Ah! I see you're surprised. Well, you shouldn't be. Your great-grandfather wrote *Notes of Nessie: the Secrets of Loch Ness*; and your grandmother, under a pseudonym, was a fairly successful romanticist around the turn of the century. You, too, I believe, have published several romances? Indeed,' and he smiled and nodded, 'it appears to be in the blood, you see?

'Like your great-grandfather, however, your Uncle Gavin McGilchrist had no romantic aspirations. He was a researcher, you see, and couldn't abide a mystery to remain unsolved. And there he was at Temple House, a bachelor and time on his hands, and a marvellous family tree to explore and a great mystery to unravel.'

'Family tree?' I said. 'He was researching the biography of a family? But which fam—' And I paused.

Asquith smiled. 'You've guessed it, of course,' he said. 'Yes, he was planning a book on the McGilchrists, with special reference to the curse . . .' And his smile quickly vanished.

It was as if a cold draught, coming from nowhere, fanned my cheek. 'The curse? My family had . . . a curse?'

He nodded. 'Oh, yes. Not the classical sort of curse, by any means, but a curse nevertheless – or at least your uncle thought so. Perhaps he wasn't really serious about it at first, but towards the end—'

'I think I know what you mean,' I said. 'I remember now: the deaths by stroke, by drowning, by thrombosis. My mother mentioned them on her own deathbed. A curse on the McGilchrists, she said, on the old house.'

Again Asquith nodded, and finally he continued. 'Well, your uncle had been collecting material for many years, I suspect since the death of your father; from local archives, historical annals, various chronicles, church records, military museums, and so on. He had even enlisted our aid, on occasion, in finding this or that old document. Our firm was founded one hundred and sixty years ago, you see, and we've had many McGilchrists as clients.

'As I've said, up to a time roughly a year ago, he was as hale and hearty a man as you could wish to meet. Then he travelled abroad; Hungary, Romania, all the old countries of antique myth and legend. He brought back many books with him, and on his return he was a changed man. He had become, in a matter of weeks, the merest shadow of his former self. Finally, nine weeks ago on March 22nd, he left his will in our hands, an additional set of instructions for us to follow in the event you couldn't be found, and the sealed envelope which he mentions in his will. I shall give that to you in a moment. Two days later, when his gillie returned to Temple House from a short holiday—'

'He found my uncle dead,' I finished it for him. 'I see . . .
And the strange circumstances?'

'For a man of his years to die of a heart attack . . .'
Asquith shook his head. 'He wasn't old. What? – an out-
doors man, like him? And what of the shotgun, with both
barrels discharged, and the spent cartridges lying at his feet
just outside the porch? What had he fired at, eh, in the dead
of night? And the look on his face – monstrous!'

'You saw him?'

'Oh, yes. That was part of our instructions; I was to see
him. And not just myself but Mr Lee also. And the doctor,
of course, who declared it could only have been a heart
attack. But then there was the post-mortem. That was also
part of your uncle's instructions . . .'

'And its findings?' I quietly asked.

'Why, that was the reason he wanted the autopsy, do you
see? So that we should know he was in good health.'

'No heart attack?'

'No,' he shook his head, 'not him. But dead, certainly.
And that look on his face, Mr McGilchrist – that terrible,
pleading look in his wide, wide eyes . . .'

3. The House

Half an hour later I left Mr Asquith in his office and saw
myself out through the anteroom and into the hot, cobbled
road that climbed to the great grey castle. In the interim I
had opened the envelope left for me by my uncle and had
given its contents a cursory scrutiny, but I intended to study
them minutely at my earliest convenience.

I had also offered to let Asquith see the contents, only to
have him wave my offer aside. It was a private thing, he
said, for my eyes only. Then he had asked me what I

intended to do now, and I had answered that I would go to Temple House and take up temporary residence there. He then produced the keys, assured me of the firm's interest in my business – its complete confidentiality and its readiness to provide assistance should I need it – and bade me good day.

I found Carl Earlman leaning on the esplanade wall and gazing out over the city. Directly below his position the castle rock fell away for hundreds of feet to a busy road that wound round and down and into the maze of streets and junctions forming the city centre. He started when I took hold of his arm.

'What—? Oh, it's you, John! I was lost in thought. This fantastic view; I've already stored away a dozen sketches in my head. Great!' Then he saw my face and frowned. 'Is anything wrong? You don't quite look yourself.'

As we made our way down from that high place I told him of my meeting with Asquith and all that had passed between us, so that by the time we found a cab (a 'taxi') and had ourselves driven to an automobile rental depot, I had managed to bring him fully up to date. Then it was simply a matter of hiring a car and driving out to Temple House . . .

We headed south-west out of Edinburgh with Carl driving our Range Rover at a leisurely pace, and within three-quarters of an hour turned right off the main road onto a narrow strip whose half-metalled surface climbed straight as an arrow toward the looming Pentlands. Bald and majestic, those grey domes rose from a scree of gorse-grown shale to cast their sooty, mid-afternoon shadows over lesser mounds, fields and streamlets alike. Over our vehicle, too, as it grew tiny in the frowning presence of the hills.

I was following a small-scale map of the area purchased from a filling station (a 'garage'), for of course the district was completely strange to me. A lad of five on leaving Scotland – and protected by my mother's exaggerated fears at that, which hardly ever let me out of her sight – I had never been allowed to stray very far from Temple House.

Temple House . . . and again the name conjured strange phantoms, stirred vague memories I had thought long dead.

Now the road narrowed more yet, swinging sharply to the right before passing round a rocky spur. The ground rose up beyond the spur and formed a shallow ridge, and my map told me that the gully or re-entry which guarded Temple House lay on the far side of this final rise. I knew that when we reached the crest the house would come into view, and I found myself holding my breath as the Range Rover's wheels bit into the cinder surface of the track.

'There she is!' cried Carl as first the eaves of the place became visible, then its oak-beamed gables and greystone walls, and finally the entire frontage where it projected from behind the sheer rise of the gully's wall. And now, as we accelerated down the slight decline and turned right to follow a course running parallel to the stream, the whole house came into view where it stood half in shadow. That strange old house in the silent gully, where no birds ever flew and not even a rabbit had been seen to sport in the long wild grass.

'Hey!' Carl cried, his voice full of enthusiasm. 'And your uncle wanted this place pulled down? What in hell for? It's beautiful – and it must be worth a fortune!'

'I shouldn't think so,' I answered. 'It might look all right from here, but wait till you get inside. Its foundations were waterlogged twenty years ago. There were always six inches of water in the cellar, and the panels of the lower rooms were mouldy even then. God only knows what it must be like now!'

'Does it look the way you remember it?' he asked.

'Not quite,' I frowned. 'Seen through the eyes of an adult, there are differences.'

For one thing, the pool was different. The level of the water was lower, so that the wide, grass-grown wall of the dam seemed somehow taller. In fact, I had completely forgotten about the dam, without which the pool could not exist, or at best would be the merest pebble-bottomed pool and not the small lake which it now was. For the first time it dawned on me that the pool was artificial, not natural as I had always thought of it, and that Temple House had been built on top of the dam's curving mound where it extended to the steep shale cliff of the defile itself.

With a skidding of loose chippings, Carl took the Range Rover up the ramp that formed the drive to the house, and a moment later we drew to a halt before the high-arched porch. We dismounted and entered, and now Carl went clattering away – almost irreverently, I thought – into cool rooms, dark stairwells and huge cupboards, his voice echoing back to me where I stood with mixed emotions, savouring the atmosphere of the old place, just inside the doorway to the house proper.

'But this is *!' he cried from somewhere. 'This is for me! My studio, and no question. Come and look, John – look at the windows letting in all this good light. You're right about the damp, I can feel it – but that aside, it's perfect.'*

I found him in what had once been the main living-room, standing in golden clouds of dust he had stirred up, motes illuminated by the sun's rays where they struck into the room through huge, leaded windows. 'You'll need to give the place a good dusting and sweeping out,' I told him.

'Oh, sure,' he answered, 'but there's a lot wants doing before that. Do you know where the master switch is?'

'Umm? Switch?'

'For the electric light,' he frowned impatiently at me. 'And surely there's an icebox in the kitchen.'

'A refrigerator?' I answered. 'Oh, yes, I'm sure there is . . , Look, you run around and explore the place and do whatever makes you happy. Me, I'm just going to potter about and try to waken a few old dreams.'

During the next hour or two – while I quite literally 'pottered about' and familiarized myself once again with this old house so full of memories – Carl fixed himself up with a bed in his 'studio,' found the main switch and got the electricity flowing, examined the refrigerator and satisfied himself that it was in working order, then searched me out where I sat in the mahogany-panelled study upstairs to tell me that he was driving into Penicuik to stock up with food.

From my window I watched him go, until the cloud of dust thrown up by his wheels disappeared over the rise to the south, then stirred myself into positive action. There were things to be done – things I must do for myself, others for my uncle – and the sooner I started the better. Not that there was any lack of time; I had three whole months to carry out Gavin McGilchrist's instructions, or to fail to carry them out. And yet somehow . . . yes, there was this feeling of *urgency* in me.

And so I switched on the light against gathering shadows, took out the envelope left for me by my uncle – that envelope whose contents, a letter and a notebook, were for my eyes only – sat down at the great desk used by so many generations of McGilchrists, and began to read . . .

4. The Curse

'My dear, dear nephew,' the letter in my uncle's uneven script began, '—so much I would like to say to you, and so little time in which to say it. And all these years grown in between since last I saw you.

'When first you left Scotland with your mother I would have written to you through her, but she forbade it. In early

1970 I learned of her death, so that even my condolences would have been six months too late; well, you have them now. She was a wonderful woman, and of course she was quite right to take you away out of it all. If I'm right in what I now suspect, her woman's intuition will yet prove to have been nearer the mark than anyone ever could have guessed, and—

'But there I go, miles off the point and rambling as usual; and such a lot to say. Except – I'm damned if I know where to begin! I suppose the plain fact of the matter is quite simply stated – namely, that for you to be reading this is for me to be gone forever from the world of men. But gone . . . *where*? And how to explain?

'The fact is, I cannot tell it all, not and make it believable. Not the way I have come to believe it. Instead you will have to be satisfied with the barest essentials. The rest you can discover for yourself. There are books in the old library that tell it all – if a man has the patience to look. And if he's capable of putting aside all matters of common knowledge, all laws of science and logic; capable of unlearning all that life has ever taught him of truth and beauty.

'Four hundred years ago we weren't such a race of damned sceptics. They were burning witches in these parts then, and if they had suspected of anyone what I have come to suspect of Temple House and its grounds . . .

'Your mother may not have mentioned the curse – the curse of the McGilchrists. Oh, she believed in it, certainly, but it's possible she thought that to tell of it might be to invoke the thing. That is to say, by telling you she might bring the curse down on your head. Perhaps she was right, for unless my death is seen to be *entirely natural*, then certainly I shall have brought it down upon myself.

'And what of you, Nephew?

'You have three months. Longer than that I do not deem safe, and nothing is guaranteed. Even three months might be dangerously overlong, but I pray not. Of course you are at liberty, if you so desire, simply to get the thing over and done with. In my study, in the bottom right-hand drawer of my desk, you will find sufficient fuses and explosive materials to bring down the wall of the defile on to the house, and the house itself into the pool, which should satisfactorily put an end to the thing.

'But . . . you had an enquiring mind as a child. If you look where I have looked and read what I have read, then you shall learn what I've learned and know that it is neither advanced senility nor madness but my own intelligence which leads me to the one, inescapable conclusion – that this House of the Temple, this Temple House of the McGilchrists, is accursed. Most terribly . . .

'I could flee this place, of course, but I doubt if that would save me. And if it did save me, still it would leave the final questions unanswered and the riddle unsolved. Also, I loved my brother, your father, and I saw his face when he was dead. If for nothing else, that look on your father's dead face has been sufficient reason for me to pursue the thing thus far. I thought to seek it out, to know it, destroy it – but now . . .

'I have never been much of a religious man, Nephew, and so it comes doubly hard for me to say what I now say: that while your father is dead these twenty years and more, I now find myself wondering if he is truly at rest! And what will be the look on *my* face when the thing is over, one way or the other? Ask about that, Nephew, ask how *I* looked when they found me.

'Finally, as to your course of action from this point onward: do what you will, but in the last event be sure you bring about the utter dissolution of the seat of ancient evil known as Temple House. There are things hidden in the great deserts and mountains of the world, and others sunken under the deepest oceans, which never were meant to exist in any sane or ordered universe. Yes, and certain revenants of immemorial horror have even come among men. One such has anchored itself here in the Pentlands, and in a little while I may meet it face to face. If all goes well . . . But then you should not be reading this.

And so the rest is up to you, John Hamish; and if indeed man has an immortal soul, I now place mine in your hands. Do what must be done and if you are a believer, then say a prayer for me . . .

Yr. Loving Uncle—
Gavin McGilchrist.'

I read the letter through a second time, then a third, and the shadows lengthened beyond the reach of the study's electric lights. Finally, I turned to the notebook – a slim, ruled, board-covered book whose like might be purchased at any stationery store – and opened it to page upon page of scrawled and at first glance seemingly unconnected jottings, references, abbreviated notes and memoranda concerning . . . Concerning what? Black magic? Witchcraft? The 'supernatural'? But what else would you call a curse if not supernatural?

Well, my uncle had mentioned a puzzle, a mystery, the McGilchrist curse, the thing he had tracked down almost to the finish. And here were all the pointers, the clues, the keys to his years of research. I stared at the great bookcases lining the walls, the leather spines of their contents dully agleam in the glow of the lights. Asquith had told me that my uncle brought many old books back with him from his wandering abroad.

I stood up and felt momentarily dizzy, and was obliged to lean on the desk until the feeling passed. The mustiness of the deserted house, I supposed, the closeness of the room and the odour of old books. Books . . . yes, and I moved shakily across to the nearest bookcase and ran my fingers over titles rubbed and faded with age and wear. There were works here which seemed to stir faint memories – perhaps I had been allowed to play with those books as a child? – but others were almost tangibly strange to the place, whose titles alone would make aliens of them without ever a page being turned. These must be those volumes my uncle had discovered abroad. I frowned as I tried to make something of their less than commonplace names.

Here were such works as the German *Unter-Zee Kulten* and Feery's *Notes on the Necronomicon* in a French edition; and here Gaston le Fe's *Dwellers in the Depths* and a black-bound, iron-hasped copy of the *Cthäat Aquadingen*, its harsh title suggestive of both German and Latin roots. Here was Gantley's *Hydrophinnae*, and here the *Liber Miraculorem* of the Monk and Chaplain Herbert of Clairvaux. Gothic letters proclaimed of one volume that it was Prinn's *De Vermis Mysteriis*, while another purported to be the suppressed and hideously disquieting *Unaussprechlichen Kulten* of von Junzt – titles which seemed to leap at me as my eyes moved from shelf to shelf in a sort of disbelieving stupefaction.

What possible connection could there be between these ancient, foreign volumes of elder madness and delirium and the solid, down-to-earth McGilchrist line of gentlemen, officers and scholars? There seemed only one way to find out. Choosing a book at random. I found it to be the *Cthäat Aquadingen* and returned with it to the desk. The light outside was failing now and the shadows of the hills were long and sooty. In less than an hour it would be dusk, and half an hour after that, dark.

Then there would only be Carl and I, and the night. And the old house. As if in answer to unspoken thoughts, settling timbers groaned somewhere overhead. Through the window, down below in the sharp shadows of the house, the dull green glint of water caught my eye.

Carl and I, the night and the old house—
And the deep, dark pool.

5. The Music

It was almost completely dark by the time Carl returned, but in between I had at least been able to discover my uncle's system of reference. It was quite elementary, really. In his notebook, references such as 'CA 121/7' simply indicated an item of interest in the *Cthäat Aquadingen*, page 121, the seventh paragraph. And in the work itself he had carefully underscored all such paragraphs or items of interest. At least a dozen such references concerning the *Cthäat Aquadingen* occurred in his notebook, and as night had drawn on I had examined each in turn.

Most of them were meaningless to me and several were in a tongue or glyph completely beyond my comprehension, but others were in a form of old English which I could transcribe with comparative ease. One such, which seemed a chant of sorts, had a brief annotation scrawled in the margin in my uncle's hand. The passage I refer to, as nearly as I can remember, went like this:

> Rise, O Nameless Ones;
> It is Thy Season
> When Thine Own of Thy Choosing,
> Through Thy Spells & Thy Magic,
> Through Dreams & Enchantry,
> May know Thou art come.
> They rush to Thy Pleasure,
> For the Love of Thy Masters—
> —the Spawn of Cthulhu.

And the accompanying annotation queried: 'Would they have used such as this to call the Thing forth, I wonder, or was it simply a blood lure? What causes it to come forth now? When will it next come?'

It was while I was comparing references and text in this fashion that I began to get a glimmer as to just what the book was, and on further considering its title I saw that I had probably guessed correctly. 'Cthäat' frankly baffled me, unless it had some connection with the language or being of the pre-Nacaal Kthatans; but 'Aquadingen' was far less alien in its sound and formation. It meant (I believed), 'water-things', or 'things of the waters'; and the – *Cthäat Aquadingen* was quite simply a compendium of myths and legends concerning water sprites, nymphs, demons, naiads and other supernatural creatures of lakes and oceans, and the spells or conjurations by which they might be evoked or called out of their watery haunts.

I had just arrived at this conclusion when Carl returned, the lights of his vehicle cutting a bright swath over the dark surface of the pool as he parked in front of the porch. Laden down, he entered the house and I went down to the spacious if somewhat old fashioned kitchen to find him filling shelves and cupboards and stocking the refrigerator with perishables. This done, bright and breezy in his enthusiasm, he enquired about the radio.

'Radio?' I answered. 'I thought your prime concern was for peace and quiet? Why, you've made enough noise for ten since we got here!'

'No, no,' he said. 'It's not *my* noise I'm concerned about, but yours. Or rather, the radio's. I mean, you've obviously found one for I heard the music.'

Carl was big, blond and blue-eyed; a Viking if ever I saw one, and quite capable of displaying a Viking's temper. He had been laughing when he asked me where the radio was, but now he was frowning. 'Are you playing games with me, John?'

'No, of course I'm not,' I answered him. 'Now what's all this about? What music have you been hearing?'

His face suddenly brightened and he snapped his fingers. 'There's a radio in the Range Rover,' he said. 'There has to be. It must have gotten switched on, very low, and I've been getting Bucharest or something.' He made as if to go back outside.

'Bucharest?' I repeated him.

'Hmm?' he paused in the kitchen doorway. 'Oh, yes – gypsyish stuff. Tambourines and chanting – and fiddles. Dancing around campfires. Look, I'd better switch it off or the battery will run down.'

'I didn't see a radio,' I told him, following him out through the porch and on to the drive.

He leaned inside the front of the vehicle, switched on the interior light and searched methodically. Finally he put the light out with an emphatic click. He turned to me and his jaw had a stubborn set to it. I looked back at him and raised my eyebrows. 'No radio?'

He shook his head. 'But I heard the music.'

'Lovers,' I said.

'Eh?'

'Lovers, out walking. A transistor radio. Perhaps they were sitting in the grass. After all, it is a beautiful summer night.'

Again he shook his head. 'No, it was right there in the air. Sweet and clear. I heard it as I approached the house. It came from the house, I thought. And you heard nothing?'

'Nothing,' I answered, shaking my head.

'Well then – damn it to hell!' he suddenly grinned. 'I've started hearing things, that's all! Skip it . . . Come on, let's have supper . . .'

Carl stuck to his 'studio' bedroom but I slept upstairs in a room adjacent to the study. Even with the windows thrown wide open, the night was very warm and the atmosphere sticky, so that sleep did not come easily. Carl must have found a similar problem for on two or three occasions I awakened from a restless half-sleep to sounds of his moving about downstairs. In the morning over breakfast both of us were a little bleary-eyed, but then he led me through into his room to display the reason for his nocturnal activity.

There on the makeshift easel, on one of a dozen old canvasses he had brought with him, Carl had started work on a picture . . . of sorts.

For the present he had done little more than lightly brush in the background, which was clearly the valley of the house, but the house itself was missing from the picture and I could see that the artist did not intend to include it. The pool was there, however, with its encircling ring of quartz columns complete and finished with lintels of a like material. The columns and lintels glowed luminously.

In between and around the columns vague figures writhed, at present insubstantial as smoke, and in the foreground the flames of a small fire were driven on a wind that blew from across the pool. Taken as a whole and for all its sketchiness, the scene gave a vivid impression of savagery and pagan excitement – strange indeed considering that as yet there seemed to be so little in it to excite any sort of emotion whatever.

'Well,' said Carl, his voice a trifle edgy, 'what do you think?'

'I'm no artist, Carl,' I answered, which I suppose in the circumstances was saying too much.

'You don't like it?' he sounded disappointed.

'I didn't say that,' I countered. 'Will it be a night scene?'

He nodded.

'And the dancers there, those wraiths . . . I suppose they *are* dancers?'

'Yes,' he answered, 'and musicians. Tambourines, fiddles . . .'

'Ah!' I nodded. 'Last night's music.'

He looked at me curiously. 'Probably . . . Anyway, I'm happy with it. At least I've started to work. What about you?'

'You do your thing,' I told him, 'and I'll do mine.'

'But what are you going to do?'

I shrugged. 'Before I do anything I'm going to soak up a lot of atmosphere. But I don't intend staying here very long. A month or so, and then—'

'And then you'll burn this beautiful old place to the ground.' He had difficulty keeping the sour note out of his voice.

'It's what my uncle wanted,' I said. 'I'm not here to write a story. A story may come of it eventually, even a book, but that can wait. Anyway, I won't burn the house.' I made a mushroom cloud with my hands. 'She goes – up!'

Carl snorted. 'You McGilchrists,' he said. 'You're all nuts!' But there was no malice in his statement.

There was a little in mine, however, when I answered: 'Maybe – but I don't hear music when there isn't any!'

But that was before I knew everything . . .

6. The Familiar

During the course of the next week Scotland began to feel the first effects of what is now being termed 'a scourge on the British Isles,' the beginning of an intense, ferocious and prolonged period of drought. Sheltered by the Pentlands, a veritable suntrap for a full eight to ten hours a day, Temple House was no exception. Carl and I took to lounging around in shorts and T-shirts, and with his blond hair and fair skin he was particularly vulnerable. If we had been swimmers, then certainly we should have used the pool; as it was we had to content ourselves by sitting at its edge with our feet in the cool mountain water.

By the end of that first week, however, the drought's effect upon the small stream which fed the pool could clearly be seen. Where before the water had rushed down from the heights of the defile, now it seeped, and the natural overflow from the sides of the dam was so reduced that the old course of the stream was now completely dry. As for our own needs: the large water tanks in the attic of the house were full and their source of supply seemed independent, possibly some reservoir higher in the hills.

In the cool of the late afternoon, when the house stood in its own and the Pentlands' shade, then we worked; Carl at his drawing or painting, I with my uncle's notebook and veritable library of esoteric books. We also did a little walking in the hills, but in the heat of this incredible summer that was far too exhausting and only served to accentuate a peculiar mood of depression which had taken both of us in its grip. We blamed the weather, of course, when at any other time we would have considered so much sunshine and fresh air a positive blessing.

By the middle of the second week I was beginning to make real sense of my uncle's fragmentary record of his research. That is to say, his trail was becoming easier to follow as I grew used to his system and started to detect a pattern.

There were in fact two trails, both historic, one dealing with the McGilchrist line itself, the other more concerned with the family seat, with the House of the Temple. Because I seemed close to a definite discovery. I worked harder and became more absorbed with the work. And as if my own industry was contagious, Carl too began to put in longer hours at his easel or drawing board.

It was a Wednesday evening, I remember, the shadows lengthening and the atmosphere heavy when I began to see just how my uncle's mind had been working. He had apparently decided that if there really was a curse on the McGilchrists, then that it had come about during the construction of Temple House. To discover why this was so, he had delved back into the years prior to its construction in this cleft in the hills, and his findings had been strange indeed.

It had seemed to start in England in 1594 with the advent of foreign refugees. These had been the members of a monkish order originating in the mountains of Romania, whose ranks had nevertheless been filled with many diverse creeds, colours and races. There were Chinamen amongst them, Hungarians, Arabs and Africans, but their leader had been a Romanian priest named Chorazos. As to why they had been hounded out of their own countries, that remained a mystery.

Chorazos and certain of his followers became regular visitors at the Court of Queen Elizabeth I – who had ever held an interest in astrology, alchemy and all similar magics and mysteries – and with her help they founded a temple 'somewhere near Finchley.' Soon, however, couriers from foreign parts began to bring in accounts of the previous doings of this darkling sect, and so the Queen took advice.

Of all persons, she consulted with Dr John Dee, that more than dubious character whose own dabbling with the occult had brought him so close to disaster in 1555 during the reign of Queen Mary. Dee, at first enamoured of Chorazos and his followers, now turned against them. They were pagans, he said; their women were whores and their ceremonies orgiastic. They had brought with them a 'familiar,' which would have 'needs' of its own, and eventually the public would rise up against them and the 'outrage' they must soon bring about in the country. The Queen should therefore sever all connections with the sect – and immediately!

Acting under Dee's guidance, she at once issued orders for the arrest, detention and investigation of Chorazos and his members . . . but too late, for they had already flown. Their 'temple' in Finchley – a 'columned pavilion about a central lake' – was destroyed and the pool filled in. That was in late 1595.

In 1596 they turned up in Scotland, this time under the guise of travelling faith-healers and herbalists working out of Edinburgh. As a reward for their work among the poorer folk in the district, they were given a land grant and took up an austere residence in the Pentlands. There, following a pattern established abroad and carried on in England, Chorazos and his followers built their temple; except that this time they had to dam a stream in order to create a pool. The work took them several years; their ground was private property; they kept for the main well out of the limelight, and all was well . . . for a while.

Then came rumours of orgiastic rites in the hills, of children wandering away from home under the influence of strange, hypnotic music, of a monstrous being conjured up from hell to preside over ceremonial murder and receive its grisly tribute, and at last the truth was out. However covertly Chorazos had organized his perversions, there now existed the gravest suspicions as to what he and the others of his sect were about. And this in the Scotland of James IV, who five years earlier had charged an Edinburgh jury with 'an Assize of Error' when they dismissed an action for witchcraft against one of the 'notorious' North Berwick Witches.

In this present matter, however, any decision of the

authorities was pre-empted by persons unknown – possibly the inhabitants of nearby Penicuik, from which town several children had disappeared – and Chorazos's order had been wiped out *en masse* one night and the temple reduced to ruins and shattered quartz stumps.

Quite obviously, the site of the temple had been here, and the place had been remembered by locals down the centuries, so that when the McGilchrist house was built in the mid-eighteenth century, it automatically acquired the name of Temple House. The name had been retained . . . but what else had lingered over from those earlier times, and what *exactly* was the nature of the McGilchrist Curse?

I yawned and stretched. It was after eight and the sinking sun had turned the crests of the hills to bronze. A movement, seen in the corner of my eye through the window, attracted my attention. Carl was making his way to the rim of the pool. He paused with his hands on his hips to stand between two of the broken columns, staring out over the silent water. Then he laid back his head and breathed deeply. There was a tired but self-satisfied air about him that set me wondering.

I threw the window wide and leaned out, calling down through air which was still warm and cloying: 'Hey, Carl – you look like the cat who got the cream!'

He turned and waved. 'Maybe I am. It's that painting of mine. I think I've got it beat. Not finished yet . . . but coming along.'

'Is it good?' I asked.

He shrugged, but it was a shrug of affirmation, not indifference. 'Are you busy? Come down and see for yourself. I only came out to clear my head, so that I can view it in fresh perspective. Yours will be a second opinion.'

I went downstairs to find him back in his studio. Since the light was poor now, he switched on all of the electric lights and led the way to his easel. I had last looked at the painting some three or four days previously, at a time when it had still been very insubstantial. Now—

Nothing insubstantial about it now. The grass was green, long and wild, rising to nighted hills of grey and purple, silvered a little by a gibbous moon. The temple was almost luminous, its columns shining with an eerie light. Gone the wraithlike dancers; they capered in cassocks now, solid, wild and weird with leering faces. I started as I stared at those faces – yellow, black and white faces, a half-dozen different races – but I started worse at the sight of the *thing* rising over the pool within the circle of glowing columns. Still vague, that horror – that leprous grey, tentacled, mushroom-domed monstrosity – and as yet mainly amorphous; but formed enough to show that it was nothing of this good, sane Earth.

'What the hell is it?' I half-gasped, half-whispered.

'Hmm?' Carl turned to me and smiled with pleased surprise at the look of shock on my blanched face. 'I'm damned if I know – but I think it's pretty good! It will be when it's finished. I'm going to call it *The Familiar* . . .'

7. The Face

For a long while I simply stood there taking in the contents of that hideous canvas and feeling the heat of the near-tropical night beating in through the open windows. It was all there: the foreign monks making their weird music, the temple glowing in the darkness, the dam, the pool and the hills as I had always known them, the *Thing* rising up in bloated loathsomeness from dark water, and a sense of realness I had never seen before and probably never again will see in any artist's work.

My first impulse when the shock wore off a little was to

turn on Carl in anger. This was too monstrous a joke. But no, his face bore only a look of astonishment now – astonishment at my reaction, which must be quite obvious to him. 'Christ!' he said, 'is it that good?'

'That – *thing* – has nothing to do with Christ!' I finally managed to force the words out of a dry throat. And again I felt myself on the verge of demanding an explanation. Had he been reading my uncle's notes? Had he been secretly following my own line of research? But how could he, secretly or otherwise? The idea was preposterous.

'You really do *feel* it, don't you?' he said, excitedly taking my arm. 'I can see it in your face.'

'I . . . I feel it, yes,' I answered. 'It's a very . . . powerful piece of work.' Then, to fill the gap, I added: 'Where did you dream it up?'

'Right first time,' he answered. 'A dream – I think. Something left over from a nightmare. I haven't been sleeping too well. The heat, I guess.'

'You're right,' I agreed. 'It's too damned hot. Will you be doing any more tonight?'

He shook his head, his eyes still on the painting. 'Not in this light. I don't want to foul it up. No, I'm for bed. Besides, I have a headache.'

'What?' I said, glad now that I had made no wild accusation. 'You? – a strapping great Viking like you, with a headache?'

'Viking?' he frowned. 'You've called me that before. My looks must be deceptive. No, my ancestors came out of Hungary – a place called Stregoicavar. And I can tell you they burned more witches there than you ever did in Scotland!'

There was little sleep for me that night, though toward morning I did finally drop off, slumped across the great desk, drowsing fitfully in the soft glow of my desk light.

Prior to that, however, in the silence of the night – driven on by a feeling of impending . . . something – I had delved deeper into the old books and documents amassed by my uncle, slowly but surely fitting together that great jigsaw whose pieces he had spent so many years collecting.

The work was more difficult now, his notes less coherent, his writing barely legible; but at least the material was or should be more familiar to me. Namely, I was studying the long line of McGilchrists gone before me, whose seat had been Temple House since its construction two hundred and forty years ago. And as I worked so my eyes would return again and again, almost involuntarily, to the dark pool with its ring of broken columns. Those stumps were white in the silver moonlight – as white as the columns in Carl's picture – and so my thoughts returned to Carl.

By now he must be well asleep, but this new mystery filled my mind through the small hours. Carl Earlman . . . It certainly sounded Hungarian, German at any rate, and I wondered what the old family name had been. Ehrlichman, perhaps? Arlmann? And not Carl but Karl.

And his family hailed from Stregoicavar. That was a name I remembered from a glance into von Junzt's *Unspeakable Cults*, I was sure. Stregoicavar: it had stayed in my mind because of its meaning, which is 'witch-town.' Certain of Chorazos's order of pagan priests had been Hungarian. Was it possible that some dim ancestral memory lingered over in Carl's mind, and that the pool with its quartz stumps had awakened that in his blood which harkened back to older times? And what of the gypsy music he had sworn to hearing on our first night in this old house? Young and strong he was certainly, but beneath an often brash exterior he had all the sensitivity of an artist born.

According to my uncle's research my own great-grand-father, Robert Allan McGilchrist, had been just such a man.

Sensitive, a dreamer, prone to hearing things in the dead of night which no one else could hear. Indeed, his wife had left him for his peculiar ways. She had taken her two sons with her; and so for many years the old man had lived here alone, writing and studying. He had been well known for his paper on the Lambton Worm legend of Northumberland: of a great worm or dragon that lived in a well and emerged at night to devour 'bairns and beasties and foolhardy wanderers in the dark.' He had also published a pamphlet on the naiads of the lochs of Inverness; and his limited edition book, *Notes on Nessie – the Secrets of Loch Ness* had caused a minor sensation when first it saw print.

It was Robert Allan McGilchrist, too, who restored the old floodgate in the dam, so that the water level in the pool could be controlled; but that had been his last work. A shepherd had found him one morning slumped across the gate, one hand still grasping the wheel which controlled its elevation, his upper body floating face-down in the water. He must have slipped and fallen, and his heart had given out. But the look on his face had been a fearful thing; and since the embalmers had been unable to do anything with him, they had buried him immediately.

And as I studied this or that old record or consulted this or that musty book, so my eyes would return to the dam, the pool with its fanged columns, the old floodgate – rusted now and fixed firmly in place – and the growing sensation of an on-rushing doom gnawed inside me until it became a knot of fear in my chest. If only the heat would let up, just for one day, and if only I could finish my research and solve the riddle once and for all.

It was then, as the first flush of dawn showed above the eastern hills, that I determined what I must do. The fact of the matter was that Temple House frightened me, as I suspected it had frightened many people before me. Well, I had neither the stamina nor the dedication of my uncle. He had resolved to track the thing down to the end, and something – sheer hard work, the 'curse,' failing health, *something* – had killed him.

But his legacy to me had been a choice: continue his work or put an end to the puzzle for all time and blow Temple House to hell. So be it, that was what I would do. A day or two more – only a day or two, to let Carl finish his damnable painting – and then I would do what Gavin McGilchrist had ordered done. And with that resolution uppermost in my mind, relieved that at last I had made the decision, so I fell asleep where I sprawled at the desk.

The sound of splashing aroused me; that and my name called from below. The sun was just up and I felt dreadful, as if suffering from a hangover. For a long time I simply lay sprawled out. Then I stood up and eased my cramped limbs, and finally I turned to the open window. There was Carl, dressed only in his shorts, stretched out flat on a wide, thick plank, paddling out toward the middle of the pool!

'Carl!' I called down, my voice harsh with my own instinctive fear of the water. 'Man, that's dangerous – you can't swim!'

He turned his head, craned his neck and grinned up at me. 'Safe as houses,' he called, 'so long as I hang on to the plank. And it's cool, John, so wonderfully cool. This feels like the first time I've been cool in weeks!'

By now he had reached roughly the pool's centre and there he stopped paddling and simply let his hands trail in green depths. The level of the water had gone down appreciably during the night and the streamlet which fed the pool was now quite dry. The plentiful weed of the pool, becoming concentrated as the water evaporated, seemed thicker than ever I remembered it. So void of life, that water, with never a fish or frog to cause a ripple on the morass-green of its surface.

And suddenly that tight knot of fear was back in my

chest, making my voice a croak as I tried to call out: 'Carl, get out of there!'

'What?' he faintly called back, but he didn't turn his head. He was staring down into the water, staring intently at something he saw there. His hand brushed aside weed—

'Carl!' I found my voice. 'For God's sake get out of it!'

He started then, his head and limbs jerking as if scalded, setting the plank to rocking so that he half slid off it. Then – a scrambling back to safety and a frantic splashing and paddling; and galvanized into activity I sprang from the window and raced breakneck downstairs. And Carl laughing shakily as I stumbled knee-deep in hated water to drag him physically from the plank, both of us trembling despite the burning rays of the new-risen sun and the furnace heat of the air.

'What happened?' I finally asked.

'I thought I saw something,' he answered. 'In the pool. A reflection, that's all, but it startled me.'

'What did you see?' I demanded, my back damp with cold sweat.

'Why, what would I see?' he answered, but his voice trembled for all that he tried to grin. 'A face, of course – my own face framed by the weeds. But it didn't look like me, that's all . . .'

8. The Dweller

Looking back now in the light of what I already knew – certainly of what I should have guessed at that time – it must seem that I was guilty of an almost suicidal negligence in spending the rest of that day upstairs on my bed, tossing in nightmares brought on by the nervous exhaustion which beset me immediately after the incident at the pool. On the other hand, I had had no sleep the night before and Carl's adventure had given me a terrific jolt; and so my failure to recognize the danger – how close it had drawn – may perhaps be forgiven.

In any event, I forced myself to wakefulness in the early evening, went downstairs and had coffee and a frugal meal of biscuits, and briefly visited Carl in his studio. He was busy – frantically busy, dripping with sweat and brushing away at his canvas – working on his loathsome painting, which he did not want me to see. That suited me perfectly for I had already seen more than enough of the thing. I did take time enough to tell him, though, that he should finish his work in the next two days; for on Friday or at the very latest Saturday morning I intended to blow the place sky high.

Then I went back upstairs, washed and shaved, and as the light began to fail so I returned to my uncle's notebook. There were only three or four pages left unread, the first dated only days before his demise, but they were such a hodge-podge of scrambled and near-illegible miscellanea that I had the greatest difficulty making anything of them. Only that feeling of a burgeoning terror drove me on, though by now I had almost completely lost faith in making anything whatever of the puzzle.

As for my uncle's notes: a basically orderly nature had kept me from leafing at random through his book, or perhaps I should have understood earlier. As it is, the notebook is lost forever, but as best I can, I shall copy down what I remember of those last few pages. After that – and after I relate the remaining facts of the occurrences of that fateful hideous night – the reader must rely upon his own judgement. The notes then, or what little I remember of them:

'Levi's or Mirandola's invocation: "*Dasmass Jeschet Boene Doess Efar Duvema Enit Marous*." If I could get the pronunciation right, perhaps . . . But what will the Thing be? And will it succumb to a double-barrelled blast? That remains to be seen. But if what I suspect is firmly founded . . . Is it a tick-thing, such as von Junzt states inhabits the globular mantle of Yogg-Sothoth? (*Unaussprechlichen Kulten*, 78/16) – fearful hints – monstrous pantheon . . . And this merely a parasite to one of *Them*!

The Cult of Cthulhu . . . immemorial horror spanning all the ages. The *Johansen Narrative* and the *Pnakotic Manuscript*. And the Innsmouth Raid of 1928; much was made of that, and yet nothing known for sure. Deep Ones, but . . . different again from this Thing.

Entire myth-cycle . . . So many sources. Pure myth and legend? I think not. Too deep, interconnected, even plausible. According to Carter in SR, (AH '59) p. 250–51, *They* were driven into this part of the universe (or into this time-dimension) by "Elder Gods" as punishment for a rebellion. Hastur the Unspeakable prisoned in Lake of Hali (again the lake or pool motif) in Carcosa; Great Cthulhu in R'lyeh, where he slumbers still in his death-sleep; Ithaqua sealed away behind icy Arctic barriers, and so on. But Yogg-Sothoth was sent *outside*, into a parallel place, conterminous with all space and time. Since Y-S is everywhere and when, if a man knew the gate he could call Him out . . .

Did Chorazos and his acolytes, for some dark reason of their own, attempt thus to call Him out? And did they get this dweller in Him instead? And I believe I understand the reason for the pool. Grandfather knew. His interest in Nessie, the Lambton Worm, the Kraken of olden legend, naiads, Cthulhu . . . Wendy Smith's burrowers feared water; and the sheer *weight* of the mighty Pacific helps keep C. prisoned in his place in R'lyeh – thank God! Water subdues these things . . .

But if water confines It, why does It *return* to the water? And how may It leave the pool if not deliberately called out? No McGilchrist ever called It out, I'm sure, not willingly; though some may have suspected that something was there. No swimmers in the family – not a one – and I think I know why. It is an instinctive, an ancestral fear of the pool! No, of the unknown *Thing* which lurks beneath the pool's surface . . .'

The thing which lurks beneath the pool's surface . . .

Clammy with the heat, and with a debilitating terror springing from these words on the written page – these scribbled thought-fragments which, I was now sure, were anything but demented ravings – I sat at the old desk and read on. And as the house grew dark and quiet, as on the previous night, again I found my eyes drawn to gaze down through the open window to the surface of the still pool.

Except that the surface was no longer still!

Ripples were spreading in concentric rings from the pool's dark centre, tiny mobile wavelets caused by – by what? Some disturbance beneath the surface? The water level was well down now and tendrils of mist drifted from the pool to lie soft, luminous and undulating in the moonlight, curling like the tentacles of some great plastic beast over the dam, across the drive to the foot of the house.

A sort of paralysis settled over me then, a dreadful lassitude, a mental and physical malaise brought on by excessive morbid study, culminating in this latest phenomenon of the old house and the aura of evil which now seemed to saturate its very stones. I should have done something – something to break the spell, anything rather than sit there and merely wait for what was happening to happen – and yet I was incapable of positive action.

Slowly I returned my eyes to the written page; and there I sat shivering and sweating, my skin crawling as I read on by the light of my desk lamp. But so deep my trance-like state that it was as much as I could do to force my eyes from one word to the next. I had no volition, no will of my own with which to fight that fatalistic spell; and the physical heat of the night was that of a furnace as sweat dripped from my forehead onto the pages of the notebook.

'. . . I have checked my findings and can't believe my previous blindness! It should have been obvious. It happens when the water level falls below a certain point. It *has* happened every time there has been extremely hot weather – when the pool has started to *dry up*! The Thing needn't be called out at all! As to why it returns to the pool after taking a victim: it must return before daylight. It is a fly-the-light. A haunter of the dark. A wampyre! . . . but not blood. Nowhere can I find mention of blood sacrifices. And no punctures or mutilations. What, then are Its "needs?" Did Dee know? Kelly knew, I'm sure, but his writings are lost . . .

Eager now to try the invocation, but I wish that first I might know the true nature of the Thing. It takes the life of Its victim – but what else?

I have it! – God, I know – and I wish I did not know! But that *look* on my poor brother's face . . . Andrew, Andrew . . . I know now why you looked that way. But if I can free you, you shall be freed, If I wondered at the nature of the Thing, then I wonder no longer. The answers are all there, in the *Cthaat A.* and *Hydrophinnae*, if only I had known exactly where to look. Yibb-Tstll is one such; Bugg-Shash, too. Yes, and the pool-thing is another . . .

There have been a number down the centuries – the horror that dwelled in the mirror of Nitocris; the sucking, hunting thing that Count Magnus kept; the red, hairy slime used by Julian Scortz – familiars of the Great Old

Ones, parasites that lived on *Them* as lice live on men. Or rather, on their life-force! This one has survived the ages, at least until now. It does not take the blood but the very essence of Its victim. *It is a soul-eater!*

I can wait no longer. Tonight, when the sun goes down and the hills are in darkness . . . But if I succeed, and if the Thing comes for me . . . We'll see how It faces up to my shotgun!'

My eyes were half-closed by the time I had finally scanned all that was written, of which the above is only a small part; and even having read it I had not fully taken it in. Rather, I had absorbed it automatically, without reading any immediate meaning into it. But as I re-read those last few lines, so I heard something which roused me up from my lassitude and snapped me alertly awake in an instant.

It was music: the faint but unmistakable strains of a whirling pagan tune that seemed to reach out to me from a time beyond time, from a hell beyond all known hells . . .

9. The Horror

Shocked back to mental alertness, still my limbs were stiff as a result of several hours crouched over the desk. Thus, as I sprang or attempted to spring to my feet, a cramp attacked both of my claves and threw me down by the window. I grabbed at the still . . . and whatever I had been about to do was at once forgotten.

I gazed out the open window on a scene straight out of madness or nightmare. The broken columns where they now stood up from bases draped with weed seemed to glow with an inner light; and to my straining eyes it appeared that this haze of light extended uniformly upwards, so that I saw a revenant of the temple as it had once been. Through the light-haze I could also see the centre of the pool, from which the ripples spread outward with a rapidly increasing agitation.

There was a shape there now, a dark oblong illuminated both by the clean moonlight and by that supernatural glow; and even as I gazed, so the water slopping above the oblong seemed pushed aside and the slab showed its stained marble surface to the air. The music grew louder then, soaring wildly, and it seemed to me in my shocked and frightened condition that dim figures reeled and writhed around the perimeter of the pool.

Then – horror of horrors! – in one mad moment the slab tilted to reveal a black hole going down under the pool, like the entrance to some sunken tomb. There came an outpouring of miasmal gases, visible in the eerie glow, and then—

Even before the thing emerged I knew what it would be; how it would look. It was that horror on Carl's canvas, the soft-tentacled, mushroom-domed terror he had painted under the ancient, evil influence of this damned, doomed place. It was the dweller, the familiar, the tick-thing, the star-born wampyre . . . it was the curse of the McGilchrists. Except I understood now that this was not merely a curse on the McGilchrists but on the entire world. Of course it had seemed to plague the McGilchrists as a personal curse – but only because they had chosen to build Temple House here on the edge of its pool. They had been victims by virtue of their *availability*, for I was sure that the pool-thing was not naturally discriminative.

Then, with an additional thrill of horror, I saw that the thing was on the move, drifting across the surface of the pool, its flaccid tentacles reaching avidly in the direction of the house. The lights downstairs were out, which meant that Carl must be asleep . . .

Carl!

The thing was across the drive now, entering the porch, the house itself. I forced cramped limbs to agonized activity, lurched across the room, out onto the dark landing and stumbled blindly down the stairs. I slipped, fell, found my feet again – and my voice, too.

'Carl!' I cried, arriving at the door of his studio. 'Carl, *for God's sake!*'

The thing straddled him where he lay upon his bed. It glowed with an unearthly, a rotten luminescence which outlined his pale body in a sort of foxfire. Its tentacles writhed over his naked form and his limbs were filled with fitful motion. Then the dweller's mushroom head settled over his face, which disappeared in folds of the thing's gilled mantle.

'Carl!' I screamed yet again, and as I lurched forward in numb horror so my hand found the light switch on the wall. In another moment the room was bathed in sane and wholesome electric light. The thing bulged upward from Carl – rising like some monstrous amoeba, some sentient, poisonous jellyfish from an alien ocean – and turned toward me.

I saw a face, a face I knew across twenty years of time fled, *my uncle's face!* Carved in horror, those well remembered features besought, pleaded with me, that an end be put to this horror and peace restored to this lonely valley; that the souls of countless victims be freed to pass on from this world to their rightful destinations.

The thing left Carl's suddenly still form and moved forward, flowed toward me; and as it came so the face it wore melted and changed. Other faces were there, hidden in the thing, many with McGilchrist features and many without, dozens of them that came and went ceaselessly. There were children there, too, mere babies; but the last face of all, the one I shall remember above all others – *that was the face of Carl Earlman himself!* And it, too, wore that pleading, that imploring look – the look of a soul in hell, which prays only for its release.

Then the light won its unseen, unsung battle. Almost upon me, suddenly the dweller seemed to wilt. It shrank from the light, turned and flowed out of the room, through the porch, back toward the pool. Weak with reaction I watched it go, saw it move out across the now still water, saw the slab tilt down upon its descending shape and heard the music fade into silence. Then I turned to Carl . . .

I do not think I need mention the look on Carl's lifeless face, or indeed say anything more about him. Except perhaps that it is my fervent prayer that he now rests in peace with the rest of the dweller's many victims, taken down the centuries. That is my prayer, but . . .

As for the rest of it:

I dragged Carl from the house to the Range Rover, drove him to the crest of the rise, left him there and returned to the house. I took my uncle's prepared charges from his study and set them in the base of the shale cliff where the house backed onto it. Then I lit the fuses, scrambled back into the Range Rover and drove to where Carl's body lay in the cool of night. I tried not to look at his face.

In a little while the fuses were detonated, going off almost simultaneously, and the night was shot with fire and smoke and a rising cloud of dust. When the air cleared the whole scene was changed forever. The cliff had come down on the house, sending it crashing into the pool. The pool itself had disappeared, swallowed up in shale and debris; and it was as if the House of the Temple, the temple itself and the demon-cursed pool had never existed.

All was silence and desolation, where only the moonlight played on jagged stumps of centuried columns, projecting still from the scree- and rubble-filled depression which had been the pool. And now the moon silvered the bed of the old stream, running with water from the ruined pool—

And at last I was able to drive on.

10. The Unending Nightmare

That should have been the end of it, but such has not been the case. Perhaps I alone am to blame. The police in Penicuik listened to my story, locked me in a cell overnight and finally conveyed me to this place, where I have been now for more than a week. In a way I supposed that the actions of the police were understandable; for my wild appearance that night – not to mention the ghastly, naked corpse in the Range Rover and the incredible story I incoherently told – could hardly be expected to solicit their faith or understanding. But I do *not* understand the position of the alienists here at Oakdeene.

Surely they, too, can hear the damnable music? – that music which grows louder hour by hour, more definite and decisive every night – the music which in olden days summoned the pool-thing to its ritual sacrifice. Or is it simply that they disagree with my theory? I have mentioned it to them time and time again and repeat it now: that there are *other* pools in the Pentlands, watery havens to which the thing might have fled from the destruction of its weedy retreat beside the now fallen seat of the McGilchrists. Oh, yes, and I firmly believe that it did so flee. And the days are long and hot and a great drought is on the land . . .

And perhaps, too, over the years, a very real curse has loomed up large and monstrous over the McGilchrists. Do souls have a flavour, I wonder, a distinctive texture of their own? Is it possible that the pool-thing has developed an appetite, a *taste* for the souls of McGilchrists? If so, then it will surely seek me out; and yet here I am detained in this institute for the insane.

Or could it be that I am now in all truth mad? Perhaps the things I have experienced and know to be true have driven me mad, and the music I hear exists only in my mind. That is what the nurses tell me and dear God, I pray that it is so! But if not – if not . . .

For there is that other thing, which I have not mentioned until now. When I carried Carl from his studio after the pool-thing left him, I saw his finished painting. Not the whole painting but merely a part of it, for when it met my eyes they saw only one thing: the finished face which Carl had painted on the dweller.

This is the nightmare which haunts me worse than any other, the question I ask myself over and over in the dead of night, when the moonlight falls upon my high, barred window and the music floods into my padded cell:

If they should bring me my breakfast one morning and find me dead – *will my face really look like that?*